"A ONE-SITTING BOOK . . . LACED WITH LOVE AND TERROR."
—Los Angeles Herald Examiner

In the first cool desert night, the telephone line repairman was beginning his work high above the ground when he saw, hanging down from a wire ten feet away, a bat watching him.

He looked down at his bike on the ground . . . he could see it was alive. At first, he thought, with toads, milling and hopping. Then he saw the whole bottom half of the pole was covered by them, and they were climbing up, and he knew what they were and what they were after . . . The line, in a matter of seconds, was solid with bats.

NIGHTWING

"HIGH EXCITEMENT! . . . MORE THAN A MERE SHOCKER . . . IT IS A FULL BOOK, AN ALTOGETHER FIRST-RATE WORK."
A. B. GUTHERIE, JR.

NIGHTWING

MARTIN CRUZ SMITH

A JOVE/HBJ BOOK

Copyright © 1977 by Martin Cruz Smith
Published by arrangement with W. W. Norton & Company

First Jove/HBJ edition published June 1978

Library of Congress Catalog Card Number: 77-5035

Printed in the United States of America

Jove/HBJ books are published by Jove Publications, Inc.
(Harcourt Brace Jovanovich) 757 Third Avenue,
New York, N.Y. 10017

FOR KNOX AND KITTY

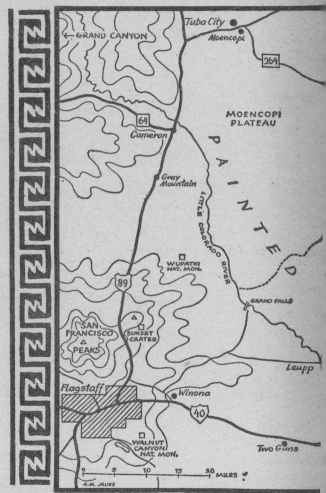

← GRAND CANYON

Tuba City

Moencopi

264

MOENCOPI PLATEAU

64

Cameron

P A I N T E D

Gray Mountain

LITTLE COLORADO RIVER

WUPATKI NAT. MON.

89

GRAND FALLS

SAN FRANCISCO PEAKS

SUNSET CRATER

Leupp

Flagstaff

Winona

40

WALNUT CANYON NAT. MON.

Two Guns

0   5   10   15   20 MILES

A.M. JAUSS

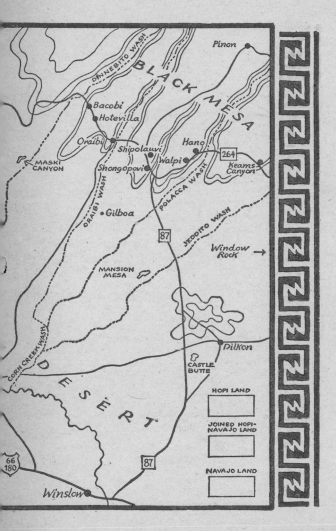

DINNEBITO WASH

BLACK MESA

Pinon

Bacobi
Hotevilla
Oraibi
Shipolauvi
Hano
264
Walpi
Keams
Canyon

MASKI
CANYON

Shongopovi

POLACCA WASH

ORAIBI WASH

Gilboa

87

JEDDITO WASH

Window
Rock →

MANSION
MESA

CORN CREEK WASH

Dilkon

CASTLE
BUTTE

D E S E R T

HOPI LAND

JOINED HOPI-
NAVAJO LAND

87

NAVAJO LAND

66
180

Winslow

When was I born?
Where did I come from?
Where am I going?
What am I?

—*the Hopi questions*

CHAPTER ONE

The Red Man tobacco sign—an Indian profile with a corroded eye—stared west. Two pick-up trucks rusted in a bower of yellow creosote bushes. Out of a headlight socket flicked the quick ribbon of a lizard tongue.

It was noon in the Painted Desert. A hundred degrees.

The tobacco sign and car hoods welded together in upright rows were the walls of Abner Tasupi's shed. A square of sheet steel was the roof. Sometimes, Abner fixed cars and, sometimes, he sold Enco gasoline straight from a drum. Usually, the drums were empty and he spent the day listening to his transistor radio. They had Navajo disc jockeys on a Gallup station. While he hated Navajos, there were no Hopi disc jockeys. There were lots of Hopis up on the Black Mesa, but not a one that dared come visit him.

Well, one.

Youngman Duran sat in the shed between the erupting springs of a car seat. A half-empty jug of Gallo port nestled between his legs.

"I'm sorry," Abner apologized to his only friend, "but they got to die."

"Anyone I know?"

Stripped down to underpants and a leather kilt, Abner squatted in the center of the dirt floor grinding cornmeal. He was past ninety and his brown body was hard like an insect's. His gray hair, cut short above the

11

eyes, hung down to frame a flat face with broad cheekbones and wide, peeling lips.

"Come on, Abner, you can tell me. Hell, I'm not a deputy for nothing."

Youngman was a third of Abner's age. His hair was shorter, pitch-black and tucked under a dirty Stetson. Sweat ringed the crown of his hat and sweat stains from his armpits and back merged to turn most of his khaki shirt into a dark sponge. He shifted his seat, trying to get comfortable without sticking himself with a seat spring. Youngman hated port wine but real alcohol was hard to find on the reservation. Besides, he liked Abner.

Abner gathered ground cornmeal in his hands and started pouring it inside of the door and, moving backwards, around the corners of the room.

"Everyone you know."

Youngman pulled out a pack of damp cigarettes.

"Well, that's a start, Abner, that's a start."

The shed always struck Youngman as a flood mark where the junk of different civilizations was left high and dry. A box of sparkplugs and points. Tire irons and jacks. Soup and bean cans on a drum converted into a stove. T-shirts stuffed into holes in the wall, where ears of blue corn hung from braided husks. On an orange crate shelf stood a line of kachina dolls, each a foot tall, one crowned with wooden rays of the sun, another wearing eagle fluffs, the crudely carved kind fifty to a hundred years old or more.

"You know, you get $1,000 for one of those dolls in Phoenix. Might as well do it before someone comes and steals 'em."

"No one comes around here, Flea." Abner finished pouring corn. "I don't worry about that."

"Well, they figure you're going to hex 'em, Abner."

On a steamer truck were mason jars of peyote and datura, ground jimson weed. Youngman resisted the

12

temptation to dig in. He'd been strung out before; he'd spent seven years trying to stay strung out. But that was the Army. Now he only smoked a little grass and drank wine. The highs weren't so high, but he didn't come so close to touching bottom. Abner was different. Abner was a priest. And Abner was right, people stayed away from him.

"Just what the hell do you mean, everyone's going to die? You're lucky you're talking to me. Anyone else would take you serious, Abner. You know that."

The lid was off the datura jar. The steamer trunk was bandaged with travel stickers reading "Tijuana," "Truth or Consequences," "Tombstone." There could as well have been one that said "Mars." Abner had picked up the trunk in a pawn shop, he'd never been further than Tuba City.

"It's a hot day and the Gallo brothers worked real hard, Abner. Have some."

Abner shook his head. Old man's been in the datura, Youngman thought. A fat dose of ground seeds was poison. A small dose of dried roots lifted the brain like a car on a jack. There were a lot of ways to die on a reservation. Drink. Datura or locoweed. Sit in the middle of the highway at night. Just let the time go by while the seconds accumulated like sand in an open grave.

Abner opened the trunk.

"Damn it. You promised me you'd never make medicine around me, Abner."

"You don't believe in it," Abner smiled back.

"I don't but I don't like it, either. I just want to sit down with you and get a buzz on. Like usual."

"I know what you want to do," the old man kept smiling. "Too late for that now."

"Look, we'll go take a ride. We can shoot some rabbit maybe."

Abner lifted a blanket from the bottom of the orange crate. Under it was a rabbit in a cage, nose pressed

13

against the slats. Youngman didn't know Abner to indulge in luxuries like fresh meat. Mostly the old man lived on pan bread, chilis, corn, and maybe a dried peach.

Inside the trunk were what Abner'd always called his "secret goods." Paho sticks. Feathers. Jars of dried corn, yellow, red, and blue. Abner poured small mounds of the corn on top of the trunk in front of the kachinas.

"It's just I don't want them coming after you," Youngman said, "because they're going to send me to deal with you. Those people are nuts. They believe your routine."

From another part of the trunk, Abner rummaged through a Baggie of feathers until he came up with the black-and-white tail feathers of a shrike. He stood a feather in each mound of corn. The effect was of an altar. Abner stepped back to appreciate his handiwork.

"I want to leave the center for the Pahana tablet. Nice, huh?"

"What's the Pahana tablet?"

"You don't know?"

"No."

"You don't know much, then." Abner rubbed his hands.

"I know you're tripping on that dream dust of yours. How much datura did you eat? Tell me."

"Not much," Abner shrugged his thin shoulders without turning around to answer. "You'll need a lot more, Flea."

Youngman was disappointed. "Making medicine" was the perfect example of a fool's errand. No amount of "medicine" had yet made a poor, ignorant Indian rich, hip, and white. At least, not in Arizona. As for kachina dolls, everyone knew they were kids' toys, nothing else.

14

The row of kachinas stared woodenly back with expressions of painted mischief.

"Yeah. I need a handful of uppers, some speed, a snort of coke, smokin' acid, and a can of Coors just to start feeling the Spirit."

"Even so," Abner maintained, "you're a good boy."

Youngman scratched between his eyebrows. There were times when he felt that he and Abner were conversing through an incompetent translator, although they were both using Hopi with the same white corruptions. Mentally, he kicked himself. He shouldn't have stopped by Abner's decrepit shack, he should have gone straight on to the Momoa ranch like he was supposed to.

Abner brought out a soda bottle stoppered with aluminum foil. He removed the foil and poured into his palm a kind of sand Youngman had never seen before. It was very fine and black and shiny as eyes. When his hand was full, Abner squatted and, letting a thin stream of the black sand slip between his fingers and thumb, drew a swastika in a corner of the floor. The lines were ruler straight and the angles could have been done with a T-square. Empty, his hand was smudged with oil.

Damn it, Youngman thought. The last thing he wanted to do was arrest the old man.

"You been around the Peabody mine, Abner? That's not sand."

"You're really a good boy. Not too dumb, either." Abner refilled his hand and started another swastika. "No, it ain't from Peabody."

A month before, Abner had been caught dumping cartons of rattlesnakes into the Black Mesa stripmine. The guards would have shot him if Youngman hadn't arrived in time to make the arrest himself. And then let Abner go.

"Tell me not to worry about you, uncle."

"Don't worry." Abner concentrated on his drawing.

15

"It'll work. I didn't get this from any white mine, I got it from the dead people."

The black sand had a viscous quality, almost liquid. Youngman sipped wine. Abner drew two more swastikas, forming a perfect square of them, the corners perfectly aligned to the four directions, Youngman had no doubt.

"What are you up to, Abner?"

Abner went to his steamer trunk and filled his arms with bottles of black powder, which he carried to the center of the square of swastikas. He squatted and opened one of the bottles, filled his hand, and started drawing again. A funny thing about priests, old and feeble as they got, once they hunkered over their so-called medicine they might as well be locked into place by magnets; it took two men to budge them. All a matter of balance, of course. The new pattern Abner drew was a curl of black sand that grew into a spiral.

"Don't you get angry at me, Flea." Abner refilled his hand. "But I think about this a lot and I just decided something had to be done about this world. First of all, there are the goddamn Navajos. Those bastards gotta go. Then, I think, all the Federal Courts and the Indian Bureau. Them, too." Powder hissed from Abner's hand, widening the spiral. "They're killing us, Flea. They are, always have been. Now it's them and the companies. Peabody Coal. El Paso Gas. I'm going to fix them, Flea. It's all up to me and I'm going to take care of them, Flea."

Abner stopped to open another bottle.

Youngman had to smile at the continued sound of his own Hopi name. He never heard it except from Abner.

"You're going to stop El Paso Gas?"

"I'm not sorry about that, just about the people."

"Sure."

That would shake El Paso's corporate structure, Youngman thought, knowing that a spaced-out 90-year-

16

old Hopi medicine man out in the middle of the desert was going to take them on. I'll drink to that, he added to himself.

"I seen the shovels digging up the Black Mesa," Abner spat out the door. "I hear about them taking the water."

"Water's going to Los Angeles. Hey, Abner, why don't you lay off your medicine and share some of this juice." Youngman offered the wine. Abner shook his head.

"Then Los Angeles has to go, too. Them and Tucson, Phoenix, Albuquerque. All them cities."

"A lot of people. You tell anyone else about this?"

Abner twisted on his knees, his arms outstretched like the points of a compass, and the black spiral swung around itself once, then a second time, curved delicately to the right, and veered into a larger circle in the opposite direction.

From where he sat, Youngman could see the stripped trucks outside. Oxidized carapaces like the remains of prehistoric animals. Hell of a lot of fossils in this country, he thought. Including Indians. He twisted the cap back on the wine.

"How're you going to do it, Abner? Get a rifle and start popping cars on the highway? Dynamite? How're you going to stop everybody?"

"Not stop them, end them." Abner looked up. He had small, powerful eyes, black centers with mottled whites. "I'm going to end the world."

The two whorls of black sand were complete. The smaller curled around itself three times, the larger one four. Together, they were a pair of serpentines five feet across. Although Abner had had to stop and begin again many times between handfuls of sand, there was no sign of a break or a falter. Not the slightest flaw in the concentric lines. In the dark of the shed, Abner's art was as pure and glistening as a double-coiled snake.

Nervous, Youngman looked out the door, past the trucks and his jeep. The sky was as blue as water, as deep as turquoise set in a silver conch. Air moved like a dancer with a dragging foot over the sandy ground, rattling dry seed pods. On the northern horizon stood the wall of the Black Mesa. To the south, Phoenix was two hundred miles distant; east, Albuquerque was 150. They could have been on different planets. That's what he'd been after, Youngman reminded himself, a different planet. He dug the last cigarette out of his pack.

Abner went to his trunk for bottles of a bright red sand.

"How're you going to end the world?"

"Different." Abner gestured for Youngman to give him a puff on the cigarette. "First world was ended by fire. People were led wrong by a woman and a snake. The Creator sent down flames and opened up the volcanoes. Everything was on fire and burned up, except for a few good Hopis."

Abner started drawing a ring of the red sand within the swastikas and around the double serpentine.

"Second world was good until people got too prosperous, too fat. They only cared about getting rich. The Creator saw what was happening and he stopped the world from turning. The earth went out of its orbit and everything froze, everything was covered with ice. Everyone died except the few good Hopis."

Youngman blew out a sigh of smoke. The story was the litany of his youth, heard over and over again.

"Third world was perfect." Abner measured out the arc of red sand. "Cities were full of jewels and feather rugs. People forgot the simple way. Women became whores. Men started fighting, flying from city to city to make war. The Creator got fed up. He put a few good Hopis in hollow reeds and covered the world with rain and water."

From the altar, the dolls listened with rigid attention.

18

A cloud-faced star god. A horned corn god. A round-headed clown. A dancer holding a plumed serpent. Dumb witnesses on a steamer trunk.

The red ring was done. Abner got a bottle of white sand and another of orange.

"At last, the land rose and the Creator let the Hopis come ashore in the desert." He opened the bottle of orange sand first. "He said, 'This is your Fourth World now. Its name is Tuwaqachi, World Complete. Its color is sikyangpu, yellow-white. Its direction is north, towards the Black Mesa. Its caretaker is Masaw, the god of death. From now on, you will have to follow the simple way.'"

The figure Abner drew between the serpentine and the ring was the outline of a running dog.

"Coyote Clan," he told Youngman. "You."

"Swell," Youngman said, uncomfortably.

Abner unstoppered the bottle of white sand and stepped carefully to the other side of the serpentine.

"So, we have worlds before and worlds after. For us, after the Fourth World there will be a Fifth."

"Maybe," Youngman suggested, "maybe, you're rushing things a little."

"The prophecies, you mean? Well, this world is supposed to end with atomic bombs, that's what some of the other priests say. I've been waiting for it but I don't think it's going to happen very soon. You can't depend on that. So, I'm going to end it now."

"When?"

"Today."

On the edge of the red ring, Abner finished the white outline of a bird. Then he excused himself and went out of the shed behind a bush to urinate. Youngman waited, wishing for nothing more than another cigarette. Abner returned, sniffing.

"It's a good day, huh? How's the machine running?"

"The jeep? It's okay. Look, I have to go see the Mo-

19

moas now but then I'm going on into the hills. You want to come with me?"

Abner shook his head and chuckled. His eyes were slightly glazed.

"You didn't go out there to take a leak," Youngman said. "You ate some more of that junk."

"Want some?"

"No."

"You will." Abner went on chuckling.

The old man had acted strange before. Never as bad as this. Even if he grabbed Abner and took him into the mesa, though, who would dare help? Who wouldn't run?

"The other priests know about your plans?"

"I asked them over. Some of them, they're busy making up tourist junk. Some of them, they wanta watch game shows on TV. I'll do it without them."

Abner unstoppered another bottle of black sand. He swayed delicately as he stepped around his painting, but he was steady enough when he bent over to draw a final figure within the ring of red. Painstakingly, he let the oily sand shape itself into a man without a head. A ragged cape hung from his shoulders; from the cape extended fingers. Abner opened a leather pouch and took out small bones, which he placed as a necklace. Where eyes and a mouth would have been, he put round corn cob sections. Under the eyes, trails of broken mirror glass, so that the headless figure seemed to be staring and crying at the same time.

"Almost done." Abner stood up, satisfied.

He wiped his hands on a rag and rummaged in his trunk until he came up with a buck knife and a leather belt. Putting a foot on one end of the belt, he snapped it taut along his leg as a strap and slapped the knife blade back and forth across it.

"If you're going to end the world, one more day won't make a difference," Youngman said. "Wait until tomorrow."

"Radio said maybe rain tomorrow night."

"So?" Youngman almost laughed.

"New clouds coming, Flea," Abner said seriously. "Dreamed them up. My clouds don't like rain."

Abner felt the edge of his knife. Then he crossed to the rabbit cage, lifted the animal out and strung it by its rear legs with a leather thong from the top of the shed door. The rabbit jerked from side to side and rolled its eyes.

"What do your clouds like?" Youngman asked.

Abner grabbed the rabbit by the base of the ears and twisted its head back, stretching the neck. He laid the knife across the white fur of the neck, and then his arm dropped.

The old man stared hesitantly, standing awkwardly in the frame of light, one hand still gripping the squirming rabbit. Reflection made the blade luminous. Youngman felt the stare like a blind hand running over his face, as if recognition had suddenly been lost.

"What do they like?" he repeated.

The rabbit clawed the air. The knife blinked, turning in Abner's hand.

The old man was crazy, Youngman thought. Senile. Finally over the edge after a lifetime of datura, grass, peyote, and bad booze. Tripped on stories, prophecies, lies, and frustration. Not that Youngman especially loved Abner, he told himself, any more than a man could love a gnarled ironwood tree or a stone chimney. When the tree fell or the chimney split, though, there had to be a sense of loss. As if a touchstone had been taken away. But a medicine man plotting war in a junkyard shed against the offices of the Indian Bureau, against the power shovels and million-dollar bankrolls of the mining companies? That was not only pathetic, it was downright comic. Abner still thought the Hopis were the Chosen People. They weren't chosen, they were marked for erasure.

Abner's eyes said he wanted to answer and that he couldn't.

"You won't believe me, Flea," he finally said.

"Then why did you start raving about all this?"

"Because you're my friend. You're part of it and you have to help. Don't worry," Abner became more reassuring, "we'll kill them all."

"Just tell me what to do."

"Later, when I'm dead."

The wind that penetrated the shed grew an edge. Youngman thought about re-opening the wine.

"If you can wait that long, Abner, I guess I can."

As Youngman stood, the glossy coils of the serpentine seemed to shift. An illusion in the shadow. For Abner, though, from the altitude of datura, Youngman guessed the spirals were moving and gaining speed. He was still nagged by the suspicion that Abner might take a gun and start sniping at cars on the highway.

"But if you're ending the world different this time," Youngman added, "I'd be curious how."

"Different."

"No floods, fire, ice, bombs. Guns, then? How?"

"This time, Masaw will end it," Abner said. "I'll see him tonight."

"Tonight, you're going to see him? The god of death, huh?"

Abner's concentration slipped to his painting and the unfinished figure with crying eyes and round mouth and no head inside a ring of red sand. The black body and cape shone, soft as fur.

"If I do things right," he said.

Youngman lifted his hat and ran a hand through his hair. He felt helpless.

"Okay," he gave up. Leaving the shed, he stopped in the doorway next to Abner and the hanging rabbit, half in shadow, half in light. "If anyone can do it, you can."

22

On the way to his jeep, he heard the rabbit's whimper cut short.

He had been born into the Coyote Clan, the only son of an unemployed construction worker and a perpetually angry woman. Joe Duran, bear-sized, arms like posts, never brooded over lack of work. Once for a year he hauled bricks at White Sands for the Air Force, an experience he felt bestowed on him enough of labor's honors. What Joe Duran did best was drink and hunt. He could go up the Dinnebito Wash with five rounds and stagger home with four kills. "Saved the last round for myself," he'd tell Youngman. The third thing he did best was clown. Whenever clowns were needed for a ceremonial, Joe Duran was always the first tapped. Disguised in white powder, he would stumble drunkenly through a line of priests, or run after women spectators waving a wooden penis, or walk suicidally backwards along the edge of the mesa. Which struck everyone as terribly funny, although it was no different from the way Joe Duran acted any other day, and in time, of course, he drove his angry wife crazy. Youngman remembered watching his father wearing clothes backwards and standing on his immense hands on the highest point of the mesa, laughing while Youngman's mother pitched knives and rocks. Finally, as a last grasp for sanity, she took up with a Navajo in Window Rock. Joe Duran followed them, killed them with his deer rifle, kicked the dead Navajo out of bed, lay down beside his wife and blew his own brains out. It was a common melodrama of reservation life.

Youngman was trucked off to mission school. Life there was comfortable enough. He had food, friends, a bed. In class, he stayed as mute as he could, watching. The teachers listed him as "slow, possibly retarded." Until the age of fourteen, when several sets of oil paints were donated to the school.

23

He had a glib facility, a hunter's eye for color. He didn't speak much more than he had before, but he would sit in front of an easel every waking minute, painting landscapes, nothing but landscapes. They were shown and, to his surprise, they were bought. Youngman experimented with watercolors, tempera, and acrylic, obsessed not so much with art as with the revelation that he could make money. In one step he strode past every other Indian he knew, and past his father in particular. Within two years, he developed a technique with acrylic and varnish that gave his desert landscapes a hard, jewel-like finish that was totally cynical and artificial. Youngman, alone, knew what he was doing. Not painting the desert. Killing it. On his canvas, birds were as bright and dead as souvenir pins, and falling rain had the quality of rocks. It was a style only whites could appreciate, but they were paying. At the galleries in Santa Fe and Phoenix, they paid a lot.

Flattered by whites, he responded in kind. He cut his hair and dressed in sports jackets. Found himself becoming a good-looking man though not pretty, his features were too angular for that. Only occasionally was he betrayed by a dark hostility in his eyes, his mother's gift.

The University of New Mexico offered Youngman a full art scholarship. This was the second step up, Youngman told himself. He could be anything.

The summer before his first year at the university, Youngman returned to the reservation. The Snake Dance was being held at Shongopovi. For fun, Youngman joined the runners whose race across the desert signaled the start of the ceremony. For the first time in seven years, he wore a leather kilt and moccasins. He had always had stamina. Midway through the race, his moccasins were soaked through with blood. The pain encouraged him. He overtook the local boys at the base of the canyon and sprinted up the narrow trail to win.

The Snake Clan was about to award Youngman the prize when they were stopped by a priest of the Fire Clan.

"This boy is not Hopi. Give the prize to a Hopi. Otherwise, all my clan will leave." The priest was Abner.

"I am Hopi and I won," Youngman protested.

"You are empty. I see inside you and nothing is there. This prize is only for real people."

Humiliated, Youngman returned to Albuquerque, to college. But college was not what he'd expected. In most subjects he was stupefyingly ignorant even for an Indian. Of history, literature, science, or social studies, he knew next to nothing. Worse, he came to the fast dead end of his talent. As long as he painted the desert, however fraudulently, the images came easily. Faced with anything else, even an elementary life class, he revealed himself as a complete incompetent. It was as if he knew a single song with a single variation and otherwise was dumb. But there were a number of ways to take out his frustration. The university had other Indians, mostly Navajos who regarded a Hopi as inferior. Youngman picked fights with Navajo gangs, with white football players, with just about anybody. After a single year of failing grades, he was drafted. After one year in the Army, he was courtmartialed and put in the stockade at Leavenworth, where he served the next six years of his life.

At the age of twenty-seven, Youngman was released and went to Los Angeles. He joined the Mexicans working as Indian extras in films, mixed colors for paint stores, and delivered cars for Hertz. One morning, delivering a rented Continental to Burbank, he was driving through the canyons that segment L.A. into an archipelago of concrete islands. Pulling off the freeway, he left the car to walk into the canyon, which had the color and texture of crumpled brown paper. Sitting still, he watched the shadows slide like cats over the hills.

Day cats that leisurely stretched and curled on the warm earth. And still he sat. Towards sunset, thousands of fire-control sprinklers fanned the parched walls of the canyon with water bought and diverted from the rivers of Arizona. Round as marbles, the water rolled through the air and shattered in the last rays of the sun. One drop after another, million after million, exploding unheard against the moans of the freeway. Water that fell as rain in the Rockies, that flowed as the Colorado River through the Grand Canyon, heading for the desert but rerouted to a sprinkler system. He laughed until he nearly cried.

Youngman delivered the car ten hours late, was fired and, the following morning, returned to the reservation, not much better off than when he'd left.

His first year back he spent relearning how to live. He taught himself again his own first language, which dry holes would yield water to a digging stick, how to mend clothes with a bone needle and to tell the difference between the tracks of a running deer and an unwary one.

At the end of the year, a pick-up truck of old men pulled into his camp.

"You're still here," they said. "We expected you to be gone long ago."

"I'm still here."

"Are you going to stay?"

"Yes."

"Then we will have to do something about you. You're a troubled person. Never at rest. We can't tell you to leave because we know our obligations. So we are going to put you to work. From now on you're a deputy. You go up to Hotevilla tomorrow and sign up. Maybe, someday, we can get some good out of you."

The old chiefs got back into their pick-up and left.

That was two years ago. Being deputy consisted largely of disarming drunks and making sure no tourists brought cameras into the pueblos when dances were held. Youngman had all the time he wanted to escape into the wilderness. He stayed out of trouble because he had the obligation to uphold the law. The old chiefs weren't so dumb.

Youngman downshifted and climbed the jeep through a copse of junipers onto a dirt road. The Momoa ranch was in the hills above Dinnebito Wash. As the road wound its way up, the temperature dropped. Scrub gave way to more junipers, oaks, and piñon trees. In the hills was water, and water was wealth.

"You finally come," Joseph Momoa welcomed the deputy. "Where the hell you been?"

Joe Momoa and his family had five thousand acres of timber and grassland that included two springs and pasturage for five hundred cattle and seven hundred sheep. His house was paneled in redwood and sat under a television aerial as large as a radar dish. The barn had been converted into a six-car garage and game room. Joe himself had been converted into a prosperous Mormon, along with his wife and his sons Joe Jr. and Ben. The Momoa men were alike in their aggressive bulk, flannel shirts, and flashy Acme boots. Joe drove an air-conditioned pick-up. His sons hot-dogged it on candy-colored motorcycles. Among Hopis, they were Rockefellers.

"What have you got to show me?" Youngman asked.

"You'll see."

Joe led the way on a sloping path under piñon branches. Bastard doesn't even walk like an Indian any more, Youngman thought with a sense of irony. For more years than he cared to dwell on, he hadn't walked like an Indian himself.

"Piñon nuts oughtta bring in $10,000 this year," Joe said automatically.

"How much in pines?"

Joe shot a scowl over his shoulder. Pines grew above

27

the Momoa spread and every year hundreds of the trees were trucked out secretly and illegally.

"That's your problem," Joe Jr. said, one step behind Youngman.

They descended to a meadow of corrals and pens. Youngman could see sheep milling in their area. Cattle were lined up at their trough. The dogs on guard cowered at the sight of the Momoas.

"Now, you take a look at that." Joe pointed to the middle corral.

At first, Youngman thought the corral was empty, but as he came through the gate he saw three quarter-horses lying on their sides. Their eyes were open and rolling. One struggled to its knees and Youngman could see that what first appeared to be a dark blanket over its back was caked blood and flies.

"Get a horse blanket," he ordered Ben Momoa.

"Pa?" Ben took a step back.

"Do what he says." Joe took a blanket from the top rail of the corral and threw it to his son.

The kneeling horse lolled its head in the manner of an animal drugged by locoweed. Flies heavy with blood bounced into the air as Ben waved the blanket at them. Youngman brushed the flies away from his face.

"What the hell happened?" he asked.

"You tell us," Joe said.

The withers and haunches of the horse looked as if they had been shredded by a straight razor wielded by a madman. Youngman patted the horse's head, ran his hand down the mane and stopped short. From neck to tail the horse's back was pink flesh, dry blood and hanging strips of skin. The cuts weren't deep.

"Keep waving that," Youngman told Ben.

"I'm gettin' sick."

Not deep, more like gouges from a V-shaped leather punch. And there were more than Youngman could count. Some blood had dried in streaks down the

28

horse's legs and belly, but the horse had lost a lot more blood than that. The animal was groggy, but not in apparent pain. Youngman checked the tail. It was brown with dried blood; it should have been totally matted.

"Well?" Joe demanded.

Youngman looked at the horse's hooves. They were smooth, not the way they'd be if the horse had struck out at anything. Youngman walked over to the other horses. They were in worse shape. The flies on them formed moving, buzzing hunchbacks. He examined their hooves, too. They were as smooth as marble, but the horses were dying from loss of blood. Three horses, half their skin flayed off, that didn't fight back.

"I don't know," Youngman said.

He took a deep breath, stepping away from the mutilated horses. They didn't even try to swat at the flies. Youngman scanned the ground.

"Ever let your dogs in here?"

"With horses? Never."

Youngman could see nothing but hoof marks in the dirt. No deep ones, nothing suggesting excitement, nothing suggesting that anything but horses had been in the corral.

"Found the horses like this this morning?"

"Right."

Youngman looked up at the clear blue sky. Eagles? Ridiculous. As his eyes dropped, he noticed something he should have seen before. Where blood stained the ground were wider, blacker stains. He picked up some of it between his fingers. It was sticky and smelled of ammonia.

"Jesus." He wiped his fingers on clean dirt. "Well, I can't figure it. Any of it."

"Coyotes," Joe said firmly.

"Coyotes? Your sheep, maybe. Or a calf. Not horses, no way. You'd've heard your dogs. The whole corral'd

29

be torn up. There'd be tracks. No coyote bites like that."

"Then a cat," Joe insisted.

"No."

"Then what?"

"I told you I don't know."

"There's nothing left, damn it. I lost three horses, I'm going' to have to shoot 'em. This is $600 in quarter-horse ripped up here an' I want some action. I want you to start up a hunt an' I don't mean some half-assed trackin'. A real hunt. The Navajos have a helicopter. You get it an' we'll go over these hills an' shoot every coyote an' cat we see."

"You're not going to get the animal that attacked your horses that way," Youngman answered.

"I say I will, an' even if I don't we'll clean up these hills the way they should of been a long time ago."

"Look, I know how you feel about losing some horses."

"The hell you do, Duran. You don't have a horse to your name. Now you get on the stick an' fix up a heli-copter for my boys an' me. We got the rifles. Lots of 'em."

Youngman could see it. A helicopter over Dinnebito Wash, with the Momoa boys blasting away like machine gunners at anything that moved. Wouldn't they have a good time.

The kneeling horse slumped onto its side. Flies set-tled on it in thick spirals.

"No Navajos, no helicopter," Youngman said.

"Tribal council meets in two weeks." Joe's face red-dened. "I'll tell 'em about your drinkin'. I can smell it on you."

"Get a vet's report on the horses." Youngman walked away. "If he says a cat did this, or a coyote, we'll talk about it again."

"Junior!" Joe yelled.

30

Joe Jr. stepped in Youngman's way. He had forty pounds on Youngman, but after a moment's glare Joe Jr. swallowed it and moved aside.

"What we need here is a real deputy," Joe Momoa shouted after Youngman, "not a bum. Real deputies like the Navajos have. An' I know you, Duran. You're not even a real Hopi."

At the house, Youngman got into his jeep. Instead of taking the road down the way he'd come, he drove higher into the hills. Without much effort he put the Momoa family out of his mind, but the sight of the horses lingered. There were mountain lions in the hills. The heights were their refuge. The cats were running away from man, not towards him.

Piñon trees and junipers fell away and in their place stood forests of Chihuahua pines, then Ponderosa pine as straight as the teeth of a comb and thickets of alder. The air developed a cold edge.

Momoa was right in a way. Properly speaking, Youngman wasn't Hopi, he was Tewa Pueblo. The Tewas were the tribe that had driven the Spanish out of New Mexico. Two hundred years ago, when the peaceful Hopis were being overrun by Navajos and Apaches, the Hopis asked the Tewas to come and fight the Hopis' war. The Tewas came, and fought, and stayed. The name of the Tewa hero was Popay. Flea. The same as Youngman's.

By the time Youngman reached the shoulders of the hills, dusk was filling in the wash. The desert was a faint purple. Sun still hit the tops of the hills and would for another hour. Youngman replaced his boots with moccasins Abner had made for him. He gathered his rifle and bedroll and hiked for twenty minutes until he came to a stream which he followed to a spring, where he lay down on a moss-covered rock and dipped his face in the water.

As he lifted his head, he saw a rabbit watching him

31

from under a pine branch. Youngman's hand slipped into his rifle sheath. He could have the rabbit for supper and take the legs to Abner in the morning. The rabbit brushed a forepaw across its whiskers. With his elbow on the rifle stock, Youngman levered a bullet into the breech. He slid the rifle out. The rabbit hopped forward, a perfect target against a green background. Water rolled down Youngman's face, off his chin. Abner already had a rabbit, it occurred to Youngman, and he wasn't so hungry himself.

"Scat!"

After a supper of Monterey Jack and tortilla, Youngman draped his roll over his back to keep warm. The stars overhead were sharp and hard. Once, he swung a flashlight beam around the stream to catch the eyeshines of the nocturnal animals congregating there. Spider eyes were silver, toad eyes were red. Moving, they made tiny trails of lightning.

Youngman hadn't been forced to stay in the Army; Hopis could choose conscientious objector status. But he stayed and screening tests showed he had a highly developed sense of spatial relationships, so he was upped to sergeant, trained to read aerial photographs through three-dimensional viewers, and shipped to Andersen Air Force Base in Guam. Every day, and every night, three-plane squadrons of eight-engine B-52's flew off Guam to North Vietnam, each plane carrying twenty tons of bombs. Their targets were picked from photographs taken by reconnaissance U-2's shuttling back and forth from Thailand and Guam. Day photos could be transformed into maps with code numbers and coordinates. Night photos were infrared puzzles and no one was better than Youngman at deciphering the mottled reds, greens, and blues that signified the heat of human activity, the cool of forest canopies, and the chill of water at night. The enemy could burn refuse, or hose down power stations. Youngman was never fooled, and the long-distance rain that he sent out was always accurate. It was a fascination to him, a game. A year into his tour he received his first service decoration and a rest-and-recreation leave in Bangkok, where he was offered Vietnamese finger necklaces and scalps at reasonable prices. And a purse of private parts sewn together.

That night in Bangkok, while Youngman slept between two whores, he heard his father laughing. So that was the joke, Youngman thought. That was the joke all along. Joe waving a wooden penis. Dancing backward, one leg over the mesa edge. The finger necklace. Standing on his hands. The bombers easing their weight from the runway. The wrinkled purse. The beautiful maps of fire. The deer rifle in the mouth. People liked to kill each other. That was funny.

"No." Youngman sat up between the whores.

He returned to Guam and, a month later, was court-martialed for deliberately misreading recon photos and sending night raids of B-52's to bomb the China Sea. Youngman's answer was that he'd decided to take the war seriously, and he didn't feel like making war any more. He could have gotten twenty years, but bombers habitually dropped their loads into the sea either because a raid had been aborted or, just as often, because a pilot was near the end of his six-month tour. Also, Youngman's unusual assignment from the Army to Guam muddied the jurisdiction of the court. He got two years.

At the start, it wasn't so bad. There were Indians at Leavenworth Stockade; he educated himself through the library and he had a soft job in the photographer's studio until, with a month left in Youngman's sentence, a guard emptied a water pistol full of urine on him. It was only a routine joke by a bored prison guard, but Youngman tore the slicer off a photo cropper and cut the guard's arm to the bone. When Youngman came out of the prison stockade a month later, he received two more years to serve, the first quarter in solitary, a close, unlit cell painted black. Towards the end of his second sentence, when Youngman was on a roadgrading crew, one of the other Indians bolted, idiotically since there was nothing to run to except miles of flat, freshly turned Kansas prairie. As the guard in charge of the crew raised his shotgun to fire, Youngman knocked him down and said he would bring the escaping man back. Youngman was gaining on his friend when he was cut down from the back by two loads of 30-30 pellets. He spent two months in the hospital, and received two more years. From then on, the guards left him alone and he made no more friends.

His first winter back on the reservation, he happened by Abner's garage. The Fire Clan priest had long been run off the mesa as a witch, but he recognized Youngman.

"Your car broke down someplace?" Abner stepped out of the garage wrapped in a blanket.

"Haven't got a car." Youngman set his backpack down. There was a rain barrel by the oil drums. He cracked the ice on the top to scoop up a drink.

"Long walk to the mesa."

"Not going to the mesa," Youngman answered.

"Well, there's no place to stay out here," Abner said belligerently.

"There's everyplace to stay out here."

The old man put his back to the chilled sun to see his visitor better.

"You with the Bureau or the companies now, which?"

"With no one."

"Then what are you doing?"

"Walking." Youngman turned to swing his pack to his shoulder. "Just walking. Okay?"

"Wait," Abner stopped Youngman from leaving. "Sit a second."

34

Youngman shrugged and squatted, keeping the pack balanced on his shoulder. Abner squatted facing him. After a couple of minutes, Youngman let his eyes slide from Abner's and studied the terrain, which at first seemed as flat as a drumhead and only with patience yielded the shadow of leafless bushes and the faults of arroyos. When he finally looked back at Abner the old man was grinning.

"I said a while ago you were empty inside," Abner told him. "I see now that you are real, a full person."

"So?"

"So, I got some wine inside."

From then on, Abner said, they were friends.

In the hills above Dinnebito Wash Youngman lay down and let night sounds fill his head. He fell asleep watching a star called Hotomkam travel west.

While the sun had been setting, a baby was born. Blind and hairless, it fell into a cradle formed by the membrane between its mother's legs. Instinctively, it chirped through milk teeth while its mother spread her baby's wings and sniffed scent glands that would distinguish it from all other infants in the dark. Only then did she allow it to climb to a waiting nipple. As it fed, she watched with bright eyes and oversized ears as the rest of the colony stirred from their torpor. Life was spreading. In the next niche, a male wrapped his wings around a female, his stomach to her back and his teeth dug into the nape of her neck, copulating. The female's own weight locked the tendons of her toes into a grip on the cave roof that even death could not release. Nearby, two males fought, screaming and drumming their wings against the roof. They circled each other, hair stiff around their jowls, until they rushed together, using their wings as clubs. One fight set off others, circles of tension that grew as daylight faded. The large members of the colony, the females, looked on with mild interest.

35

The mating couple disengaged, the male to join other males, the female to preen. A week-old baby unfolded stubby wings and chattered. The great colony's mating, fighting, and births coincided until the shaft of light that fell through the cave roof narrowed to a thin stream and a different, greater need took hold. Others of their order might seek the twilight; these would wait for the dark. In the manner of upside-down spiders, wings mantled, padded claws reaching for rock, all the hundreds of adults moved sideways or backwards towards the ebbing light at the sinkhole. Squat faces fringed with whiskers concentrated on the mark of a dissolving day. As that mark faded, a ten-year-old female unfurled her wings and flew upward. One after another, the rest followed, in seconds more than a thousand streaming up through the sinkhole, climbing and trumpeting cries that directed them to their proper position in the flight. Biologically, they were miracles of evolution. Fourteen-inch wings, their membranes five times more sheer than surgical gloves, propelled them as fast as swallows. Downy fur, gray on the back and brown in front, cut wind resistance. Color-blind eyes magnified the light of emerging stars so that the canyon glowed for them and, ahead, the desert was brushed with silver. They drifted above the canyon ridge like a cloud but as they reached the desert they flew ever lower, until they were a tide flowing a bare three feet above the desert floor. In front and around them spread a net of silent cries and echoes that returned to large, tender ears marked by a separate tragus. Each bat flew so close to its companions that their tide seemed a solid mass, and yet the tide flowed unchecked through cactus and brush. The terrain was new to the bats but not altogether different from their Mexican home. Hungry, their flattened spade-shaped noses soaked up the animal smells on the night wind. A stream of moths approached the bats, scattered and escaped. The bats swung into the wind, where smells were rich and traveled far. A nighthawk following the moths changed its course, abruptly wheeling upward and away. Unlike birds, the bats couldn't soar. They only flew and they flew only for the Food, their wings beating air fourteen times a second in a steady, purposeful rhythm until the warm smell they sought tinged the air. Minute particles of sweat and plasma transferred from the air to the folds of their nostrils. The tide swung again and the all-but-silent screams increased in urgency. A thousand mouths opened, revealing the distinctive chin and long canines and, unlike teeth of any other bat or animal in Creation, incisors which were as curved and sharp as blades. Biologists called the bats Desmondontidae, a name suggesting those teeth and despair. Vampires.

CHAPTER TWO

The morning sun warmed Abner's shed, a dirty-white Public Health Service van, and five tourists who anxiously watched Youngman's jeep drive up. Youngman put most tourists in two categories. Soul-toters, who tended to be young, scruffy, and desperate to "get into" Indian religion. And camera-toters, who were older, cleaner, and only desperate to get back to air conditioning. The three women and two men beside the van were definitely of the second category, although a little bit better dressed than most, in expensive casual outfits. One of the men had been sick down the front of his pastel shirt. Youngman got out of his jeep. He didn't see Abner.

When he asked if he could be of any help, one of the women put her hand over her mouth.

"Abner's giving you trouble?" Youngman tried a smile on her. "Don't pay him any mind, he's that way with everyone."

"No, he's . . .," The man with the spoiled shirt pointed towards the shed. "God help him."

By now, Youngman wasn't listening. He ran around the van, past the creosote bushes with their rusting trucks, and into the shed.

The doorway and the ground around it where the rabbit had been killed were splattered with blood. A trail of blood went around the sand painting and through the ring of red sand to the drawing of the caped

38

man, where the blood painted in a head around the mouth and crying eyes. At the figure's right hand, the red border was broken, swept aside and marked by a prayer stick decorated by shrike feathers. Another prayer stick pinned a cigarette pack Youngman had thrown away the day before into the figure of the coyote. And in the center of the painting, sprawled over the double serpentine, lay Abner, dead, still in his kilt, wearing a mask of raw rabbitskin. His own skin, from his feet to the crown of his head, was sliced away so completely that bone showed at his fingers and knees.

Youngman wasn't the only person staring with disgust and awe. Just inside the door was another tourist in a windbreaker, a short man with a confident bearing and a smooth, marbled face. On the other side of the painting was the Health Service nurse, a blonde girl in faded jeans.

"When did you get here?" Youngman asked her.

"Ten minutes ago."

The tourist knelt by Abner. He cleared his throat and took a Bible from inside his windbreaker, but before he could speak Youngman hauled him up by his collar.

"No missionary work here."

"Red or white," the man held up his Bible, "a person deserves a final blessing."

"He was a priest of the Fire Clan," Youngman said.

"Maybe he was Christian as well."

"Not even dead." Youngman turned to the girl. "Did they touch anything?"

"No," she answered angrily. "And they're not missionaries."

"We're with a foundation." The tourist adjusted his jacket. "We only try to help—"

"Same thing." Youngman cut him off. "Why are you here?"

"Miss Dillon volunteered to show us around the reservation and take us to your famous Snake Dance. We arrived a few days early so we thought we'd get some camping in as well. I'm John Franklin." Franklin had an amplified baritone, the kind that carried well in a boardroom. In Abner's shed it was too loud.

"Did you examine the body?" Youngman asked the girl.

"There was nothing I could do for Abner, so I looked for tracks. In case we have a rabid coyote running loose. I didn't know when you were going to be around. That's why we stopped here, so I could ask about you."

"Did you find any tracks?"

"None." Anne Dillon had a tanned, oval face with deep-set eyes. She was almost as good a hunter as Youngman and he knew it well.

"I took a look at the body," Franklin interjected. "The blood looks quite fresh to me. This attack of wild dogs or whatever must have occurred right before we arrived."

With his boot, Youngman nudged Abner's leg.

"He's stiff. About ten hours dead."

Youngman led the way back to the van, where the other missionaries huddled as if the morning weren't already warming up to its regular oven quality.

"Everything is all right," Franklin reassured them. "I believe this is the Deputy Duran that Miss Dillon mentioned."

"What kind of cameras do you have?" Youngman asked.

Franklin had a Nikon and the rest had similar 35mm cameras, except for Mrs. Franklin, a frightened lady with blue-rinsed hair, who held up an SX-70.

"That's what I want. A flash attachment, too, if you have it."

Youngman took the Polaroid alone into the shed. He took two pictures of Abner and four pictures of the

40

shed, left them to develop behind the altar on the trunk and returned to the van.

"Thanks." He handed back the camera and $8. "That's for the film and bulbs."

"You don't have to—"

"I think you better go now." He made a cigarette while they got into the van, Anne behind the steering wheel. He watched them drive away until they were out of sight, then he killed the cigarette and went to the shed.

"Damn it, Abner."

Youngman stood for ten minutes, only his eyes moving. He blocked the sound of the wind and stripes of light that came through the walls and, most of all, any memory of the white campers, because Abner had done his best to turn his junkyard garage into a sacred kiva and it was in terms of a kiva that Youngman had to think and see.

In front of the altar was a wooden plaque of bread, raw meat, tobacco, and cornmeal; some of the cornmeal was scattered over the floor. A fire had been built next to the altar. In the ashes, Youngman found the pine needle strings and juniper bark. He dropped the charred bark when he saw the rabbit in a corner of the shed. The rabbit was flayed but not dressed, and the throat was slit for the blood to drain out alive, paint for Abner's god.

The truth was, the deputy understood the rabbit and the painting little better than Franklin had. Youngman had been away from the reservation too long and part of him, no matter how long he stayed now, would always be white. He'd lost the thread. He didn't believe in anything, let alone the gods of a medicine man who pumped gas. All he knew was that Abner said he was going to end the world.

He squatted by Abner and lifted the mask. Abner's mouth gaped full with clotted datura. If death was gruesome, Abner didn't know; or he had known and been prepared. Anyway, he couldn't have felt a thing.

"Uncle," Youngman asked, "what are you up to? What the hell are you doing?"

Abner gazed up at his friend, all eyes and teeth. The skin that wasn't sliced was punctured by small claw marks. Despite rigor mortis, some of the wounds were still damp.

Sniffing, Youngman recoiled. The same smell as in Joe Momoa's corral. Around Abner's body, the serpentine was stained with ammoniac pitch.

Abner's eyes were dry. Relaxed pupils had folded into slits. Goat eyes.

"I don't get it, Abner. I don't know what or why. You don't want to help me?"

Abner's teeth, like most reservation Indians', were thin posts corrupted by decay. The jaw held a stiff grin.

"Okay, uncle." Youngman closed the eyes.

He wrapped the body in a sheet and carried it to the back of the jeep. He returned to the shed for the photographs. Proper police procedure preserved the site of any suspicious death. For whom and for what, he asked himself. He was about as much police as there was, unless Arizona troopers were called in. For a dead Indian, they'd come in one week, maybe two. It wasn't a murder. There were animals in the desert. Things happened.

The sand painting was beautiful, complete and beautiful and totally mysterious. From where Youngman had moved Abner, in the middle of the rank stain, was the sprawled negative silhouette of a body.

"Son of a bitch." Youngman kicked the sand painting. Red grains, blue grains, yellow and white sprayed the walls. When the ground looked like a desecrated work of art, he began kicking the black outline of the silhouette. Ammoniac pitch stuck to his boots. He picked up loose sand and poured it over the outline. The outline faded, but showed through the sand. He

42

looked up. A desert skink was watching him from an orange crate shelf on the wall. Fly wings protruded from the lizard's jaws. It jumped as Youngman ripped the shelf from the wall. He broke the shelf over his knee, dropped the halves onto the stained floor, and lit a match. And snuffed it between his fingers. Wasn't going to do any good to burn the place down.

"Dead. Just plain dead."

As Youngman came out of the shed, he heard the coughing of thunder north from the mesa. A ladder of dark clouds climbed into the sky. Within the clouds, lightning exploded like bombs. A wind scurried ahead of the storm.

The deputy put his jeep in gear and pulled out toward the clouds. A ball of sagebrush bounced by in the opposite direction.

The faces you could see in clouds, Youngman thought. Sad faces with gray and blue cheeks. Puffed up. Eyes closed and ready to cry. Just water, no atomic rain. No end of the world.

"You blew it," he said to the man in the sheet. "You didn't end the world, only yourself. A man your age ought to know the difference."

The thunderheads kept climbing. The hot air of the desert was a wall that the clouds had to scale, until there were two walls, one warm and invisible and the other a cool, boiling blue. The invisible wall retreated, the dark one advanced, casting twenty miles before it an opalescent shadow.

Beneath the feet of the clouds was a washboard road, a clapboard store, an outdoor freezer, and a mud-and-log hogan. Gilboa was the name of the place. It wasn't a town any more. The U.S. Postal Service no longer delivered mail; the half dozen inhabitants of Gilboa had to go to Shongopovi on the mesa for letters. Maps ignored it, as did the utilities and telephone companies. For that matter, the washboard road vanished at either end about ten miles out, erased by wind and sand.

Fat globules of water rode on the wind. The real storm hadn't begun yet. Youngman stopped in front of the hogan, picked up Abner in his arms, and went inside. After he laid the dead man out on the floor, he reached up and twisted a hanging light bulb.

The deputy's office consisted of a roll-top desk and chair. Two-way radio. A metal locker for his gun shells, two bottles of Jim Beam, plastic bag of marijuana, and underwear. Dirt, a lot of dirt because he was away from his office for weeks at a time. Two maps—one of the reservation, another an Arizona State Highway map—were pinned to the wall. They rustled from the breeze Youngman let in to air the hogan out.

He slid up the desk's ribbed top and took a report form out of one of the pigeonholes. The forms were bought surplus and the rubber-stamped heading "Phoenix Police Department" was crossed out in pencil. He found a leaky ballpoint in another pigeonhole.

NAME—Abner Tasupi. OCCUPATION—garage owner. D.O.B.—unknown. RACE-SEX—Indian male. CRIME—death. Under MODUS OPERANDI, Youngman entered "attack of undetermined animal, possibly rabid." Then he went out to his jeep.

Dust devils wove back and forth over Gilboa's road. A hundred yards away and across the road, lightning illuminated Selwyn's Trading Post. The store was a tombstone of past aspirations. From the clapboard wall a peeling sign promised "Tourist Rooms-Gas-Candy-Dry Goods-Indian Curios." The tin Coke sign had a broken thermometer. The twin screen doors were patched with electrical tape.

The front of the store carried flour, pinto beans, cheese, blankets and cloth, axe and hoe heads, buck knives and ammo. An eyeless elk was mounted over the counter. Under the counter were pawned jewelry and

44

whiskey in pints. Selwyn was in the rear room with John Franklin and the other whites. An old Hopi woman and four half-breed girls were on the floor, pots and ropes of clay at their feet. Anne was away in her van, searching for firewood before the rain hit.

Selwyn had once been a Quaker missionary. He wore his white hair long, touching the velour shirt which draped open over his gut. A turquoise necklace nestled in the hair of his chest.

"You don't have to tell me these people need help. Next you're going to tell me the desert is dry. I know! Excuse me." Selwyn burped against the back of his hand. "Look, I've dedicated my life to these Indians. Speaking absolutely frankly, I personally have poured love and blood over them."

"That's very admirable." Mrs. Franklin launched a smile into Selwyn's alcoholic haze.

"What do I get in return? A spit in the eye. Look, you folks can hallelujah lizards and get more gratitude. Now I told the Bureau people when they came through a dozen year ago or so, throw your money away on going to the moon. I was willing to testify as an expert. Pardon." He frowned at a piece of tobacco he picked from his tongue because he couldn't remember when he'd smoked last. "There wouldn't be a Gilboa if it wasn't for me. Did you know that? It's my generator provides the power here, not just for me but for that freezer they throw their goddamn deer in and for that bum they have for a deputy. You see it? They hate me 'cause I help them. I sell them food on credit. They hate me more for that. And this is the best example of all. These stupid women are making pots. Pots! I mean, every trading post in Navajo country has women in the back making blankets. Now blankets sell, damn it, for $2,000, $3,000 a rug. My luck, all these savages know how to make is pots. For Christ's sake," he rubbed his eyes, "hasn't anyone got a fag?"

When there was no answer, he opened his eyes and followed his visitors' gaze to the deputy leaning in the doorway.

"Good." The trading post owner left the missionaries for Youngman. "You always have a fag."

Youngman had heard all Selwyn's complaints many times. The "stupid" women making pots were Selwyn's wife and daughters.

"Sure." He tapped out a cigarette for Selwyn. Youngman could see Franklin's group bracing for a fight. Incredible. Like his store, Selwyn was a wreck in the desert, barely anchored enough in the sand not to roll into an arroyo or whatever else could serve as a gutter. Who would tolerate any white so collapsed except Indians? "There you go." Youngman held a match to the shaking cigarette.

"Thanks," Selwyn muttered. "These biblethumpers they send out now can give hemorrhoids to your ears."

"That so?"

"Telling me about Indians, for Christ's sake. Stick around. They'll get their asses out of here and we'll have a taste."

Selwyn's wife giggled and Franklin cleared his throat because Selwyn's voice had strayed to normal speaking level.

"We'd intended to buy some supplies for our campout," Franklin said. "With our change in schedule, we didn't have a chance to in Flagstaff."

"I gotta go," Youngman told Selwyn. "But I need some cornmeal, rope, a white sack."

"Who died?"

"Abner."

"Shit, you don't say."

"That was that Indian gentleman we saw this morning?" Franklin asked and was ignored.

"You're not going to give him a regular funeral, are you?" Selwyn asked Youngman.

46

"Why not?" Franklin was outraged.

"Because he was a goddamn witch, that's why!" Selwyn wheeled on Franklin.

"You don't believe in that, surely."

"Believe? Brother Franklin, you don't know where the hell you are, do you? Hey, honey," Selwyn shouted to his wife, "any witches out here?"

The woman dropped her giggling. She folded her hands on her lap and studied her pots.

"Witches?" Selwyn laughed. "Well, the saints and apostles stop at the reservation line. What do you think this place is fit for? Indians, drunks, bums. Jesus, I was full of 'thees and thous' and the Spirit when I came out here forty years ago. Bet I was just as big an asshole as you, Brother. That's hard to believe, too. Full of the Word, I was. Then one day, I found some of my congregation axing up an old woman. That was something. 'Why are thee killing this woman?' I ask. Almost got myself axed trying to stop them. Well, the reason they did her in was because the night before she'd turned herself into a wolf and killed a man."

"You didn't believe them."

"Of course not. I'm not one of these ignorant savages. On the other hand, well, I stay away from haunted pueblos, you know, and when the Indians ax up a witch, which they do every year or so, I keep my mouth shut." Selwyn paused. "You people keep giving me these pathetic looks. Don't look at me, look around you. You give yourself some eyestrain trying to see to the end of that sand and you go get yourself lost in those canyons. While you're there, you ask yourself what kind of gods live in a place like that."

"We aren't totally unenlightened persons," one of the other campers spoke up mildly. "Every society believes in a different Creator. Whatever names they give Him, the Creator is always much the same throughout the world."

"Yeah? You mean the Skeleton Man."

"Who?"

"Skeleton Man. Masaw. You call him what you want. Pluto. Satan. I know a man," Selwyn's eyes glistened like yellowed china, "thinks this is hell on earth right here. Maybe you'll come to think so, too."

"Deputy, if this man we found this morning was a so-called witch," Franklin said, "is there any possibility that he was killed?"

"Not Abner," Selwyn answered for Youngman. "He was too big a witch. Sure, they'd chase him off the mesa. But they'd no sooner touch him than cut off their own hands. He'd come right out of the grave for them. Come like a wolf, or a—"

"The man you found," Youngman interrupted, "was an old hermit. That's all. Nobody killed him, and if I hear any rumors that someone did I'll know where those rumors started. Right, Selwyn?" He gripped the store owner above the elbow. "Excuse us, please."

Youngman pulled Selwyn into the front room.

"You get yourself something to drink, old man."

"I talk too much when I'm sober."

"You're not sober, you're just not drunk enough. You know better than to start babbling about witches. 'Come out of his grave . . .' Jesus." He found a pint under the counter, unscrewed the top and poured whiskey into Selwyn's mouth. A gust of wind made the screen doors slap open. Liquor rolled down the side of Selwyn's chin as he started.

"Just the wind," Youngman said.

"He could."

"Then you say yourself a prayer tonight."

"He could do a lot of things."

"Not any more."

Lightning jigsawed over Gilboa. As a bolt hit the outdoor freezer, the inside of the store turned silver, then black from the backflow of electricity. The generator

48

started again. The lights inside the store cast a waxy glow. Youngman hurried to pick up the goods he'd come for.

"Put it on my bill."

"What else?" Selwyn was feeling better. "Maybe I can still get one of those sob sisters in there to buy a pot."

Like sails, the clouds split. In half an hour, they'd drop three inches of water, a quarter of the year's total rainfall, enough to turn arroyos into rapids and break open the armored seeds of smoke trees, ironwood and blue paloverde. Gilboa's road turned into rutted mud and waves spewed from the jeep's tires as Youngman drove the hundred yards to his hogan.

A Land Rover was parked in front of the office. He had to run through the mud before putting his shoulder to the door.

Abner was still lying in the corner but the sheet was pulled back and kneeling over the exposed body was another white man.

"You missionaries don't give up easy." Youngman shut the door.

The white looked up. He was Youngman's age, deeply tanned, with close-cut red hair, wide blue eyes, wide smile, dressed in rough khakis and big, so big that the body at his feet looked like a doll. His hands were covered by rubber gloves and, instead of a Bible, they held a scalpel and a glassine envelope.

"Won't be a minute." The voice was modestly official.

"You won't be a second. Stand up."

Reluctantly, the visitor did as he was told, stooping to prevent his head from touching the ceiling. He rolled the glove off his right hand and held it out to Youngman.

"I apologize for what this must look like. My name's Hayden Paine." He held his hand out for ten seconds before dropping it. "Well. Just give me a chance to clean up and I'll explain everything."

"If I were you, I'd start talking now."

Paine smiled, totally at ease despite his bloody gloves, the closeness of the hogan, and the drumming of the rain.

"I'm stopping at all the law enforcement and health offices on the reservation. This will satisfy you, I believe." He handed Youngman a folded paper. While Youngman read it, Paine crouched by an aluminum case. He removed his second glove and dropped both into a plastic bag, washed his hands with alcohol and cotton, and taped the glassine packet.

"To Whom It May Concern," Youngman read the letter, "Mr. Hayden Paine is conducting a medical survey that may be of great benefit to our nation. He has full authority to travel the reservation, and to call on the assistance of all officers of the reservation in conjunction with his survey." The letterhead had an embossed seal of a sun, mountains, and crossed sheaves of corn. It was signed by "Walker Chee, Chairman of the Navajo Tribal Council."

"I have more identification if you want it." Paine locked his case.

"I don't want it. You're on the wrong reservation."

"This is Hopi territory, I know, but—"

"You haven't explained anything yet. You were desecrating a body when I came in and you still haven't told me why."

"The medical survey, as explained in—"

"There's no explanation in the letter. What kind of survey?"

Paine showed no more than a slight social embarrassment. He took the letter back.

"It's very technical, Sheriff."

"Deputy."

"Deputy. I'm doing a serologic study of antibodies.

50

By identifying antibodies in the blood samples of the local population, I'll be able to identify diseases endemic to this area. Some diseases can't be found any other way. It's a complicated process and if I tried to explain it further, I doubt you'd understand. No layman would," Paine added quickly. "All I can say is that this kind of study is necessary to raise the level of health here. I've been having the most trouble getting samples from the older people on the reservation and when I saw the body here I took the opportunity. I meant no discourtesy to the dead man or to you, believe me. If anything, I need your help."

Paine's voice had risen to a shout as the drumming of the rain increased in volume, punctuated by kicks of thunder. Paine waited impatiently for the din to fade. Youngman liked the rain; anyone who lived in a desert would. More than that, the downpour forced Paine to be quiet. It forced him to drink his own rain of words. To Indians, words were a white weapon. Indians always found it interesting to watch a white try to be silent. Youngman folded his arms and waited. Silence could be informative.

Paine maintained a broad smile. He was about thirty. His tan was a veneer marred only by a smudge of lost sleep around the eyes. A minute passed under the hard rain.

Paine sighed. He had a big chest and heavy arms, light copper hairs down to the wrists, which were marked by curved scars. A bolt hit outside, probably on the Land Rover, Youngman thought. Paine only glanced aside at the crash. Confident and self-controlled. The storm continued to work to its climax. It wasn't so much rain that opened desert seeds as violence. Paine's smile had relaxed to amusement.

The blue eyes were clear as pools, untroubled and unruffled. Totally neutral. There was no pigment in blue eyes, Youngman remembered. It was all refraction.

Dead eyes, Abner called them. Used to call them. Paine held the mutual gaze patiently, still amused. Water ran under the floor boards of the hogan. Five more minutes passed while lightning concentrated on the meager elevation of Selwyn's store.

Selwyn's generator faltered. The bulb in the hogan dimmed to the power of a cigarette, and at that level slowly pulsed with each feeble beat of the gas-powered generator. Youngman watched Paine's eyes slide towards the body. Paine's hands curled into fists and uncurled. The eyes slid back. Youngman saw the blue eyes shadow and the pupils narrow to points. He picked up his rifle. The bulb faded to a single orange filament.

Youngman reached into Paine's shirt pocket and took out the glassine envelope. Paine's hand clamped around the deputy's wrist.

"I need it!" Paine shouted.

The muzzle of Youngman's rifle burrowed under Paine's jaw. Paine rocked slightly back, his head against the wall. His fingers let go of Youngman, who screwed the barrel into the jaw.

"You lied," Youngman said in a flat voice. He was sure the other man understood. "I don't know what about, but you lied."

He took two steps back and lowered his aim to the doctor's belt buckle. Paine gestured with his hand and stopped himself at the glint of the hammer's rise.

"You're making a mistake! Deputy, I need that sample! You don't know what you're doing! Please!"

Youngman's foot shoved the aluminum case over the floor.

"Go play with the Navajos. They'll believe anything."

Paine's expression said he couldn't hear Youngman over the thunder, so Youngman opened the hogan door. The storm spilled in. The road outside was a shallow river.

"You could be next," Paine warned. At least, Young-

52

man thought that was what he said because with the door open not even a shout was intelligible. Paine gathered his case and went into the rain, having to stop to unlock the Land Rover. Youngman watched from the hogan doorway and noticed the Health Service van pull in behind his jeep. Why, Youngman asked himself, would anyone lock his car in a place like Gilboa? He waited until the Land Rover moved away, lights on and wipers thrashing the windshield. At a distance of fifty feet, only its rear lights could be seen through the rain.

Anne Dillon threw open the door of the van. Youngman climbed in, as wet as if he'd stood under a shower, and dropped his hat and rifle onto the firewood on the back seat.

The van was better insulated than Youngman's office. A person could talk.

"I see you're still busy promoting tourism." She turned to Youngman. "I'm sorry about Abner."

"So am I."

"But what I came for was an apology."

"I apologize."

"That's not good enough. I finally get these foundation people to come all the way out here from the midwest and the very first thing you do is insult them and embarrass me. Since when are you the guardian of all that's sacred around this place? You made a fool of me. Then you apologize and I'm supposed to forgive you."

"Well, you'll try. You'll try like hell."

Anne's eyes were blue, but rayed with spots of brown. Sometimes, very analytical eyes.

"You know, Youngman, that's an incredibly cruel thing to say. I don't have to love you. I can try like hell to stop doing that."

"What does it matter?" he asked.

"What does that mean?"

"I mean, you've got one more week before you leave the reservation for good and go back to your trust fund

53

and backgammon or whatever rich folks do in Phoenix. I thought we were going to have the week together but it looks like you're busy with your birdwatchers, or missionaries, whoever they are. What is it they do anyway? Give money to the needy? Or only to the romantically needy? Where does their money come from?"

"Some religious groups, mostly corporations."

"Better yet. A romantic tax deduction. That's tops. Speaking as one of the needy, you understand. So do that, have your kicks. Better yet, share your kicks with them. White Goddess of the Hopi, saint of eye salve."

"If we'd had the whole week together, is this what you were going to tell me?"

"What else?"

He watched the rain smashing into the windshield because she was staring at him. It took him a while to notice her eyes welling.

"No," Youngman said. "I wouldn't have said any of that. I'm a jerk, and I'm goddamn jealous."

She pulled him against herself. Her fingers dug into his back and he felt a tear hot on his neck.

"Jealous I accept," Anne whispered. "The rest you can stuff."

"I'll have a whole week to stuff it."

"I wish they hadn't come, now. They're waiting for me."

As they kissed, his hand slipped into her shirt and brushed a breast softly so that its tip hardened against his palm.

"It won't be a whole week with them, just four days," she said.

Anne shifted, stretching out on the seat.

"Maybe I should go with you." Youngman covered her.

"Um, that kind of romantic needy they're not ready for. That's just my hang-up. Can they see from the trading post?"

54

"They can't see a thing."

Anne had come to the reservation two years before, using volunteer paramedical service as her escape from Phoenix and a family fortune that was based on buying desert cheap and selling it dear as test range acreage to the Air Force. Life for the Dillons was the Southwestern dream: Arabian horse shows, golf in Scottsdale, a box at the Sombrero Playhouse, and monogrammed tennis balls from Neiman-Marcus. In Anne's eyes, the dream was a kind of sleeping sickness that infected everyone she knew. This whole class of sleepwalkers lived out their lives seemingly unconscious of Chicano barrios, black slums, and Indian poverty. By the time she was in college she'd diagnosed one peculiar syndrome of this "sleep," the idea prevalent in this privileged class that somehow they were the true natives and that everyone else, particularly the poor of different colors, was an interloper. Hence, Chicanos were more likely to be called Mexicans. Blacks were Nigras. A dead Indian was an interesting item of Western Lore, but a live Indian was a social ill. And it was easy to live out this dream because accepting the rights of these less fortunate groups—especially the land and water rights of the Indians—led inevitably to uncomfortable sensations of guilt. Phoenix did not believe in guilt, it was not part of the lifestyle.

Guilt. Anne worked out of Hotevilla Pueblo on the mesa. Driving a hundred miles at a time throughout the mesa and into the desert to provide antibiotics and basic surgery to outlying pueblos, she had a great deal of time to consider social guilt as a motivation. Early on, she decided it stank. Indians stank, the pueblos stank, and the chronic running sores she dealt with day after day had a tendency to stink. After six months she thought she was ready to quit and trade in her jeans for tennis whites. From nothing less than perversity, she stayed for another six months and curious things happened. Either

55

Indians stopped stinking, or she stopped smelling them. Increasingly she found herself surprised to be treated as a white by white tourists visiting the reservation. And she met Youngman.

Their paths had crossed a number of times before, enough to form an unspoken dislike between them. On this occasion she'd gone to the hill country around Moencopi, an area claimed by both the Hopis and Navajos, to treat a boy bitten by a rabid coyote. Navajo police and Youngman arrived to destroy the animal, which had taken refuge in a storehouse. While the Navajos waited outside the storehouse with their rifles, the Hopi deputy went in with a blanket and a pistol. At the cost of one bite through the blanket, he shot the coyote. For the next four days, Anne treated the boy and the deputy with a series of painful injections in the abdomen. On the very first day she told Youngman he deserved the pain for going into the storehouse instead of waiting. He answered that the family's chickens and rabbit pens were at the top of the storehouse and if the coyote had broken into them half the family's yearly food supply would have been wiped out. She was on hand with medicine, so what did he have to lose? Except pain.

Within a month, she was meeting Youngman regularly at different places on the mesa and in the desert. They reversed the usual order of a relationship, starting with the physical release of sex, and then talking and releasing loneliness. Love, each felt, came in spite of them. Now, with her leaving the Health Service and the reservation, love was nothing less than a burden, the embarrassing souvenir.

She clung to him, holding him inside her. But the storm was fading into squalls. Cold, liquid shadows ran over her arms.

"I've got to go. You can wait another four days, can't you?"

"Selwyn's girls haven't seduced me yet."

"Not for lack of trying. They'd kill me if they had a chance."

"Well, watch out for falling pots." -

"I really have to go." Anne kissed him and pushed him up.

They sat up and pulled their clothes back together. The rain was easing, almost over.

"Who was that you kicked into the street?"

"Nobody. He had some phony story about a study of antibodies in the blood to find diseases."

Anne buttoned the rest of her shirt in silence.

"How do you know it was phony?" She brushed her hair back.

"I just did."

"Youngman, that's exactly the study the Health Service was supposed to do years ago. And you kicked him out? Don't you know how many Hopis I have to treat for pernicious anemia or blood parasites?"

She felt her anger rising, she couldn't help it.

"It was a phony story," Youngman repeated.

"How many go blind every year from venereal disease, or deaf from aural atresia? Why didn't you let me talk to him? He didn't have any accreditation?"

"A letter from Window Rock," Youngman admitted. He didn't mention what Paine was doing to Abner, he didn't want any defense.

"Oh, that was it. He only had a letter from the Navajos and that wasn't good enough for you. Thank you very much. Maybe I would have had a different opinion."

With every word, she felt him withdrawing and shutting her out. What's the use, she thought. Together, they were the perfect example of centrifugal force. Why was she exhausting herself against it? Youngman fumbled in the glove compartment for cigarettes.

"Smoke your own," Anne said.

"Yours are stale."

"So?"

"Might as well smoke them now."

Besides his stubbornness, his habits of poverty also irritated her. In fact, smoking up stale cigarettes was one of his prison traits.

"You don't trust Navajos, you don't trust whites. Are you paranoid? You hate outside help so much, why do you tolerate me?" she asked.

"I love you."

"It's that simple?"

"What could be simpler?"

"Well, I'm leaving this place for good in seven days, Youngman. Are you coming with me?"

"To Phoenix?"

"It doesn't have to be Phoenix. It can be anywhere. Mexico, if you want."

"And what would I do there?"

"You happen to be one of the very few Hopis who could make it off the reservation. You know photography, painting. I have enough money for the two of us until you get started."

"You could stay here, you know."

"I have stayed. I've been the audience for all your battles against the imaginary slights of anyone who tries to help you. Like the way you treated Franklin."

"He's going to help me?" Youngman laughed.

"His foundation represents, among other sources, a number of drug companies. What the Hopi people need is a donation of medical supplies and money for a clinic of your own. I was hoping that the last thing I did before I left was guarantee that donation, but so far I've spent most of the morning apologizing for you."

"Don't!" Youngman's face darkened. "Don't ever apologize for me to those people."

Anne looked out the side window, towards a rainbow that was already fast evaporating. She was more de-

58

pressed than angry. "Those people" were the pahans, Anglos, whites. By some fluke, Youngman didn't include her with her own type. The day would come of course, when he would . . . and she was begging him to follow her off the reservation? How crazy was she?

"Maybe it is just sex," she whispered to herself.

"Maybe." Youngman's hearing was too good.

She was damned if she was going to cry in front of him again, so she found the key and started the engine.

"We'll desert camp for a couple of days and go on to Joe Momoa's to fish. We'll come down to the Snake Dance with the Momoas. I'll see you there."

"Don't go."

"Why not?" Anne rested her hands on the steering wheel.

Youngman didn't know. He'd said it quickly, not as a conclusion of any thought but from a sudden rush of images through his mind. Joe Momoa's horses, a sand painting, Abner's eyes, a stain of black pitch. The smell of that pitch.

"Look," Anne touched Youngman's hand. "When I get back we'll go off for a couple of days alone."

"It's not that."

"Then what?"

Mostly the smell. Once inhaled, it seemed to work into the blood.

"Something Abner said yesterday."

"Oh." She could see them. Two Indians drunk under the sun. "That's it?"

"Why don't you just go to the mesa now and wait for the dance? If they want to see a lot of Indians, that's the place to go."

"They want to go camping." Anne shook her head and put the van into gear. When she said nothing else, Youngman climbed out and shut the door.

He looked through the window. His black hair hung

damp across his forehead. From the driver's seat of the van, he seemed hardly bigger than a boy.

Anne could think of nothing else to say except that he was wrong. He was too bitter, too silent, too lean, too dark. Too Indian.

Youngman watched her drive to Selwyn's and then went back into the hogan.

The dead were supposed to be buried before sundown. Youngman didn't believe in that sort of stuff but Abner did and Abner, after all, was the dead man.

Youngman pulled up a floor board where there was still a pool of water underneath and washed Abner's hands and face. With the white paint from Selwyn's, he decorated Abner's arms and legs with dotted lines and over Abner's left eye drew a half moon, the insignia of a priest. He combed Abner's hair and strung feather fluffs to the hair, wrists, and ankles. He filled the dead man's palms with cornmeal. Luckily, rigor mortis was past because he had to bind the fingers tight around the cornmeal. He rubbed the rest of the cornmeal over Abner's face, which was difficult where the flesh was shredded. With his knife he cut holes into the white cotton sack so that it made a "cloud mask" for Abner's head. Nothing went to waste in the desert, not even the dead; they were obligated to return as rain. After he wrapped Abner in the sheet, he bent and tied the legs into a kneeling position. Abner made a small corpse. Youngman carried him under one arm and a planting stick with the other out to the jeep.

Youngman drove about fifteen miles out of Gilboa until he reached a rise crowned yellow by paloverde trees. There he dug down through two inches of wet soil and three and a half feet of dry sand, laid Abner in the grave in an upright position facing east, and sat down for a smoke.

"Well, uncle, you should have some family here to

say a few words. I guess you're stuck with me. Frankly, I'd rather ask you some questions than give a speech. I sure as hell don't know if you were a good man or not. To tell you the truth, I don't even know how important that is.

"You fool them. Don't come back as a cloud. You come back as a cactus, huh."

Within the eyeholes of the cloud mask Abner's lids were shut. A pink spot appeared on the mask around the cheek. As that spot blossomed, other spots grew. Abner was still bleeding.

"Hey, old man, you're dead," Youngman said.

Not only the mask was turning red, the sheet was as well. Points of rosy red that spread. Youngman didn't have the nerve to lift the mask so he lowered himself into the grave and pulled open the sheet. All the wounds that covered Abner's chest and arms were wet and running. Maybe the ride in the jeep opened the cuts, Youngman told himself. But dead cuts don't bleed. He reached inside the sheet to Abner's wrist, which was wet and cold and had no pulse. Then he saw Abner's hand. It had snapped the string that had closed it and lay open on clots of blood-soaked cornmeal.

As the sun set, an evening wind followed, swaying the branches of the paloverde trees like yellow froth. Youngman filled in the grave and covered it with stones to discourage scavengers. On top of the stones he stood a planting stick, the symbolic ladder from the grave to the spirit world. Wind rattled the stick against the rocks.

"Relax, Abner. Let go of that stick." The stick stilled. "Try being dead for a while. You might prefer it."

Youngman drove the same way back to Gilboa. He stopped once to look behind. By then, the last flush of sunlight was hitting the rise, turning the paloverde trees a brilliant red.

According to the Koran, Jesus created the first bat. During the fast of Ramadan, when no believer may eat from sunrise to sunset, Christ was in the hills outside Jerusalem and couldn't see the western horizon. Taking clay in his hands he made a winged creature into which he blew life. This creature—a bat—flew into a cave from which it emerged each nightfall to flutter around Jesus and tell him of the setting sun.

The ancient Egyptians regarded bats because of their nipples as examples of maternal care. The Chinese character for bat was also used for "happiness," and some South Pacific peoples prized bats as sexual totems.

But in the New World, the bat was god. His Mayan name was Zotzilaha. Whole cities and peoples bore his name and throughout Mexico temples carried his image: a striding man with the wings, face, teeth, and tongue of a bat, holding a severed human head in one hand and a heart in the other. Zotzilaha, the Bat God who controlled fire, was transformed into the Aztec's supreme Sun God, Huitzilopochtli, who demanded sacrificial mounds of human hearts cut out by priests attired in bat-skin capes. In 1519, the year prophesied for the return of a lost White Brother, Cortez arrived in Mexico. Armed with a prophecy, and aided by rebellious tribes, he took Montezuma prisoner. The Spanish chronicled attacks of "bloodsucking" bats, but by then the Aztec Empire had fallen.

Gods die, peoples change, and nature persists. For centuries after Cortez, the vampire bats held sway in the Mexican jungle and in the last twenty years, for no reason discernible to man, had been reported moving steadily north. It was a migration of the night, recorded only by random and unscientific accounts of slaughtered goats, cattle, even people in the Sónora mountains.

Now in a new environment of desert and mesas, the

vampires hunted as they always did, with patience and intelligence. They passed over two flocks of unsheared sheep and a dead rabbit, poisoned and set out for coyotes. Arroyos were dark ribbons in the moonlight. Tiger salamanders stirred in the damp beds of the arroyos, feeding off insects and being fed on by night snakes. The bats slipped untouched by the spines of fifty-foot saguaros. The petals of night-blooming cereus spread milky white.

A different sound mixed with the high-pitched chatter of the bats. It traveled on the breeze from miles away, a nasally plaintive country-and-western song. As one, the thousand bats veered, their own chatter increasing in intensity, the membranes of their powerful wings stroking faster. This certain kind of sound, they knew, meant Man. Man and his animals, conveniently gathered. A lake of life.

Two miles ahead, Isa Loloma, fourteen years old, his arms and back aching from a day of shearing sheep and binding their greasy wool, sat in the cab of a Dodge pick-up sipping from a warm can of orange soda and listening to his transistor radio. The truck had no engine. Its wheel hubs sat on blocks. Its whole purpose was simply to scare away coyotes and that purpose it served very well. Isa's nights were long and lonely.

The night played tricks. Sometimes the Navajo station out of Gallup would fade and in its place would come stations from Houston or Kansas City. Voices would talk to him about steak palaces and local astronauts. Then he only had to lay his hands on the truck's steering wheel and close his eyes to imagine that he was driving his own Eldorado down the freeway of some Anglo city, that he was wearing a custom shirt with mother of pearl snaps and sitting on an alligator skin wallet stuffed with $20 bills.

Tonight, the Gallup transmission droned steadily on. Every Piggly Wiggly Supermarket in Bernalillo County, the voice from the ether said, was pleased to honor food stamps. There was going to be a social dance at the Tuba City Chapter. Sports results were brought courtesy of Massey-Ferguson tractors.

Isa made the soda last. When his eyelids started to grow heavy, he climbed out of the truck and rubbed his legs and ran in place to start his blood moving. Still yawning, he drew his father's old Browning Auto-5 shotgun from the blanket on the cab seat. The sheep were quiet. He'd take one turn around the flock and come back for a nap.

Something fluttered by him. A nighthawk, he thought. The only problem with sheep was during the spring, when coyotes came in for the lambs, or during shearing if the clipping was done badly and cut up the sheep, then the smell of blood would make coyotes bold. But Isa was a good clipper. He left the sheep shorn down to their pink skin without a nick.

He walked for about fifty yards before he became very awake. He could hardly see the sheep, although he heard a constant rustling. The sheep were there, he knew they wouldn't leave the grass. There was that rustling, a busy, papery rustling that came from every direction. He fought a first, childish impulse to run. And then, just a few feet in front of him, he saw the pale blur of a sleeping sheep's head. Baby, he scolded himself.

Strangely, he could make out the legs but not the body of the sheep. He could see the head of another sheep, but not its body either. A wing grazed the boy's long hair, fanning his cheek. Something touched his foot. There was a rusted flashlight with weak batteries in his pocket. He aimed the flashlight at the nearer sheep. A pale, yellow beam picked out the steadily breathing nostrils of the sheep. The light slid back over the curly head.

At first, the sheep's flanks seemed to be covered by a

gray blanket. Then two of the bats raised their eyes to the beam and he saw the blanket was a dozen bats lying on a sheet of blood. The next sheep had its own blanket of bats and, as Isa swung the flashlight around, he saw that all the sheep were covered in the same manner, sleeping under the feeding. The bats were larger than any he'd ever seen before and the ones he'd disturbed only glared at him with open mouths. He shined the light downwards and kicked off a bat that was climbing up his pants.

With all his strength, Isa swung his father's shotgun at the sheep.

The bats, as a community, were first aroused by the explosion of the shotgun. Two bats were dead. Those closest scattered, only to land a short distance away. The community as a whole drew in, ringing the source of the noise. There were no leaders, except in that the communal instincts would first be carried out by the most aggressive individuals, the females, among a very aggressive species of animal. The instincts were to protect the Food and to repel an aggressor, which they could clearly see was a single man. In a sense, then, more Food. The ring drew tighter.

The Food was a marvelous thing. There were few animals in the world, and no other at the bats' level of intelligence, whose every organ and sense were so designed and attuned solely for the taking of sustenance, and perhaps this was true because no other animal was so uniquely surrounded by it. From every other warm-blooded animal they could feel the pulsing of the Food, or taste it in the air so rich with sweat and exhalations. As a result, to the bats there were no natural enemies, not even man. There could be no enemies, when all was the Food.

A bat darted by the boy, easily dodging the stroke of a shotgun stock. Another bat flashed by him, slicing his nose. The boy turned in a circle, flailing the air. The agitation, his labored breathing and the pounding of his heart, excited the bats. A whirlpool of them swirled around him, just out of reach of the shotgun. From straight above, one dived and tore open his ear. He fell and at once his back was covered with bats, which clung to his shirt as they ripped through to the skin. Another bat landed on his hand and the boy dropped the shotgun, rose, and began to run.

They followed the running boy until he reached the truck, dived through its door and rolled the window up. For a while, the bats clustered on the hood and windshield. Then, one by one, they returned to the sheep. To the feast.

CHAPTER THREE

"When I die and go to hell," Selwyn squinted at the sun, "that place is going to look awful familiar."

He clutched the flask in his breast pocket as Youngman steered around a hole in the road. Selwyn's wife Esther and one of his half-breed daughters rode in the back of the deputy's jeep. The teen-age girl was dolled up for social attention in a black dress trimmed in red. Looming ahead was that center of the Hopi universe called the Black Mesa. From the giant mesa four fingers stretched southwards into the desert. They were called, from west to east, Third Mesa (with the pueblos of Hotevilla and Oraibi), Second Mesa (with the Shongopovi and Shipaulovi pueblos), First Mesa (Hano and Walpi), and Antelope Mesa (with the ruins of Awatovi). Seen from the road below, the mesas appeared a single, flat-topped wall of stone reaching to the horizon in either direction. Only two fragile clouds intruded on the sky.

"Did Anne tell you where she was going to camp?" Youngman asked.

"Didn't ask. She wouldn't give me the time of day or the year anyway, Romeo. She's after your balls, you know that. Rich white girl, that's the worst. I mean, she is not for you. Now, take my girl Mae here. You could do worse." He weighed Youngman's lack of interest. "Typical. They want blankets, I have pots. They want white girls . . ."

"Hey, Selwyn, you never told me. Why did you give up the missionary business?"

"Never did. It gave up on me. I got another germ, see?"

"No."

Selwyn took advantage of a relatively smooth stretch of the unpaved road to suck his flask.

"It's my theory that religion is like a disease. A great religion's like an epidemic. Take Christianity, Mohammedanism, Buddhism. Just like epidemics. Start in one place, always spread along the trade routes, flourish for a few hundred years and die out. Or get overrun by a new epidemic. I was sent here like a germ, to infect you people. Instead," he shrugged, "you infected me."

"With what?"

"A very dry mouth," Selwyn tipped his flask again.

As they neared it, Third Mesa jutted out towards the road, an escarpment of rock sheared cleanly at its top except for decaying, boxlike structures of adobe. Old Oraibi was still inhabited, barely, as if by the survivors of some disaster.

Esther nudged Youngman's back.

"I have to do Mae's legs. Pull over at Spanish Place."

Youngman pulled off the road beside a mesquite tree and a weathered tin sign that read, "Warning. No outside visitors allowed in Oraibi. Because of your failure to obey the laws of our tribe as well as the laws of your own, this village is hereby closed."

Selwyn went behind the sign to urinate. Mae's white cotton leg wrappings had come undone, revealing a pair of 59¢ athletic socks. While Esther wound the traditional wrapping again, Youngman stretched his legs up on the windshield and smoked.

There was nothing much to distinguish this strip of the highway from any other, although some Hopis said it was here that they greeted a Conquistador named Pedro de Tovar and his troops in 1540.

He was supposed to be the Pahana, the White Brother whom the Hopis had left a thousand years before, when they first began their long diaspora out of Mexico. Oraibi was established in 1100; the other pueblos followed as other clans arrived at the Black Mesa. Together, they waited for the bearded white brother whose arrival would signify the completion of the world. Pahana didn't arrive the year he was expected; in the person of Cortez, he was busy bringing down the Aztec Empire. Keeping watch, the Hopis cut a notch in a stick for each year their Brother was late.

There were twenty notches when de Tovar appeared on the horizon. Hastily, the Hopis prepared for this epic culmination. Fire Clan and Bear Clan priests ran down to the desert and drew a line of welcoming blue cornmeal before the horses and armored men. De Tovar looked on in confusion, and so it fell to the Catholic priest to make a decision. "Why are we here?" he yelled. "Santiago!" the troopers answered, lanced the Hopis in their way, and rushed up the mesa, quickly subduing the pueblos.

For the greater glory of God, the Hopis were made Christians and slaves. They were sent down mines in search of gold, silver, mercury, and oil-saturated shale that burned like coal. Indians found conducting pagan rites were whipped and torched with burning turpentine. For 140 years, the Hopis endured their error about de Tovar, until the Tewa called Popay sent to them a knotted cord indicating the night of rebellion throughout the pueblos of the Southwest. At the Black Mesa, the moment of revolt was signaled by the call of a screech owl. The Castillo soldiers were slaughtered at the church doors, the priests were knifed at the altar, their steel pikes were buried and the church razed to its last stone. In all, over 500 Spanish died during their retreat to Mexico, and although the Hopis were subsequently overrun by Spanish and Mexicans and Americans the tribe became infamous for its reluctance to convert again.

They settled down to wait for the real, the true Pahana.

Selwyn emerged from behind the sign zipping his fly.

"The Bible says that Jesus went into the wilderness and there he fasted for forty days." He shook his pants. "Sort of interesting exactly how long the Son of God could take living like a Hopi, huh?"

"You're a cynical bastard, Selwyn."

"Not compared to you. I just talk that way. Booze keeps me innocent."

"Except for your kidney."

Two cars came flashing up the road to the mesa. The first was a new Buick Le Sabre, shiny in spite of its patina of dust. As the car went by, Youngman caught sight of its driver, a square-faced Indian in a business suit talking on a car phone as he steered. A sticker on the bumper read *"Dine Bizeel."* "Navajo Power."

"Walker Chee!" Mae looked in awe after the car of the Chairman of the Navajo Tribal Council.

"Headpounder." Youngman used the Hopi epithet for Navajos, earned by the Navajos' old habit of crushing the skulls of their prisoners.

The second car was a Cadillac. Behind the wheel was a man unknown to Youngman, a white in shirtsleeves and a tie. He glanced at the Indians on the side of the road, sunglasses making one decisive swipe.

Inside the Land Rover, after a night of signal tracking, Paine was asleep. Sweating and dreaming in the morning heat.

He was back in Mexico.

He and his father were immunologists under contract to the Instituto Nacional de Investigaciones Pecuarias, working out of the agency's Vampire Bat Research Station in Mexico City. The research station's aim was to
70

control *derriengue,* rabies transferred by vampire bites. The Paines' particular mission was to find why the vampires were largely immune to the lethal virus they carried.

Paine's closed eyelids glistened. He was back in the Sierra Madre del Sur, near the Guatemalan border. In the cave. He and his father and Ochay were following the beams of their helmet lamps, feeling their way along a ridge two hundred feet above the cavern floor. The cavern wormed its way half a mile into the mountain. Its general shape was ovoid, the walls below the ridge smoothly curved to the floor, the walls above arched another hundred feet up to giant stalactites and the bat roosts. Paine was team leader and point man. He was attached to a nylon rope strung through saw-toothed pitons he hammered into the limestone wall. Joe Paine and Ochay were close behind, unattached, moving hand over hand along the rope, both men bearing a red canister of poison on their backs. No vinyl overalls this trip because of the climbing, only goggles and gas masks to endure ammonia rising from the bat dung. Without a mask, a man could survive a maximum ammonia concentration of 100 parts per million for an hour; near the mouth of the cave they'd registered the concentration at 4,000.

"Deeper, we're not there yet," Hayden Paine said.

Dr. Joseph Paine was getting too old for this kind of work. Gray hair sprouted like owl feathers from under his sailor's cap and the oppressive weight of the canister bowed his knees. As a point of pride, though, he refused to restrict himself to lab work in the capital. Besides, he could control his son.

Ochay probably wouldn't have come without the old man along. All the Mexicans from the station knew the son was a crazy glory seeker who chose the largest roosts in the most inaccessible mountains. Of the ten original members of the team, only Ochay and Hayden

Paine had escaped bites or falls or ammonia exposure. The whole expedition would have been scrapped if the old man hadn't arrived.

In the lead, Paine dug in the crampons of his boots. The ridge of slick limestone was twenty inches across; a glistening stalactite, half-born from the wall, completely blocked the way.

Behind Paine, his father pulled his mask away to talk.

"That's it for today. We can tie the canisters here and come back tomorrow."

Paine ignored the advice. With his left hand he swung his axe hard around the protrusion into the wall on the other side. He tugged the axe handle. It seemed solid enough. Clutching it, he swayed around the stalactite and stretched himself to where the ridge continued. As he hammered a fresh piton, the echoes of his blows resounded along the recess of the cavern. A few bats squealed in complaint.

Two million bats occupied the cave. White Ghost bats. Carnivorous Spear-Nosed bats. Nectar-sucking bats. Minute insectivorous bats of a dozen varieties. Meat-eating Vampyrum Spectrums with three-foot wingspreads. Fishing bats. And the colony all the others roosted far away from, the true Vampires, Desmodus.

"Pass the tanks," Paine ordered.

Joe Paine and Ochay hooked the canisters to the rope. From the far side, Paine watched the tanks jiggle around the stalactite and with anxious tenderness he pulled the poison onto the ridge.

"Come on."

"I can't make it," Ochay answered.

"The vampires are further on."

"I can't—"

A shriek cut them off. There was a scuffle on the cave roof where the Vampyrum Spectrums hung.

Ochay's hand lantern followed the fall of a pink Spectrum infant to the floor.

The floor was a world of its own, a steaming brown soup of digested nectar, meat, insects, and blood. Twenty percent protein, it supported pools of bacteria. Over a million mites, scavenger beetles, toads, and mountain crabs to a square yard. Giant cockroaches and venomous snakes. For them all, guano was a steady rain of food, or food for their food. The fall of an unlucky bat was a bonanza for them, and seconds of agony for the bat.

"Let's go." Paine yanked the rope.

Joe Paine slid around the stalactite first and then Ochay. The latter was shaking.

"You're taking too many chances." Joe Paine clung to the wall. "Ochay—"

"If I can do it, so can he."

"But we're running out of air. I suggest—"

"But you're not the leader of this team. I am."

Paine pushed on. As they went deeper into the cave, the ridge narrowed to twelve inches, to ten, to six. Paine had to drive in a piton every second step, while his father and Ochay struggled behind with the canisters.

"He's scared," his father whispered to Paine. "You should understand that. He's scared of you. I think I'm scared of you now, too."

"I can do it without you."

"Could you?"

In overhead grottoes, shapes twisted, ears attuned to human voices. Even through his mask, Paine could smell the change in the ammonia, getting fouler, more penetrating.

"This is the last cave you go into. I'm going to see to that," Joe Paine said.

"We're almost there."

It was the end of the rope, not the diminishing air, that finally halted Paine.

"Madre de Dios," Ochay was sobbing.

Paine had brought a selection of wet and dry poisons in the expedition's trucks. For a cavern as large as this, he'd selected Cyanogas. The bottom half of each tank was compressed air, the top half a compartment of poisonous dust. He strapped the two canisters together so that they'd lie flat and lowered them by a separate rope from the last piton until their tops hung level with the ridge. After he adjusted the tank nozzles to achieve a 90-degree range, he set the timer on each nozzle at thirty minutes. When the timers ticked down, the tanks would release a hundred-foot spray of Cyanogas which, in contact with the cavern's moisture, would change into hydrocyanic acid lethal to every life form it touched, including the men who brought it. The strapping and adjustments Paine made with a mechanical deliberateness.

"Por favor . . ." Ochay pleaded.

"We're heading back," Joe Paine told his son. "Maybe when you and I get to Mexico City, we'll keep on going to the States."

Paine wasn't listening. He remained alone to make certain both timers were ticking down. When he was sure, he shined his hand lantern up to where the roof seemed to be covered by jagged brown stones. Then one of the stones spread its wings and shifted to bare its teeth at the light. Paine turned the lamp away before any more vampires were disturbed.

He released himself from the rope and knotted it to the last piton. His father and Ochay were about thirty feet away. They were making better time going than coming, already nearing the pearly stalactite they'd claimed they couldn't clear. He checked the gauge of his air tank. Twenty minutes. Just enough time.

From the sudden lack of tension on the strung rope, before he'd seen it happen Paine knew someone was gone. With his lantern, he picked out legs flailing in

74

mid-air, blackness, and the solid impact of a body hitting at the end of a long drive. Then the beam found Ochay, who'd cried all during his climb and never uttered a word when he slipped. He was sinking into the ooze.

"Spider!" Joe Paine shouted. "Spider on the rope."

The rope jerked again in Paine's hands and went slack.

"Hayden! Hurry up!"

Joe Paine hung three feet below the ridge on a thin shelf. Paine moved arm over arm along the rope.

"I'm slipping."

Paine could see his father's fingers spread flat over the slick rime of the limestone, giving ground. A tarantula, ten inches across at the legs, darted along the ridge towards Paine. He stomped it under his boot.

"Give me your hand." He reached down.

"Can't reach."

Paine wrapped the piton rope twice around his left wrist and leaned as far as he could. His father heaved himself up, stretched a hand that was too short and too wet for Paine to get a grip on. The two men looked at each other for a moment and then Joe Paine started sliding. He slid down the incline of the cave, dropping ten or fifteen feet at a time and then sliding again until, very small in the beam of Paine's lantern, he hit the bottom.

"Hayden! Throw me something!"

Paine wrenched the rope, almost losing his own balance as pitons sprang out of the soft limestone. He tied the slack rope around his axe and threw the axe down. It swayed at its limit of fifteen feet over his father's head.

"They're all over me! Jesus, they're eating me alive!"

Ochay's axe was still on the ridge. Paine slammed it deep into the limestone and hung himself by it. His own

75

axe now dangled five feet over his father. He pulled his mask off.

"Get to the wall! Climb!"

"I can't see! Hayden, they're . . . Oh, God! . . . No!"

"Climb!"

"Oh, God!"

Silence, until the last call.

"Hayden!"

He woke, shaking as if in convulsions, a cramped hand locked around the leg of a truck seat. On his hands and knees, still trembling, he crawled to the Rover's food locker and poured a quart of water over his head. He dug his fists into his eyes, erasing his father and Ochay and the others. It took him a minute to open and spill out the Valiums.

Had to sleep. Had to sleep. But, please, God, no more dreams. If he could just last until night.

"Don't forget to pick me up on the way back," Selwyn asked as he and Esther and Mae got out of the jeep at the base of the mesa, where Esther's sister's family of eight lived in an aluminum trailer, which was a runway of small children between the beer cooler and the television. Wearing gift shop headdresses, the children converged on Selwyn and began pommelling him with rubber tomahawks.

"And never intermarry," Selwyn groaned.

Youngman drove alone back into the desert where the Snake Clan was rounding up snakes.

Cecil Somiviki and his younger brother Powell were sitting on the open tailgate of Cecil's station wagon. Between them was a canvas sack that constantly shifted from the movements of the snakes inside—diamondback and prairie rattlers, bullsnakes, whipsnakes, garter snakes, but mostly small Hopi rattlers. The brothers were both stripped down to bathing suits and leather breech clouts; Cecil had a Stetson on and Powell wore sunglasses. From time to time, the older brother doused the sack with water to keep the snakes cool.

"What's new?" Cecil greeted Youngman. He was tribal sheriff and, on the side, sold propane gas to the pueblos from his station wagon.

"Abner Tasupi died."

"Son of a bitch! How'd that happen?"

"Some kind of animal attack. He was all chewed up."

"Son of a bitch!"

Powell said nothing. He was nineteen and he frowned studiously over the tribal newspaper *Qua' Toqti, The Eagle's Cry,* as if conversation was a distraction below his dignity.

"Man, he was a crazy mean fucker. Oh, he was wild. Well, that's the best thing I heard today."

"He was just an old man, Cecil."

"He was a killer. Everybody knows that. A witch."

"You don't believe that shit."

"I don't believe it, but it's true. Why do you think we kicked him out? Oh, he was always up in Maski Canyon where the ghost pueblos are. Come back after he made up some corpse poison. I bet he killed fifteen, twenty men, more. There was a man he hated, he'd turn hisself into a black dog and pull the poor bastard right over the edge of the mesa. Even the headpounders were afraid of him. By the way, that Walker Chee was around and he wants your ass."

"It's not the first time."

"This time he says you roughed up some pahan. I don't want to know about it, but stop it. And what about Joe Momoa? Why are you always rubbing folks the wrong way? You always pick the wrong folks, too. Learn to get along, for my sake."

A Snake priest came up to the station wagon. He had his arms outstretched and three or four rattlers in each hand, the diamondbacks pale and heavy, a sidewinder rough-scaled and horned, all of them twisting ineffectually. Cecil opened the sack while Powell picked up an eagle feather. As a Hopi rattler raised its mouth out of the sack, a wave of the feather made the snake duck. The priest dumped the snakes in, bummed a cigarette, and trotted back out into the desert.

"Did Momoa have a vet up at his place?" Youngman asked.

"I heard from Joe yesterday. All he said was he was going to shoot some night varmints in the Wash. Maybe he meant you." Cecil smoked; ashes drifted over his belly. "You were away, you don't know nothing about Abner. Hear about the time Arizona Public Gas sent some men down to Jeddito Wash? Abner gets wind of it. Does hisself up like Masaw. Sure. Crazy son of a bitch digs up a grave and dresses in a dead man's clothes, covers hisself in rabbit blood and goes to Jeddito to make medicine."

"Did it work?"

"What do you think? Those pahans see some nut in rags and blood shrieking his head off, you think they're gonna stick around? Shit, man."

Powell cleared his throat.

"Listen to this in the paper. 'Although the pahans have drained the Gila River dry, although the pahans have stolen four times their legal share of water from the Colorado River, although they have raped Glen Canyon and the Little Colorado River, although they have stolen wholesale the San Juan River, the water table level under Phoenix is still falling so fast the city may be a ghost town in twenty years.'"

"Asshole," Cecil yawned. "Before there's a dry swimming pool in Phoenix, they'll be up here to drain you for spit."

"That's just the kind of remark I could expect from you." Powell was the star pupil of his mission school.

78

He talked like a typewriter. "We don't have any leadership, just old men and the nonpolitical types like you two. That's why we have to join Chee; at least he's a leader who knows how to read a contract. That's why the Navajos have power plants and coal leases. Chee could get this reservation on the move again."

"Yeah, he'll move us right into a toilet an' slap the lid on if he gets the chance." Cecil rooted behind the snake sack for a couple of beers. He handed a can to Youngman. "You get anyone dumb enough to bury Abner?"

"Me."

"Oh, oh. Well, you get that shed of his then. But what about his medicine? He was into all kinds of powers no one else could handle."

"I don't believe in that stuff."

"No one does. But you better take care of it, or give it back to the Fire Clan. They're all up in Shongopovi today."

Youngman took the road up to the mesa, passing the turnaround area for Cal Gas trucks that couldn't navigate the road any further, going by orchards that produced small, wizened peaches, past corn stalks that would grow no higher than a man's chest, on up to the new plywood-and-cement houses in Shipaulovi pueblo where Cecil lived and around the edge of the mesa for two more miles. Entering Shongopovi pueblo always brought about an immense depression in Youngman. More than almost any other pueblo, Shongopovi was the home of the old "Traditional" people. Retreating from Navajos, retreating from whites, making a last stand on the very rim of the mesa.

A garbage dump. A hundred forlorn houses of stone and dirt set on rubble. Flanked by slopes of concrete outhouses. Not a blade of grass and not a real street, only flies dozing in alleys, a wrinkled face at a broken window, and shadows chipping at adobe. Inhabited ruins around a dusty plaza suspended over the desert.

No one ever took the long fall, of course. At Shongopovi, everyone shuffled into oblivion.

The sun was blinding. Youngman parked on the plaza in front of the house belonging to Harold Masito, a priest of the Bear Strap Clan, and went through a screen door into the cool, dark interior. Harold was on a sofa bed mending prayer sticks. The walls were decorated with color snapshots of his grandchildren and a needlepoint portrait of John Kennedy.

At one time, Harold had been one of the strongest men on the reservation. The muscles were gone now, leaving his big frame bent and his face shrunken around a heavy nose and jaw. He was one of the men who'd made Youngman a deputy.

"Abner is dead." Youngman sat down respectfully on a folding chair.

"Huh," Harold nodded. Carefully, he bound a fluff around the base of the stick.

"Two nights ago. You were a friend of his, so I thought you ought to know."

"That so?"

Harold went on to a different prayer stick, arthritic fingers straining to be steady.

"That's so. I had to bury him alone. He asked you and the other priests to go out to his place before he died."

"I'm not Fire Clan."

"But you used to be his friend. The least you could have done was made a visit. Two years, you didn't visit him once and now he's dead."

"You're angry."

"Hell, yes. What am I, some bum. Some bum buried Abner. That doesn't make any sense to me, uncle. Abner was somebody, he deserved a lot better than that. A lot better than everybody turning their backs on him and leaving him to die alone in the desert. Even when I was a kid, Abner was a great man."

80

"Abner was a great man," Harold said after a space of a minute. "But then he became crazy, dangerous. Before that, he was a very great man as you say. Maybe the greatest man in the world. Hungry?"

Harold went out the back screen door to where his wife was tending a horno, a stone oven. He returned with flat, steaming pan bread.

"Got no butter. You want margarine?"

"No thanks, uncle."

The old man sat on the sofa in thought. The bread cooled in his hands. Finally, Youngman lost patience.

"You treated him like dirt, worse than a pahan. You and the Fire Clan and all the elders. Now the poor guy is dead and you still act the same way. Well, why?"

"Abner was old, old," Harold sighed. "Older than me. Hard to think he's dead, but he's among friends. I was his friend, as you say. It bothers me what we did, but it was necessary. And if he's dead, like you say, then he's got friends."

"Uncle, that's not what I asked. Just give me an answer. How could you treat Abner like that?"

"You're more Tewa than Hopi. You're a warrior—"

"Knock it off, uncle." Youngman inched forward on his chair. "I was no warrior. I was a goddamn convict in Leavenworth. Abner deserved better company than that for a funeral and I want to know why that's all he got. I want a reason."

Harold picked up a prayer stick, then put it down and looked at Youngman.

"See, he talked to Masaw all the time and Masaw crawling up the mesa wall, that scared people. And Abner he'd go off to the pueblos of the dead people and come back smelling of the dead, and that was unpleasant for the rest of us."

"You mean, Abner was a witch. That's it? The whole thing? You all, all the priests, you believed that."

"You know how it is," Harold said. "Everything will

be all right as long as we tend to things. As long as we do the ceremonies right, there'll be rain and Masaw will protect us from our enemies. Okay. But Abner he went too far."

"Too far?"

"He had Masaw walking around here every night. I seen him," Harold said.

"Masaw?"

"Right. From far off 'cause if he touches you, then you're dead. You see what I'm talking about? Even Death gets hungry. It has a stomach to fill."

"I'll tell you what I saw. I saw the body of an old man. Not a witch. An old man who was a friend of mine and who had been a friend of yours and everyone else on the mesa. And if he acted crazy lately, maybe it was because all the priests up here, all his old friends made him that way."

"You did a good thing to keep him company this last year." Harold Masito averted his eyes from Youngman. "It makes me feel good to know we were right about you. Was there anything else?"

Youngman sighed.

"Well, uncle, there was. His possessions. What should I do about those, or who should I give them to?"

"I see. I'm afraid you're late. The Fire Clan priests they already went down into a kiva and they won't be up for a couple days. Anyway, they took the clan tablet from Abner a year ago."

"What tablet?" Youngman asked.

"The Fire Clan tablet. Abner can't stir up too much trouble without that."

Youngman wasn't interested in stories about a tablet and there was nothing left to do in Harold's house. He thanked Harold for talking. At the door he stopped.

"One more thing, uncle. Did you hear anything about Abner wanting to stop the world?"

"No," Harold answered curtly. He picked up a

prayer stick and a fluff. The fluff escaped from his gnarled fingers and floated upwards, slowly spinning. "You sure he's dead?"

Youngman went back out on the plaza. The sun was directly overhead, trying to melt the mesa. Youngman blinked through sunglasses at a silver water tower and his eyes fell to boys playing with a handmade top on a roof, and to the plaza. Rough ladders marked three holes spaced across the dusty plaza. The ladders led down to kivas, underground chambers. From the bow standard and horsehair on the two nearer ladders, he could tell they were occupied by Antelope and Snake priests who had already been in hiding for six days for the Snake Dance.

From a house two doors away, two men emerged. One was Walker Chee and the other was the white who'd been driving the Cadillac. Chee filled the doorway. Navajos were different from Hopis: they were bigger, fleshier, and their heads seemed squared at the corners. Chee embellished these attributes with hair razorcut to the collar of a dark, three-piece suit, a silk tie, and thick fingers studded with turquoise rings. The white took off sunglasses. His features were broad and pink, drawn with the eraser end of a pencil. Neither man noticed Youngman in the shadows.

The white frowned.

"You said the deal was set."

"Just a few more days, Piggot."

"A few more days and a few more days, that's all I've heard. I have crews standing by. What fucking game are you playing? And you were going to bring maps of the canyon. What happened to the maps?"

"The maps aren't important," Chee said.

"You know how expensive that kind of map is?"

"We don't want maps here. Not here. Back off and leave it to me."

83

"You're stalling me, chief. I'm trying to figure out why."

A village elder joined the two men and Youngman took the opportunity to try to slip away unseen. He got to the middle of the plaza.

"Deputy, I want to talk to you," Chee called.

Youngman came to a stop.

"Excuse me." Chee left Piggot and the elder and approached Youngman alone. The tribal chairman moved with proprietary ease, ushering Youngman out of earshot of anyone else. Youngman was aware of being smaller and, in comparison, grubby. There were perhaps a thousand flies buzzing around the plaza. No one of them would dare land on Chee. Chee dispensed a smile.

"You're Deputy Duran, right?" he asked softly.

"Yes."

"And you pushed around a Mr. Paine yesterday, is that correct?" Chee lowered his voice.

"I pointed out to him that he was on the wrong reservation."

Eyes began appearing in the windows around the plaza. The white man was searching the soles of his shoes.

"Are you going to tell me I'm on the wrong reservation?" Chee asked.

"Are you confused?"

"No, I'm not. That's how you and me differ. See, I got loads of my own Indians just like you. Dumb and poor. You get satisfaction out of that, fine. I heard about you before, Duran. You are the best living example of ignorance in Arizona, did you know that? You can't help yourself and you can't help anyone else. I bust my balls to bring some money to the mesa. I go to Washington, New York, Houston and show 'em an Indian doesn't necessarily have to be drunk or dumb and as soon as I get someone out here to help us some jerk like you shows up and screws me. Now you think I do it so I can get my face on a magazine cover. Great, that's your opinion. But there are three power plants and twelve proposed power plants on my reservation that say an Indian can do more than pose for nickels. And I've started the medical programs that'll mean we don't have to be the most disease-ridden people in this country. And the irrigation programs I've fought through the courts are just as much for Hopis as Navajos. So, do me a courtesy, Deputy, until you get as smart as the average toad, you hide yourself away the next time you see anyone who has anything to do with me. That a deal? And don't you eavesdrop on me ever again."

While Youngman stood and burned for an answer, Chee gestured to the white and the two men walked away from the plaza. The deputy heard the word "troublemaker" dropped, discarded the way a man would throw away an inferior item. Seconds later, the Buick and Caddy nosed into view and conspicuously squeezed through alleys to the mesa road.

Youngman could hear the soft roll of fat tires in the dirt. Why did he hate Chee? Because Chee was right?

"You're laughing," Stone Man said. "Is there anything funny?"

Stone Man was the village elder Chee had been talking to. He wore a rag around his head. His flesh was ropy. Youngman had the sense, and the fear, that he was looking at his future self.

"Not a thing, uncle. I guess all the Fire Clan priests are already in the kiva."

"Yes. I think Abner Tasupi was the last to go down."

"Abner? That's not possible."

Youngman walked across the plaza to a kiva almost on the edge of the mesa. The clan feathers on the ladder were stirred by a wind that blew straight out of the San Francisco Mountains, visible on the other side of the desert at a distance of seventy-five miles. A kiva was a link to that Underworld from which the first Hopis crawled; in other words, it was a dark, tobacco-rank chamber in which destitute people secluded themselves to prepare the ceremonies that would keep their miserable world together. Juniper bushes tied to the ladder below the entrance hole blocked Youngman's view. Stone Man followed him.

"Abner's dead."

"Oh." Stone Man concentrated. "Well, you know, I only seen him from the back. You know, I seen eight fellows go down and I just thought the last one was Abner." He watched Youngman nervously toe the stones around the opening. "You say he's dead, I must be wrong."

Paine had stayed in Mexico after his father's death. None of the Mexicans from the research station would work with him again but since the program was lavishly funded by American Agency for International Development money he was allowed to operate alone for a year. When he'd arrive in his Land Rover full of lab equipment and poisons the hill Indians would desert their village, a sight that always struck Paine as obscenely ridiculous because he came to kill death, not spread it. They'd watch, hidden, as Paine, his face strapped into a gas mask, carried into a cave canisters of barium carbonate, or arsenic trioxide, or thallium sulfate. When he left, the Indians would celebrate in the comic belief they'd driven off a demon.

Even when the Mexicans did cut off his funds, it didn't matter. Heart researchers wanted to study the vampire's circulatory system, sonar researchers wanted to test the vampire's ears, and psychologists were fascinated by the vampire's intelligence. No bat mastered a Skinner box faster than a vampire.

All the time, Paine was heading north following the survivors of the vampire colony from the cave where

Joe Paine had died. One vampire roost, however large, was generally only part of a larger vampire colony. By implanting miniature radio transmitters on captive bats, he traced the survivors to new caves. When he poisoned those caves, the survivors would move to others.

Their hours and movements became his. The distinctive marks of their feeding were the compass points of his life. A cave of their poisoned dead was his defeat, because his tracking equipment always recorded more survivors and yet more caves and Mexico itself seemed a lightless hall of caves, which at night it very much was.

In this fashion, he tracked his bats up the Sierra Madre Occidental, along the oceanside Sierra de San Francisco and north to the foothills of Sonora. The hunt took two years and he did not know whether any of the original survivors still existed, but vampires were long-lived, intelligent, and adaptable. Finally, he had pursued his prey to the end of that hall of caves to the last cave before the American border. That evening, he tracked the silent chorus of a major colony of vampires crossing the border.

No true colony of vampires had ever been reported in the United States, which was a classic puzzle to zoologists. From Northern Mexico to Argentina, through the Andean highlands to the swamps of Guyana, vampires flourished. At the U.S. border they'd always halted. No one knew why.

But Paine's bats didn't come back.

He recognized his great opportunity. Since there were no other vampire bat colonies in Arizona for his to merge with, at last he could destroy them all. Paine didn't anticipate his next problem, however. No one would believe him. County medical officers, when asked about vampire bat attacks, laughed in his face. He stopped asking about bats and used more general

87

queries about nighttime attacks and unfamiliar wounds, still without success. The vampires had disappeared.

Paine started again with the Indian reservations, working north through the Gila River, Maricopa, Apache, Colorado, and Hualapai, finishing with the largest of all, the Navajo.

He had found Walker Chee on the Black Mesa. The Navajo Tribal Chairman was leading a group of white men around the lip of what had been part of the mesa and was now the Peabody Coal Co. stripmine. The mine was an enormous inverted pyramid dug by layers, a pyramid all the more dizzying because it was such a sudden and overwhelming vacuum within which eight-story electrically powered shovels were dwarfed to the size of toys. Paine hung back by two limousines parked away from the lip as Chee strutted back and forth, pointing out elements of the operation to the visitors.

"Over there, you can just see it," Chee pointed to a chimney on the far side of the mine, "is the pulverizing plant. The Peabody people use fossil water to make a slurry of the coal and the slurry is gravity-fed by pipeline 275 miles around the Grand Canyon to the generating plants in Nevada."

One of the whites kicked a stone into the mine. He turned to Chee; he had the sort of pink head on which sunglasses became the most dominant feature.

"About the Peabody folks. You're givin' them some trouble, aren't you?"

"No trouble, Mr. Piggot. Renegotiating. We get 15 to 25 cents royalty per ton. The state of Montana gets a minimum of 40 cents. We just want to bring our royalties into line. You take oil—"

"That's why we're here," the man called Piggot said.

"We've been getting a 15 percent royalty. Arabs demand a minimum of 50 percent. . . ."

Paine watched the power shovels browsing a quarter mile deep in the pit. Steel cables dragged jaws over blasted ore. Overflowing, the jaws swung up, wheezed, rotated to dump trucks, and regurgitated tons of low-grade coal. They looked like brontosaurs lethargically feeding in a dry lagoon.

"You wanted to see me." Chee stepped aside from his group to Paine.

"Yes. I understand that all medical queries have to go through you."

"Right." The Navajo scratched his vest. It was hot by the strip mine. His eyes stayed hooked on Piggot.

"I've been doing a kind of biological survey—"

"Some other time," Chee suggested impatiently. "I have an office, you know. Make an appointment."

"Well, I have a photo to show you." Paine blocked Chee's view with a manila envelope.

"Excuse me."

"Just take a look."

"Some other—"

Paine slid the photograph from the envelope. The picture was a color blowup of a vampire bite, a clean crater two millimeters deep into richly vascularized human dermal tissue.

"Where the hell did you get that?" Chee reacted with anger.

"I—"

Chee grabbed Paine by the arm and forcibly led him another fifty feet from the lip of the mine. He started whispering furiously.

"What are you up to? Who gave that picture to you? I'm trying to do business here and all I need is some white son of a bitch like you busting up a million-dollar deal with some story about plague. You know what those men over there are going to do if they hear the word 'plague'? You ever seen a limousine vanish?"

"I didn't say anything about plague," Paine said.

The long moment that followed turned exquisite for Paine. In fact, his picture was of a Mexican Indian

89

who'd been bitten months before but he calculated swiftly and accurately.

"You have a photo like this, too," he told Chee. "You have somebody with wounds like this and he has plague. Do you know what made those wounds?"

Chee didn't answer.

"Then you're very fortunate," Paine said, "because I know, and you're going to hire me."

That encounter with Chee at the strip mine was only the first. After, were more meetings at Window Rock and on the mesa, transfers of an unpublicized autopsy report from Chee and lists of equipment demanded by Paine.

Now, in the dozing heat of midday, Paine was searching for fleas.

The desert's arroyos were still slightly dark, as if bruised by yesterday's rain. Yucca stems vibrated through waves of warm air.

The Painted Desert appealed to Paine. He appreciated the false sterility that masked such desperate adaptations of life as limbless lizards and giant saguaros. More than that, he savored the loneliness, the sense that he could go days, months if he wanted, without seeing another human soul. Other people, no matter how different, were mirrors of one's self. Paine wanted no reflections.

He drove over a sand dune to hard ground, where he stopped and climbed to the roof of the Land Rover. He'd seen one vulture earlier. This time through his field glasses he spotted two about half a mile up and two miles away, spiraling down a thermal. A third vulture joined them. Paine slipped down into the cab, throwing the glasses aside to get the truck into gear.

A matter of minutes could make his work a hundred times more difficult. Paine pushed the Rover up to 30, running over mesquite and crashing through sand drifts. Already, without glasses, he saw more vultures descend-

90

ing the thermal. A deep arroyo about six feet wide stretched in front of Paine. He swerved right, found a rise, and shoved his foot to the floor. At 40, the Rover cleared the arroyo, bounced stiffly, and continued over a drift.

Paine hit his horn. A mile off on a surprisingly green knoll was a truck in the middle of sixty or seventy vultures. Sheep carcasses covered the hill. Horn blaring, Paine drove into the scavengers, scattering them off his fenders. Red eyes staring out of black faces, the vultures hopped away, trying to gather air in their four-foot wingspread. Paine braked and jumped out of the Rover, cocking his .45 as he hit the ground. He fired, taking the head off one bird. The rest scattered in a black wave, lumbering up. Paine fired again, straight up, just to keep them moving.

Death, he'd long ago learned, was not a moment of calm. Without the squabbling of vultures, the hill still resounded with the vibrant activity of flies. When he left the vultures would return, and mice and smaller birds, a whole chorus of scavengers great and small. He only hoped he was in time.

From the back of the Land Rover he took his aluminum case, which he spread open beside a lamb that had been reduced to head, feet, and a thousand flies fighting for room to lay their eggs. He tied on a surgical mask and slipped on rubber gloves. Around his waist he strapped a belt of his own design. In addition to a holster for his automatic, the belt carried in leather-and-felt cups an odd number of jars, syringes, scalpels, operating scissors, glassine envelopes, and a jeweler' eyeglass.

The truck stationed on the hill didn't even have wheels, it was on blocks. The windows and windshield were smeared with blood from the inside. Paine grasped the handle of the door and stepped aside as he opened it.

No one fell out. There was no body in the cab, although the seat and floor were covered with dried blood. Paine was disappointed, but at least the profusion of blood stains was a good sign.

He walked among the sheep. As many as a hundred carcasses littered the hill, most of them ripped open by the activity of coyotes and vultures. The ground was torn up. He lifted a carcass with his boot and uncovered soil discolored by a dark pitch smelling of ammonia. That was better. He moved on in this pastoral setting until he found a ewe less disturbed than the rest. Although she was disemboweled, her intestines strung out on the grass, a fluttering of her nostrils showed she was still clinically alive. Paine squatted next to her. Some vultures landed to pick at farther away sheep. He paid them no attention.

The forward area of the ewe's chest was striped by shallow gouges seeping blood. Paine held a jar upside down almost flush over the wounds. Between the open lid and the wounds he stroked a paper card. A minuscule activity began developing in the jar. He moved the jar and card over all the wounds and then screwed the top on the jar. He fixed the jeweler's loupe in his right eye and held the jar up to the sky. Eight, nine fleas hopped against the glass.

There were over two hundred different species of fleas in North America alone. Magnified, the parasites of the Order Siphonaptera shared a basic equipment: wingless bodies, powerful legs, bristles in rows, and the sucking mouths that bestowed their Latin name. There were four species in the jar. Mice that had nibbled on the wounds had left rodent fleas, *Xenopsylla Cheopis,* eyeless fleas with double rows of bristles. The coyote that had ripped open the ewe had deposited two species: common Dog Fleas, rounded, with a moustache-like mouth comb; and blunt-headed, eyed Carnivore Fleas. There were two specimens of the last species.

They had eyeless, helmet-shaped heads. A mouth comb like mimic teeth. Bat Fleas.

For a moment, Paine was stunned by the magnitude of his luck. Overhead, the vultures watched him squat by other sheep and collect more specimens, and when he stowed them in his truck and drove away the birds all descended again through the rising air of the thermal to finish that work nature designed them for.

Controlling his excitement, Paine drove slowly.

Life was unfair. Usually, only the poor and geniuses realized this but Hayden Paine was admitted to the fact with his father's death. It was Joe Paine who was the really first-rate immunologist, Joe Paine who back in '44 led the Rockefeller Institute team that identified a mysterious paralytic disease killing hundreds of thousands of cattle annually as vampire-transmitted rabies. All the other authorities claimed the bat was an impossible vector. Under a microscope, the so-called *derriengue* virus didn't look exactly like rabies. Besides, rabies invariably killed its host, yet the majority of vampires thrived on the virus that infected them. It took Joe Paine to prove that the rabies virus had mutated under the influence of its bizarre host and that the vampire alone of all species on earth was not vulnerable to rabies.

Joe Paine's abilities hardly ended there. Chee was terrified of plague? In 1967, the Paines, father and son, were in Saigon to study a disease raging among the refugees of the beleaguered city. Joe Paine overcame American and Vietnamese obstructions to identify the disease as bubonic plague carried by rat-infested rice. A small item among the horrors of war: there were 5,547 cases of plague in Vietnam in 1967.

But always for Hayden Paine it came back to the caves. He suffered from claustrophobia. One step into the dark and his heart doubled its beat. The condition had come on gradually, accreting with experience. In the first year of vampire work with his father, the claustrophobia paraded as nervous energy. The second year, without understanding why—he'd been on spelunking expeditions with his father even as a boy—Paine had trouble breathing. By the end of the second year, adrenalin flowing like nitro through a bloodstream dark with lack of oxygen, he began passing out. The third year was the worst.

In an age of sophisticated torture there is no more effective tool than claustrophobia. It combines elements of suffocation, desertion, blindness, and isolation from reality. All these elements operate in a cave, except that they are reality. When Paine entered a bat cave, his heart was already racing, each beat a muffled alarm. As the light of the entrance evaporated, his lungs became twin vacuums and his limbs numbed. With every step he felt the cave closing behind him. The glow of his helmet lamp was a ghostly moon without reference to him, like a glowworm in a coffin. Past the threshold of panic, he forced himself deeper into the cave, seemingly more steady as his sanity folded in. Within goggles, his eyes bulged. Even as he tried to concentrate on the techniques of ropework or spreading a mist net of superfine thread, he tasted his hot and salty terror. Then someone would set off a flash and the cave would erupt into a whirlwind of panicked wings. When the sound of the wings and the lower-pitched cries of the bats made a dizzying roar, only then, occasionally, would Paine let go his scream of terror.

He wasn't stupid enough to think he was a coward. Unfortunately, he was intelligent enough to know the reason he returned to the caves was to mimic his father, and that in imitating a better man, he was a farce.

No matter how many caves he went into and how competent he seemed, the secret panic blossomed. Until he took risks just to keep his eyes from straying to the enveloping dark. No one knew except his father, which was why Joe Paine had to go along when others hung back.

So, unfairly, in that Mexican cave, it was the better man who'd died. Not without a parting gift, though. Like dross from a fire, Paine's panic fell away and was gone.

The desert sand had the quality of compacted ash. A desert, to Paine, was a land that was burned and constantly burning. For Paine, a relief compared to night.

After thirty miles of driving, he stopped in the shade of a canyon of stark, yellow walls and set up his laboratory. Like his belt, it was a construction of his own design. Aluminum poles screwed horizontally onto the top rear of the Rover and telescoped backwards fifteen feet to supporting poles rooted in the dirt. Over this structure he hung a fine wire mesh tent that zipped tight around the open doors of the Rover and at an entrance flap at the other end. He staked the mesh taut to the ground through eyeholes spaced every six inches; the whole effect was of a cocoon growing out of the truck. Inside this cocoon he set up tables and equipment. From the Rover's refrigerator, bowls of blood culture gelatines. Test tubes. Rubber-stopped jars of killing solution. Microscopes and slides. A square black box two feet high with a front hooded by black crepe. Alongside the box, he placed the jar of specimens from the sheep.

He pulled the black hood aside and uncoiled an extension cord from inside the box to a dry cell battery he'd placed under the table. A frosted white light panel—the type used for X-rays—glowed underneath an acetate map of the Navajo-Hopi reservation. Paine removed the map. With a clean scalpel he cut into the flesh of his little finger and milked three drops of blood onto the glowing panel. Over the blood-specked panel he set a clear plastic cover that had one circular, threaded opening. He picked up the specimen jar, shook it gently, counted the fleas at the bottom of the glass, and carefully unscrewed the lid, sliding a paper card between lid and jar. He turned jar and card over and slid the card away as he screwed the jar into the plastic cover. Then he set a microscope over the panel and pulled the crepe hood over the back of his head.

Magnified by 20X, the fleas lurched uncomfortably within the confines of the panel and cover. The heat of the glowing panel, though, spread the rich vapor of an abattoir. Antennae twitched and the hair of their palps stiffened. The sighted Dog and Carnivore Fleas were first to move towards the balloon-like drops of blood, but the blind *X. Cheopis* and Bat Flea joined the rush. There was enough for all. Sheaths pulled back from sucking stylets, which plunged into the walls of the blood.

At 50X, the bodies of the fleas were transparent. Paine watched a stream of red flow through stylet, esophagus, and pour into the stomach. The walls of the pharynx and gullet expanded and contracted, pumping the blood in. He studied Dog Flea, Carnivore Flea, and *X. Cheopis* before focusing on one of the two feeding Bat Fleas. A red stream flowed through the stylet, swirled and flowed back out again into the blood drop. The Bat Flea was sick, vomiting up its food, dying slowly from starvation. At 75X Paine could see why. A gelatinous mass was blocking the esophagus, distending it so that the valve action was malfunctioning, sucking as much blood out of the flea's stomach as it brought in. The second Bat Flea suffered from the same blockage.

Paine unscrewed the jar from the cover and slipped in a gloved hand. He tweezered one Bat Flea and crushed it in a bowl of blood culture gelatine. The second Bat Flea he picked up carefully in the tweezers and held over a slide as he squeezed the stomach. A red strip shot over the slide. Paine dropped the flea in a killing solution. He screwed the jar back on the cover.

Paine moved to another table that was almost

dwarfed by a fluorescence microscope. The microscope had ordinary compound optics built into a sway-backed system of mercury-discharge lamp, radiation shields, and ultra-violet filters that flooded the slide stage with blue-violet light. It was an ungainly, hot, and power-draining apparatus, but Chee had insisted on no more communication between Paine and the Navajo labs at Ship Rock except by radio. And the fluorescence microscope was a bacteriologic laboratory in itself.

Paine prepared a slide smear of the contents of the Bat Flea's stomach, dried it, and dyed it with fluorescent stain. He set the slide on the stage, pulled the hood over his head, turned on the lamp, and focused.

The stain was still taking effect. Paine waited, only fearing that the pounding of his heart would disturb the delicate focus. In spite of the canyon shade, the heat of the lamp rolled sweat down his neck and chest.

On the slide, invisible organisms were becoming visible against a dark background. They were short bacilli, slightly resembling safety pins.

Plague bacilli. The bats carried plague.

Chee had hired the right man.

On the way back to Gilboa, having left his wife at her brother's trailer, Selwyn was roaring drunk.

"So, big Walker Chee took you to the cleaners, huh? Did a war dance on you and hit you over the head with his Phi Beta Kappa key. You always have your leg half down a scorpion hole before you watch where you step? You're not just dealing with another savage, boy. You're fighting Peabody Coal and Kennecott Copper. My friend, you are a turtle on the superhighway of progress. Know what happens to turtles on highways?"

Youngman handed back Selwyn's bottle. He was feeling a little run over already.

"You're right, aren't you, Selwyn?"

"Right, I'm right. Watch the road. Bad enough you're

drinking my booze, don't get me killed. You know, Tonto, I can't believe Abner's dead. I think I'll drink to Abner."

"I thought you hated Abner."

"Me? Never! A wonderful guy. Weird but still a great individual."

"Not Quaker, either."

"Let's drink to the Quakers. Now, goddamn it, you stay on the road."

Youngman steered the jeep off the road and between a close-set pair of barrel cactuses. He kept on an angle away from the road while Selwyn clutched the windshield.

"Where we going?" Selwyn shouted.

"You want to drink to Abner, we'll go drink to Abner."

The jeep shook as Youngman raced over the stones of a dry wash. Ahead, the land developed those stubby rises of piñon and mesquite trees that Southwesterners like to call hills. The jeep's speed created a false breeze.

"My bladder!" Selwyn warned.

Youngman wasn't listening. He needed a blast of air in the face and the physical tension of handling a fast-moving vehicle on sliding, exploding rocks without losing control.

"Hang on."

"Holy . . . !" Selwyn exhaled as the jeep flew up a side of the wash and landed on two wheels, then four.

Youngman, more relaxed, slowed down as he wended his way through the mesquite trees. Where water was next to nonexistent, mesquite was the familiar scruffy bush, but where there was any decent water table mesquite became a true tree with olive-green leaves. Half a mile on, his eye caught the brilliant yellow of paloverde branches through a screen of mesquite, like the plumage of yellow birds.

98

"We going where I think we're going?" Selwyn muttered.

The jeep's trail of dust curled through the hills. Inch-long cholla spikes clicked under tires. To Selwyn, drunk or sober, the desert was a labyrinth. He had never understood why the Hopi weren't a tribe of people continually lost and meandering about in the wilderness. Somehow, to him, Youngman picked out one rise of paloverde trees from all the rest.

"Bring your bottle." Youngman stopped the jeep.

"I always hated that son of a bitch, you know that."

"Come on."

They leaned against each other and stumbled up through the trees. Youngman remembered that he should have brought something, a bowl of cornmeal or a candy bar, for Abner's spirit to eat. Selwyn tripped.

"You can make it," Youngman said.

"Look, if I could walk I'd be going in the other direction."

Youngman put Selwyn's arm over his shoulders and half-carried him up the slope. They ducked the low branches and waded through poppies, while Selwyn's curses grew in intensity. A real wind came up. The trees bowed.

At the top of the rise, Selwyn slipped from Youngman and fell to his knees. All around the grave were dirt and rocks, and the grave itself was empty.

"He's not dead," Selwyn said. "I knew it. The bastard rose."

Youngman walked around the hole. Not even the winding sheet was left.

"He's dead. Somebody dug him out."

"I don't see any shovel marks or any footprints. He came out. I told you he was a witch," Selwyn moaned.

"A graverobber doesn't have to leave his name. It was those bastards up on the mesa, Abner's old friends. Or that pahan who tried to get at Abner before. Paine."

"No, he rose. He's not dead, Sweet Jesus, he's not. Feel that wind. Christ, he's walking around. He's out there."

"Michael, row the boat ashore, allelujah, Michael row the boat ashore, allelujah! The river Jordan is deep and wide, allelujah, Milk and honey on the other side, allelujah!"

The song mixed with the sounds of tin plates and utensils being distributed, and the sizzle of hamburger patties in the campfire. John Franklin directed his choir with a cigarette. The campers sat on bedrolls; their silhouettes, cast by the fire, wavered over the side of the van.

"Excellent," Franklin applauded. "Wasn't that excellent, Miss Dillon?"

Anne mustered a faint smile.

"My voice isn't what it used to be. La!" One of the ladies tried a high note.

"I'm hungry. That desert air sure does it to you."

"George, you'd be hungry underwater."

Anne passed out potato chips and rolls. Since they'd started out from Gilboa, her pious charges had yet to help with the cooking or cleaning up. As long as they doled out some money to the reservation, she reminded herself.

"You can do your own toasting."

"I sure like my burgers rare."

"Is that coffee ready yet? Gee, it gets nippy here at night, doesn't it?"

"Rough it, Henry," Franklin said, a moment before Anne answered with a phrase that sounded vaguely the same.

"Hey, will you listen to that!"

Everyone fell silent. Anne had set up camp in late afternoon in an area that had seemed comfortably closed in by bouquets of ocotillos. The night dissolved the ocotillos, while the fire brought closer a grim ring of saguaro cactus. A call trailed over the desert.

"An owl," Anne said. "They roost in holes in the cactus."

Mrs. Franklin continued to stare into the dark. She hadn't recovered from the sight of that old Indian they found dead the day before. She'd seen dead folks before; Lord knew, she'd made enough calls to hospitals. But that was dying like a person. That Indian had died like some animal, well, like a pigeon in a gutter, she thought. Such things shouldn't happen. And the desert bothered her. The starkness disoriented her. She was accustomed to the soft clouds and stately green trees of her Minnesota lake country. In contrast, the desert was a graveyard, and the saguaros like tombstones.

"It is beautiful," she lied. "Do we have any more wood for the fire?"

"Leave it alone, Claire," one of the other wives answered. "It's romantic."

"Don't be a dude, Claire."

"I'm still cold," she said.

Anne walked away from the camp in search of wood. She didn't expect to find any, not even a greasewood tree, but after a day of driving in a crowded van, she was happy to be alone for a couple of minutes in the dark. A moon hung out of reach above the upraised arms of a dead saguaro. Anne was about a hundred feet from the camp when she heard a step behind her.

"It's me," Franklin said. "I thought you might need some help."

"There's no wood out here."

"I know." Franklin oozed complicity, and then shifted to concern. "Have you been giving any more thought to my offer, Miss Dillon?"

"No. I don't see myself as a secretary."

"Oh, it could be much more interesting than that. Actually, you'd be more of a personal aide. You'd love

101

the travel. There's going to be a World Council of Churches convention in London this winter. Philanthropy has a lot of fringe benefits."

"I'm not one of them."

While Franklin decoded Anne's insult, his wife called from the van.

"Never mind, John, don't bother." She watched her husband and the girl walk back. "A blanket will do."

At the fire, Anne served up hamburgers and dished out beans from a pot resting in the center of the coals. Franklin said the blessing.

"Miss Dillon," said the hungry man called Henry, "I can't help thinking about that deputy we ran into. Are all the Hopis as unfriendly as that? It seems to me after all the work you've done for his people that he was less than grateful. What's the point of donating work or money if these people are going to bite the hand that feeds them?"

Between bites there was a general echo of agreement around the campfire.

"I don't think foundations can depend on gratitude," Anne said.

"We all certainly know that," John Franklin remarked. "What we really want from you is an assessment of their character. Now, take that deputy as an example. How do you explain him?"

"I don't know what you mean, 'explain him.' "

"He's the only Hopi that we've met so far, unless you count the women making pots. He seems to be a friend of yours, you've talked about him enough."

"You'll meet other Indians." Anne tried to dodge the question. "The Momoa family, people at the Snake Dance."

She didn't like the turn the conversation was taking. Franklin wanted to punish her because she had refused his offer, and the others were joining in. Or maybe Youngman's paranoia was contagious. But the boredom
102

that had been settling in on the group was definitely gone.

"Is he a good friend?" Claire Franklin asked.

"Yes. You have to get to know him, though."

"Well, apparently you do, dear. How ever did you manage it?"

"My answers may not be your answers." That was a poor evasion, Anne realized. "See, I've lived here for a while."

"Alone?" one of the other women asked with the thrill of possible titillation in her eyes.

"We haven't lived here." Franklin gave the interrogation a more dignified tone. "We haven't had the privilege. Now, you mentioned us helping these people. In fact, I tend to doubt we would have the benefit of your company unless you thought you could put forward a case for some sort of aid. But for us to help these people, you have to help us. Tell us about your deputy."

"All I can tell you," Anne said after a moment's thought, "is that he's a desert person. A desert creature. It takes a very different kind of animal or plant to survive out here. Something very tough and self-sufficient. Well, take the bushes here as a kind of example. They grow wide apart from each other, and one of the reasons is that each bush spreads a poison around itself that will kill off another seedling. It has to be that way, because if the bushes grew closer to each other there wouldn't be enough water for either."

"He sounds more like a scorpion, the way you describe him," Franklin said.

Anne looked at their silly, food-stuffed faces. Any appetite she'd had for their company was gone.

She dropped her empty plate to the ground. "I'm going to catch the weather report."

As soon as she was in the van she closed the windows to shut out the sound of their voices. Her fingers reached for the radio, and then left it silent.

"You think there's something going on between our Miss Dillon and that deputy?" Henry's wife wondered aloud.

Anne stared through the windshield. Was Youngman like that, as impossible to approach as she'd said? Was killing love a form of self-preservation?

"I hope it doesn't rain tomorrow," Claire Franklin sighed. "A day in a van is not my idea of a vacation."

"It might rain tonight. Hear the breeze?"

"Pass the ketchup, please."

"I can hear it, but I don't feel it."

"Can you imagine, Miss Dillon and that deputy?"

"Why didn't you and Miss Dillon bring back any wood, dear?"

"It sounds like wings, actually."

"There's nothing like a hamburger cooked out of doors."

"You know, she was pestering me about that donation."

"We have enough people who need help closer to home."

"I still don't see the ketchup."

"Look at the moon."

"I don't see it."

"That's what I mean. It was there a second ago."

"Never mind, I found the ketchup."

"Just keep your hands off her, John, that's all I'm going to say," Claire Franklin whispered.

"Listen to that."

"Oh!" Mrs. Franklin jumped to her feet and swung at the air. "A bat!"

"I didn't see anything."

"For heaven's sake, dear." Franklin was disgusted. "It isn't going to nest in your hair."

"That's an old wives' tale." Henry pitched the ketchup bottle aside. "I don't know, maybe that means they only bother old wives."

104

"There's another!" Claire ducked.

"All right, all right." Franklin stood up holding a blanket. "Show me."

A muffled sound streaked over the campfire. Claire Franklin swayed, her hands up to her head. She took her hands away. A gouge ran from her left eyebrow to her right temple and from the wound, over her eyes, ran a sheet of blood.

"John!" she screamed. "Help!"

Franklin swung the blanket, and stumbled as something like a fist hit him between the shoulderblades. He felt teeth slice into his back.

"John," Henry, like the others, didn't understand what was happening. "John, boy, what's the matter?"

Then the sound, first like a scattering of dry leaves, then like a tide rushing over steps, poured over the camp. It spread and blanketed the camp. Ten, twenty bats on a body. Hundreds swirling overhead.

"Maude!" Henry pitched on the ground, two bats on his neck, and watched one rip open his hand. Beyond was his wife, on one knee, screaming in a coat of bats. A bat fixed on her cheek. Another bat landed on the ground. It drew up its wings and scuttled towards Henry like a spider.

The ground was covered with running bats. Claire Franklin rose from the ground, a statue in red. Another figure, seemingly two-headed, ran through the fire. Franklin and another man spun like maddened dancers.

"Here!" Anne shouted from the van door.

Henry staggered against the door, closing it. He leaned against the van even harder as others tried to push him down or pull him away, climbing over him and each other.

"Get back! Let me open it!" Anne shouted from inside.

They didn't hear her. She heard them. Shrieking. Anne had never seen such huge bats before and, since

105

the campers had stopped fighting the bats to fight each other, the bats swarmed over them at gross leisure. The efforts of the campers became grotesque, as if they were swimming in slow motion. Swimmers no longer identifiable one from the other. Just screams and gaping eyes and a hand that smeared blood over the window.

Anne kicked the door open. Two figures rushed in, and the second slammed the door shut and locked it.

"The others . . ."

"Shut up." Franklin pushed her away.

The others beat on the windows, but futilely. A combination of horror, confusion, and loss of blood started to take its effect. One, a woman in a coat of bats, clutched her left arm and toppled backwards. In a second, her face was covered. Smothered.

"We have to let them in." Anne struggled against Franklin.

"And let the bats in, are you crazy?"

"You can't let them die."

"You got us into this. Help me hold her, Henry."

A wet forearm reached across Anne's throat. At first, she thought they were strangling her, but they were only pulling her into the back seat, away from the door handle.

Claire crawled under the van to scrape the bats off her back. A steady stream of bats slid under the vehicle after her. Another figure knelt, hands in prayer, arms and body under clusters of bats. Finally, the screaming subsided, overlapped by the scuttling of claws on the roof of the van, and by the cries of the bats, too high-pitched for human detection but a subtle, incessant pressure on the consciousness.

Franklin started the motor and turned on the headlights.

A figure walked towards the van swinging a burning stick. His shirt and hair were on fire. A cloud of bats hovered over him.

The van started, lurched over Claire, and stalled. The burning man beat his stick against a window while the generator whined and caught. The van ripped through an ocotillo bush.

"You can't leave them," Anne said.

"Shut her up," Franklin ordered.

Anne fought off Henry. Everything she touched was raw flesh.

The van rammed a saguaro, smashing the right headlight as blood continued to pour into Franklin's eyes. But he managed to find room to gain speed. A bat or two fluttered ahead. He pushed the accelerator to the floor mat, dodging the tall saguaros and running over smaller cactus and bushes.

By chance, he found the dirt road Anne had taken to the campsite. The road was uneven but straight and the van rocked at 60, outdistancing the last of the bats.

Thank God, he thought over and over again. Thank God.

For half an hour, Franklin raced after the beam of his single headlight. Henry had lapsed into shock, while Anne numbly let her head loll with the weaving of the van. In the middle of a nightmare, she wanted no feeling. Franklin glanced at her through the rearview mirror.

"I'll do the call on the radio," he said.

"There's no radio. It's back at the camp, everything's back there."

"The least you can do is give me a cloth. I'm still bleeding."

"Then let me drive, I know the road."

"Have you turn around? No way. And when we get out of here, you leave the talking to me. Just remember, you're the one who got us into this. Did you ever see bats like that before?"

"No one ever saw bats like that before," she said in a flat voice.

"Except here," he laughed bitterly. "How's Henry doing?"

"Not much pulse, but more than the ones you left."

"Look, you can thank me that you're alive. We barely got out of there. I did what had to be done. When we reach help, I'll do the explaining."

"Go to hell."

How could bats act like that? Franklin asked himself. Rabies. The girl didn't have any medical supplies with her and, besides, she wasn't bitten. She had nothing to worry about. He was the one who needed help.

A white rag of cloud hung in the moonlight. Franklin kept wiping blood from his eyes. The road was disappearing now under stretches of windblown sand. A mesquite tree slapped at the windows.

"You don't know the way," Anne said. "You have to let me drive."

"I'm the one who may die," he blurted out, and hearing the words in his mouth became aware of the chill creeping through his body. He didn't think of the night air or of lower blood pressure, only of the rank clamminess and a smell something like ammonia. The tires skidded on sand.

"Watch where you're going," Anne warned. She leaned forward. Franklin was breathing noisily through his mouth and his eyes were glassy under red lids. "You're going into shock. You have to pull over. Do it slowly."

Clinging to the wheel as if to life, he concentrated on overtaking the single beam of light, which was narrowing and turning red.

"Slow down." Anne spoke deliberately in his ear. "You have to let me take the wheel."

As Franklin had lost the power of speech, he concentrated all the more on the ruby shaft of light. It glittered with night insects, with wings and eyes, with warm

108

promises. Incredibly, he was overtaking the light. The red road expanded and welcomed him.

"I'm going to take the wheel now." Anne reached over his shoulders. As her forearm touched his collar-bone his shirt stirred, and a bat raised its head from the damp burrow it had made in Franklin's chest to give Anne a scarlet grin.

The road curved. The van went straight, shearing off two giant saguaros at the base and ploughing through tamarisk trees before it hit a dune and rolled on its back.

CHAPTER FOUR

Isa Loloma felt cold. He was in the Months of the Hawk Moon and snow was covering him. The snow fell on his eyes and on his brain and between his ribs onto his heart.

Isa Loloma, dry and hot, fought in his fever against the straps that held him spreadeagled on a hay wagon in the sun outside Youngman's hogan. His wrists and ankles were raw. On his shoulders, the back of one hand, and, worst, on his neck were bulging, reddish buboes. Lymph nodes become swollen moons of disease, around which the rest of Isa's life would gravitate.

His parents were in the hogan.

"I went up in the morning like always to get him." Richard Loloma twisted the brim of his hat. "Sheep was all dead. I figured a cat got at them. The boy was okay except for some scratches and acting crazy. We put him to bed but he went and got a fever and those bumps, so we come in to see Abner."

"It'll ruin us probably without the sheep. I don't know, maybe we can get some new sheep," Irene Loloma said, "but he's the only boy we got."

The father turned his hat in his hands, two inches at a time, while Irene respectfully claspéd her hands against her apron, as if she and her husband were in a marble hall of justice instead of standing on dirty floor boards.

110

"Abner's dead," Youngman said. "Miss Dillon's off in the desert. Did you give him aspirin?"

"He can't keep it down."

"He's real hot," the man added. "He gets shaking and you can't hold him down."

Youngman didn't want to look at the boy. He didn't know anything about medicine. There was a clinic in Tuba City and the Lolomas could reach it by afternoon. All the same, he pulled himself from the chair. If it made them feel better, he told himself.

"You'll check him out?" the woman asked.

"Yeah, yeah."

He was hung over from Selwyn's bad whiskey and the white sun hammered on his forehead. Youngman stood by the hay cart squinting when he saw the boy's sweat and the glossy, pink swelling on the boy's neck, and then the lines of Youngman's face went flat. The boy started shaking and straining, twisting like a bow until only his shoulders and heels touched the cart. His mother reached to comfort him.

"No!" Youngman said. "Get back."

"Why? I was—"

"Don't touch him, don't get within five feet of him. Go to the trading post and get some blankets. On the way back go to the freezer. There's a cut up elk of mine in there. Wrap the meat in the blankets and bring it back to me."

"Sure," Richard Lolomas said uncertainly.

"Wait, one more thing. You get any flea bites lately, either of you?"

"No."

Youngman returned to the hogan and radioed Cecil Somiviki. Cecil's wife answered and said the sheriff was away at Shongopovi washing snakes for the dance.

Youngman sat in front of the radio. It was a Saturday. If he radioed Arizona Public Health for forty-eight hours he might get them to answer, just maybe get a doctor. The nearest town was Flagstaff. It was swimming pool and drowning season there; they weren't going to send one of their ambulances way into the reservation.

Then, there were the Navajo clinics at Tuba City and Ship Rock.

He turned to a band he'd never used before, the one to the Navajo capital.

"Calling Window Rock. This is Hopi Deputy Duran calling Navajo Police. Come in, please."

"This is Window Rock. Did you say Hopi? Over."

"I'm at Gilboa."

"We know where you operate from, Duran."

"I have a possible case of bubonic plague here."

An hour later, a white "Navajo Air" Beechcraft eight-seater, trimmed in blue with a yellow Navajo sun on the tail, taxied directly in front of the hogan. Two Navajo police in glossy black-and-white plastic helmets stood by while gloved and masked doctors removed the cold meat Youngman had laid beside the boy to keep him cool. Isa was slid onto a chrome table and zippered into a transparent oxygen tent attached to an air cooler and germ scrubber on the bottom of the table. His parents watched with fascination, as if their son were being transformed into someone alien. They kept glancing at Youngman for reassurance, but Walker Chee was in charge.

"It's not necessarily plague," Chee told Youngman. "We run a watch on all the possible carriers of the plague flea. Rats, prairie dogs, rabbits, ground squirrels. We've got it pretty much under control. Kid probably has cat scratch fever."

"Sure. I'm just a little surprised you came with the doctors, what with all the power plants you have to run a watch on," Youngman said.

"Anything I can do to help." Chee was in a turquoise jumpsuit with monogrammed pockets. He lit a small ci-

112

gar. "You were right on the ball giving us that call. I was wrong about you. A lot of guys would've let these folks go on to a medicine man and then, God forbid we have a case of the plague here, we could have had a problem of more infection. You are definitely going to get a good report out of this."

"That's wonderful," Youngman said in a monotone. He watched the doctors briskly roll the boy to the plane. Very smooth.

In spite of his dislike for Chee, Youngman had to admit he was impressed. At thirty-eight, Chee governed an area larger than many states. If his flashy smile and suits made the cover of *Business Week,* maybe it was because he deserved it. He had brought in those power plants, and medical clinics, and power shovels to rip coal out of the mesa, and uranium surveys of the desert, and a digital watch assembly plant in Ship Rock, and an Indian community college, and teams of white investors from Phoenix and Dallas. Youngman was very impressed that a man like Walker Chee, who was not a doctor, would personally supervise the care of a Hopi boy. Also, skeptical.

"Don't have any cases on your land?" Youngman asked.

"Of plague? None in the whole Navajo nation."

"Any last year?"

"Why do you ask?"

"Because I remember three years ago you had twenty cases of bubonic plague."

The doctors returned to fumigate the hay cart with sulfur dioxide.

"Let me level with you, Deputy. The life of any individual on my nation's land or your nation's is valuable to me. You can't put a price on people. But, with all the other stuff on our agenda—unemployment, education, and general health care—I just wish a couple of cases of plague were the biggest problem we had."

Finished with the cart, the doctors trotted up to Chee. One was a young Navajo, the other was older and white. The two Navajo police pushed the Loloma couple forward. Youngman recognized the bigger policeman, a muscleman called Begay.

"What's going on?" Youngman asked.

"Don't worry," Chee slapped his back, "there's enough room in the plane for all of us."

"Why?"

"Quarantine, of course. Just a couple of days at the clinic until we get lab reports. The doctors can tell you, this is standard procedure set down by the government. It's purely for your protection." Chee gave the faintest nod to his police, who slipped by the Lolomas to either side of Youngman. "Go ahead, ask the doctors."

Youngman was wearing his .38. He rested his hand on the grip as casually as he could.

"It's definitely plague, then?" he asked the white doctor.

"Hold on." Chee raised his hand. "I told you, they can't make a diagnosis now. Look, Deputy, you asked for my help here. Since I'm giving it to you, you do what I say. You hop like a bunny over to that plane."

As the sleek plane dominated Gilboa, Chee dominated other Indians. Usually, sheer force of personality was enough, but there were other ways. He took a step back, and the doctors followed suit.

"What bit him?" Youngman asked.

"Huh?"

"You say you keep a watch on flea carriers. I saw those wounds. You tell me what animal bit him."

Chee was momentarily sidetracked.

"Folks say a cat or coyotes got the sheep. Probably the same thing got him. We'll know when the kid talks."

"If he talks, and that could be too late for someone else. You talk, doctor, tell me what kind of wounds those were."

114

"Well," the pahan doctor seized the opportunity to cover anxiety with professionalism, "a good question. They can't be teeth marks because they're more like the gouges you see from claws. There aren't the puncture marks you expect from canine teeth. On the other hand, they can't be claw marks because they're far too sharp. There isn't the bruising you expect to see, and the pattern is of a single crater instead of four or five lacerations as is the usual pattern for claws. In fact, the only way I could describe them is a gouge one might receive from two grooved razors held close together."

"Cat, coyote, rat, prairie dog? Mouse? What?"

"I can't say. I never saw wounds like that before," the doctor said.

"What does all this prove?" Chee lost patience.

"I've seen wounds like that before," Youngman said. "And I've seen the stains that go with them."

Begay moved closer.

"You're going to check out where the boy was attacked, aren't you?" Youngman talked fast. "You'll never find the place without the Lolomas or me. Let's see if we can find something else. Since you want to be a help."

Paine got to the campsite too late.

" 'Wee, sleekit, cow'rin, tim'rous, beastie,' " he slid up the door of a 12″ × 20″ lucite cage next to what was left of Claire Franklin, which was dried blood, a skull crushed on a tire track, and an abdominal cavity gutted and as empty as a drum. Almost empty. " 'Thou need na' start awa sae hasty, wi' bickering brattle. I wad be laith to rin an' chase thee, wi' murd'ring pattle.' "

Paine kicked the dead woman's back, and a kangaroo mouse jumped from the stomach into the cage. The cage door slapped shut.

The rest of the three corpses were as badly mutilated by scavengers. The effect scavengers created, it always seemed to Paine, was an after-the-party air. Bits of skin and clothes were strewn here and there in the dirt like torn streamers. Bodies, a coffee pot, hamburger buns and marshmallows scattered in weary repose. Only flies and ants still at work, and a horned toad waiting for the ants. A scene for Dürer, he thought.

He opened a Coke from the campers' food chest and sat down.

"The reason I've asked you here, the topic for today is, What do you think of Death? You're all worn out, I know, but it's more than likely you have some constructive insights. Group therapy may be new to you. It's not to me, so I will lead this session. A topic we might begin with is whether from your vantage point you see death as a mere continuum of life, whether you see yourselves as now existing in part at least as a vulture or a prairie dog, a communion of flesh in the Catholic view. I realize people hate to talk about it. They avoid the subject, it's a conversation killer. If it helps I can tell you this. All the really deep, all the really great thinking on the subject of death is done during a plague. Granted, millions die during a war, but all the thinking is wasted on patriotism and strategies. Take a plague. Strategies are useless and patriotism is ridiculous. Pure death, nothing but death is finally met.

"For example, you probably recall what bad poetry Robert Frost wrote about a woodpile rotting in the woods. No real sense of life or death. Just mildew. Compare it to Nashe's *In Time of Pestilence*. 'Brightness falls from the air; queens have died young and fair; dust hath closed Helen's eye. I am sick, I must die. Lord have mercy on us.' "

Paine chugged soda down a dry throat.

"Death is an intimate thing. That's so easy to forget. Just like sex, a very intimate thing. Nowadays, people like to be deceased, not in 'death's embrace.'

"The fascinating thing about plague, you see, is that

116

it's death personified. I mean, death as a person. A lover. There was a case reported in *A Journal of the Plague Year* of a dying man who ran through the streets of London kissing pretty girls, deliberately infecting them. Killing them. People said he was mad. It's my opinion, however, that at the time he was running through the streets he had given up his soul and he was Death with two legs and two lips.

"I think you're beginning to understand. Plague is a kiss. Without that kiss, that flea bite, plague dies. Now that's the amazing part. Death can die, too. Yes, love makes us all vulnerable. Even Him."

Paine finished the Coke and dropped the aquamarine bottle on the ground. He picked up the caged mouse on his way to the Land Rover and looked at distant spires of rock.

" 'Twinkle, twinkle little bat, how I wonder what you're at. Up above the world you fly, like a teatray in the sky.' "

The Bell UH-1 "Iroquois" copter rattled fifty feet above its shadow as metal pipes rained down on the dead sheep. The center of each pipe was baited with meat, the open ends were lined with insecticide.

"Don't see those ammonia stains you're talking about." Walker Chee surveyed the carcasses through binoculars.

"We're not close enough. Go down," Youngman yelled over the engine noise.

"Not on your life!"

The copter peeled off into a wide circle. Inside, the patrolmen rolled canisters to the bays, and as the copter passed over the sheep and Isa Loloma's truck again Begay dumped more poison, bags that exploded on contact with the ground in a dust of cornmeal spiced by a lethal anticoagulant called warfarin.

"I have a meeting with Piggot at my office in one hour. Let's step on it," Chee told the pilot.

"I can show you the same bites and stains on the horses in Joe Momoa's corral," Youngman said to the doctors.

"No," Chee answered.

"Whatever attacked the boy and the sheep attacked the horses."

"Says you."

"Then what attacked them?" Youngman pointed back at the receding hill. "A cat goes after a flock, it picks out one sheep. Coyotes'll scatter sheep over kingdom come. That's eighty sheep back there, slaughtered."

"Duran," Chee shook his head, "you see one sick kid and you scream 'Plague.' You see some dead sheep and horses and you say it's a mystery. We've been dealing with plague control for years. We've done it with the Indian Bureau and experts from the Center for Disease Control in Atlanta. Plague is spread by rodent fleas. Any rodent within miles of that hill is as good as dead now. We know how to handle this problem, if you'll just let us get on with it."

"Those sheep weren't killed by prairie dogs."

"But plague is spread by rodent fleas. Get it through your head, Deputy. I haven't got time to check out every vulture lunch you find."

"Because you got to get back to your whites."

"Right. Because it was the white oil company that gave us this helicopter so we could dust those sheep for you. Because it's the white utilities give us satellite pictures to help our irrigation program. Yeah, you figured it out. Because in spite of you people, I'm going to bring some money into red hands. If you don't like it, you can always step outside."

Chee lit a cigar for his grin.

"You're scared, Duran. You're scared of anyone suc-

118

cessful, especially another Indian. I could show you some computer technology we're setting up at the clinic that would knock your eyes out, but I've changed my mind. I'm not going to have you pestering the doctors. Besides, this desert is quarantine enough for you. Just wash yourself down with some green soap and burn your clothes before you go near anyone. I can't help you."

Chee settled back, listening to the jets' whine and the rotors' strokes, a rider secure in his element. Youngman watched the ground.

Anne sawed through the distributor cable and carried it with her to sit in the shade of the overturned van. Henry was sprawled unconscious on the sand. Franklin watched through slitted eyes. Both of his legs were broken from the accident. The two smaller fingers of Anne's left hand were broken and tied together. She peeled insulation off the cable with Franklin's penknife.

He spat cactus pulp onto the ground.

"It's no use."

"It's all we have. We left everything with the bats."

When she'd peeled all the insulation off, she separated the copper strands, coiling and putting aside all but one. Beside her was the one item of use she'd found in the van, a fishing pole they'd planned to use on Joe Momoa's trout stream. One end of the single copper wire Anne formed into a quarter-inch loop, through which she passed the free end of the wire. With every movement of her broken fingers, pain throbbed to her elbow. Worse, her fingers were slippery. On her fourth try, she attached the wire loop to the end of the fishing pole and drew the free end through the pole's top eye.

Franklin looked on without interest. The trauma of his injuries was secondary to the fact that he refused to eat or drink. The mathematics of survival in the desert were simple. Without shelter or water, a healthy man would last one day. Since Franklin was only losing ten pounds of body fluid a day in the shade, he had about two more days to go. Henry, with a fever, little pulse, a coma, Anne gave hours.

"Pray for me," Franklin asked.

"No."

She put a pebble in her mouth to control her own thirst. It took her ten minutes just to hook the wire and tie on fishing leader. An experimental tug on the leader snapped the noose at the end of the pole shut.

"Yea, tho I walk through the Valley of the Shadow of Death—"

"You're wasting energy."

"Should I save it?" he said. "This is easy for you. It's always easy for heroes. I have it a little more difficult, my dear. I am a bad man," he laughed weakly, "and I believe in God. It's a contradiction that I've been able to maintain during life, but as I near death my situation becomes sharply uncomfortable."

"And you're wasting lung moisture with every word."

"The very least of my problems. You know that bat that was on my chest—"

"You were in shock long before you showed it. You wouldn't have felt a knife in your chest."

"The Bible tells us bats shall roost on false idols. It's an omen."

Anne's broken fingers had puffed up. She wrapped them up again with her middle finger for support.

"You're going to leave us, aren't you? When the sun goes down. Trading post can't be more than forty miles away and you know the way. You can make it in a couple of nights."

"Maybe they'll send someone out for us," she said.

"No. I remember you told us we wouldn't see a soul until we reached the hills. We're not expected back for three more days. What do you think, two more days before anyone gets worried? Before your deputy comes looking for you? A week, then. I'm sure you've figured this out already. You'll go tonight while you still have the strength."

Earlier, she'd climbed the dune the van had hit. From there she could see, north, the distant edge of the mesa. South, the blue haze of the San Francisco Peaks. In between, nothing, not a hogan or a shepherd, nothing but wasteland and the thick shimmer of superheated air which, where the ground was flat and barren, presented the illusion of water.

She sat and re-formed the noose at the end of the pole.

"You are a beautiful woman. You shouldn't die out here."

"I won't."

"Maybe an Indian can live out here—"

"That's right. You learn to live. You learn to live differently."

Anne removed her sweat-damp shirt and tied it into a hat. Her bare breasts, nipples dark against pale, freckled skin, shifted with each movement. She put on Franklin's windbreaker, picked up the fishing pole, and left the van.

Fifty yards away, by the shallow gully of a dry arroyo pitted with burrows, she stopped and waited ten minutes, until her presence became part of the arroyo along with a beetle climbing over minuscule boulders and a nose that repeatedly sniffed the air before emerging as a mouse on the run. Upside-down, a spider traveled seemingly on air from one side of the gully to the other. A Chihuahua whiptail lizard as long as Anne's finger dug for scorpions.

She felt the sun's hands on her back, a ball of sweat running down between her shoulder blades. The colors of the desert, when one spent enough time looking at it, were the colors of a woman. At a distance, the texture of skin stretched over the soft curves of hips, white in

121

the sun, pale dun in semi-shade, in deep shade the blue of the underside of breasts. If she were naked, Anne thought, she could become indiscernible against the skin of the desert.

The lizard's tongue flashed like a ribbon. There were no male Chihuahua whiptails, only females that reproduced by cloning as if males were as needless a luxury as leaves on a cactus. Working industriously, sensing a scorpion below, the lizard didn't see a five-foot-long whipsnake gliding over the arroyo bed.

The whipsnake slid with his head held high and moving slowly from side to side the better to gauge the distance of his strike. He was smooth-scaled, striped on the side and creamy as marble on the belly. Concentrating on his prey, he nosed the copper noose.

The lizard darted down the arroyo as Anne pulled the leader. The whipsnake swayed in the noose until Anne set it down and crushed its slim head under a rock.

Half the snake meat she'd cook, half would be eaten raw for the moisture.

She refused to die.

Sixty million years ago, as the long Day of the Dinosaurs faded, an explosion of versatility was taking place among a newer class of life called mammals. Some mammals grew great, striving to fill the niche being vacated by the dinosaurs. Others developed speed afoot or fins to swim. A few tree shrews, small insectivores gifted with nimble fingers and voracious appetites, developed loose folds of skin along their ribs that enabled them to glide between branches.

Gliding was made easier as their three outer fingers grew longer and webbed. Teeth changed, the incisors crowded out by larger canines. The collarbone extended, ribs flattened out, and the sternum became ridged to support powerful chest muscles, while the

122

heart and lungs swelled. The upper arm shrank more. Thumb and forefinger shrank. Webbed outer fingers grew still longer, the third finger as long as the animal's head and body. Gliding became flying, and there were bats. By the Age of Man, there were an estimated two thousand forms of bats.

Paine listened for them in the dark.

He sat bathed in the yellow glow of the Rover's interior light idly flipping a copy of *Playboy* he'd picked up in the office of Chee's doctor in Window Rock. The sheen of the pages transformed the nudes. Breasts were as glossy as fingernails. The centerfold blonde was as slick as soap.

On top of the Rover, a unidirectional microphone rhythmically swung back and forth 360 degrees. In the center of the mike were six aluminum tubes, each designed to vibrate sympathetically like a tuning fork to a single frequency, however soft, at a distance of a thousand yards. The calls of many different bats might make one tube hum; only the echolocating call of the vampire could make all the tubes respond. Inside the truck, the pistol grip of the microphone shaft twisted next to Paine's ear. One wire trailed from the grip to a battery and a second wire led to a distortion-free signal amplifier that, in turn, was jacked into an oscilloscope on the seat beside Paine. Across the green face of the scope was a white line as straight as a ruler.

Chee's doctor had given Paine an injection. He was full of sewage now; a sludge of 3,000 million formalin-killed plague bacilli coated with aluminum hydroxide floated through his veins. What he wanted was new ears for new voices.

The night was so full of voices. Owls, frogs, hawks, lizards, mice, insects, coyotes, the entire desert was a reservoir of mews, barks, howls, and screams. Cries heard and unheard. Which was why he had to use the oscilloscope, because human hearing ended at the meager frequency of 20,000 cycles per second.

From the magazine page a pouty face stuck out its tongue.

Animals adapted in different ways to survive. In humans adaptation was outwardly evidenced by the size of the skull and sexual apparatus. The distended penis, enlarged breasts, full lips, and buttocks. Among bats? The wings. And the ears so magnified and as convoluted as crowns. The ear tragus as separate as a dagger. A cochlea wound round and like a seashell and interlaced by muscles that allowed the ear to hear the echo clearer than the call, a call that could go to 200,000 cycles per second, ten times the range of man.

Touch was what most mammals relied on in the night, when colors changed to shades of gray. Rodents packed themselves into the security of close burrows. Humans groped, hoping for the feel of soft skin, surrounded by fantasies and limitations, blind in the dark.

Paine put the magazine aside, and smiled.

Jezebels, Ochay would have said. Every day until his death, the Mexican was either kneeling in prayer or pressing religious tracts on the other members of the team.

After his death, Ochay had his revenge. High in the Sierras, hill Indians had vandalized Paine's truck and he lost his personal library of Milton, Shakespeare and Lewis Carroll. All that was left was Ochay's New Testament, a well-thumbed copy with the most horrific judgements and prophecies thoughtfully underlined. It was Paine's only reading matter for the next six months.

All of Revelations was underlined. St. John the Divine howling in the wilderness, stuffing the luggage of future madmen. "They have as king over them the angel of the bottomless pit. . . . The rest of mankind who were not killed by these plagues did not repent of the works of their hands. . . ." Better the chains of Marley's

124

ghost than Ochay's book, Paine had thought more than once, though there were parts he did find interesting. "Then I saw an angel standing in the sun and with a loud voice he called to all the birds that fly in midheaven, 'Come, gather for the great supper of God, to eat the flesh of kings, the flesh of captains, the flesh of mighty men, the flesh of horses and their riders, and the flesh of all men, both free and slave, both small and great.' "

The oscilloscope shivered and cast a "print" of white dots. Only one microphone tube was responding; a wrong "print." The Arizona sky was full of small insectivorous bats—guano bats, cave bats, red bats, pygmy canyon bats, fringed bats, and death's head bats, which bore white "eyes and mouth" on their black belly fur—all wheeling in their nightly chase after grasshoppers and moths, blasting the air with high-intensity cries somewhere around 140,000 cps. The sensitive tubes of Paine's microphone would tremble sympathetically at 73,000 cps, because the larger vampire bats were "whispering" bats, sending out low-intensity cries not through their mouths but through their nostrils. Like breath. The microphone continued its steady sweep. The oscilloscope line returned to level.

Over the last few nights, the bats seemed to be coming from the west. The most likely origin was the San Francisco Peaks. He as good as crossed off the bat roosts of Mansion Mesa to the southeast.

Sympathy was a concept Ochay and St. John never could grasp, Paine thought. For them, the reach to God or the skid to hell, anything but the reality of the world. But sympathy was one of the most interesting of all biological phenomena.

Metal humming to batsong. Flesh with the crispness of magazine paper. Those were simple examples of mechanical sympathy. Sympathy between life forms was more subtle.

The truth was that death was no rending of the skies

125

asunder, no clash of angels, no chariots of fire. Death was a filaria worm that was brought by a fly bite, grew on the pigment in human skin, and crawled out through the eye. Or a cancer virus that seemed to leap off the slide and begin metastasizing in mid-air. Or leprosy bacilli that turned limbs into withered ornaments. The joke was that among immunologists there was no immunity, and among parasitologists there was no prevention. Did the body recoil or throw up defenses against the seductive attraction of the invader? Rarely. As a statistical fact, among researchers the flesh yielded with tender anticipation. With sympathy. Cancer researchers had the highest cancer rate. Filaria researchers went blind. The specialist in leprosy became a lazar. The very point to saying a disease or parasite was endemic to a region was that there they were everywhere, and that there was no escape. Especially when you were not trying to escape, but rather relentlessly pursuing. Where intimacy was a professional necessity. People were always amazed at immunologists who studied the progression of a disgusting disease through their own bodies. Yet, if you were going to catch it, what the hell else could you do about it? The cancer blossomed, the worms fattened, and the man pared himself for specimens. An occupational hazard. You became, quite literally as the invasion spread, exactly what you studied. "Which is why," Joe Paine used to point out in Mexico City, "we're so damn clever."

The oscilloscope line trembled, just barely.

Paine watched the microphone's rotating shaft and the needle turning in the compass. The oscilloscope line was flat, shuddered, and was flat again. A tremor, not even enough for a print. Paine tapped the compass nervously.

"We're so clever," Joe Paine used to say, "because our subject is rabies. We picked one with a cure."

Which was about the only mistake Paine could remember his father making. Because the subject was bats.

His head jerked. The oscilloscope line was flat, flat, flat . . . a tremor . . . flat, flat, flat . . . a print. A faint one of low intensity slashing down an octave with three harmonic streaks. From the west, according to the compass.

Inside the stationary sleeve of the microphone shaft, microswitches rode over cams. Four idents set the revolutions of the shaft. He twisted the sleeve one click to an arc of 180 degrees running west from north to south.

On the oscilloscope, the prints were slightly stronger and twice as frequent. Those would be the lead females, casting soft, regular, searching whispers ahead of the main group. About eight hundred yards off, he estimated, and traveling around twenty miles per hour. On a clipboard map, he noted the direction and time of contact.

Despite the cool night air, he perspired. Most bat "prints" were graceful shadows shaped like bells or diamonds. The voices of vampires were ragged, almost human. More bats came within range of the microphone. Northwest, he decided, and twisted the sleeve another click, cutting the arc to 90 degrees. The oscilloscope line was shivering almost constantly. They were coming right at him.

Paine got out of the Rover and snapped an ultra red filter on a searchlight mounted in his door. The oscilloscope started beeping, triggered by the intensity of the signals. He got into the Rover and rolled up the windows. He twisted the sleeve another click to 45 degrees, and the oscilloscope turned into a solid band of strong and nearing slashes.

Paine pulled the battery plug from the microphone shaft and directed the microphone manually by the grip. The oscilloscope image exploded into snow, overloaded by input. He switched off the scope and the interior light, picked up sensitized, electronic binoculars and switched on his searchlight. He swung the beam up.

They came over, ten at a time, then twenty, then more than he could count, about twenty-five feet above the Rover, hundreds of them, one of the biggest vampire colonies he'd ever seen. Not fluttering like insectivorous bats, but rowing easily with long wings, covering the sky, coloring it with red wings the shape of knives.

The rider steered his heavy motorcycle down the mountain road. The road was bad, half the time on the edge of a drop, and if he hadn't known it as well as he did he would have been reduced to a crawl in the dark. He maintained speed, as much from fear as anything else.

The lip of the road, weakened by rain, crumbled under his tires. He straightened out and downshifted. He was happy to have to concentrate on the road and when he reached a point where it was almost totally washed out he skillfully gunned the bike up the inside bank until he reached good road again.

He was lucky, he told himself, luckier than his brother. Someone had had to stay out by the corral at night to shoot whatever was attacking the livestock. His brother wanted to go and try out his new 30-30, which he took with a pump shotgun, two remote control lamps, and a bedroll. His brother never fired a shot. At midnight, he staggered in the kitchen door, bleeding from his head to his boots and screaming, "Bats!"

Which was crazy.

And he was luckier than his folks. The old lady took sick first. The old man had to tend both and then the old man took sick. None of which had to be serious if the storm hadn't come along and knocked out the phone line. Jesus, how many times had he told them all they should have a radio at the ranch just in case? Maybe a million. If he didn't get a doctor in time it was

128

going to be their fault. A little planning went a long way. For one thing, the whole damn road had to be repaired, graded some places, if they intended to get trucks up for the piñon harvest. He'd probably have to run everything for a while.

He slowed to pick his way through some branches that had fallen across the road. A black line like a coach whip was tangled in the branches. He stopped and twisted the bike's handlebars, swinging the beam until he found a telephone pole on the outside edge of the road. The line was the telephone wire.

He walked his bike to the pole and opened his engraved leather saddlebags. He really was lucky, but luck didn't mean a damn thing unless you were prepared. Inside the bags were the line repairman's lamp helmet, gloves, belt, and phone he'd taken when he quit Southwest Bell. It wasn't stealing; everybody took things. Nobody was going to quarrel if he saved a few lives. He strapped on the belt and helmet, tried the light, which was faint but good enough. Eagerly, he climbed the pole stakes up to the disconnected wire.

On top of the pole, he had his first misgivings. He never had been so good at line work and the helmet lamp seemed much fainter thirty feet in the air than it had on the ground. If he just took his time, though, he could still save hours off trying to reach help on his bike. There weren't any other homes with phones around Dinnebito Wash and there wasn't a public phone until you were almost in Tuba City. He hitched his belt around the pole a notch tighter. The night was so damn dark; although he often liked dark nights for hunting coons, sometimes even deer. He'd stay in a blind until he heard noise and then hit the flood lamp. The animals would freeze, their eyes orange and panicked, and he'd put a bullet right through their lights.

The gloves were stiff from disuse. He was afraid he was going to drop the line phone if he made a mistake.

129

The phone itself was simple enough: it had a dial on the grip and two wires attached to roach clips. His boots couldn't get a firm hold on the stakes and that slowed him. Also, the roach clips were so rusted shut from disuse he had to scrape them clean with his buck knife. He was about to sink the clips in the wire when he found he wasn't alone. Hanging upside down from the wire about ten feet away, a bat was watching him.

The clips slipped from his gloves but he recovered quickly. It was the biggest bat he'd ever seen, dull brown, with a squat nose and fringed head. Just a single bat, though, and after swallowing on a dry throat he laughed at himself. He hooked his knife on his belt to free both hands and clipped the phone onto the wire. The helmet beam slid up the wire. Five more bats hung on the wire.

There hadn't been any bats on the line when he first climbed the pole, he was sure. He wasn't afraid, but he did wish he'd brought up a varmint pistol. There was one in his saddlebags. He looked down at the bike. His beam barely reached the ground, but he could swear that it was alive. At first, he thought, with toads milling and hopping after the road, and then he looked straight down and saw that the whole bottom half of the pole was covered by them and they were climbing up, sideways and backwards, and he knew what they were and, however irrationally, what they were after. His heart knew and began beating on his ribs. The line swayed, tugging the phone in his hand. The line, in a matter of seconds, was solid with bats. He saw one with a baby clutched to its chest. The baby twisted its head to look at him.

"No!"

Something hit him in the center of the back and slapped him against the pole. He dropped the line phone to swing. Teeth bit through his pants. He punched downward and his arm came up sliced from

130

the elbow to the wrist. He stared at it, amazed. In a hanging march, the bats on the wire walked toward him. He tried to unhook his belt, but his gloves were too clumsy. He shook his left glove off and at once a bat covered the back of his hand. There were more on his back and others securing themselves to his legs. The bites were sharp but not terribly painful. More cold than anything else. He shook the bat off his hand and now his fingers were red and slippery. He'd always had luck on his side and if he could just get to his bike . . .

He kicked, and his other boot slipped from its stake. He hung from his belt and watched the bats crawling, head downwards, from the top of the pole. His legs kicked and churned like a man running in place for a short time, and for a long time after that they slowly rose and fell like a marathon runner staggering towards the end of his race under an unfair burden.

CHAPTER FIVE

A line of men chanted "Ho-o-hah!" against the backdrop of the desert. They were painted all in black except for white across their foreheads and mouths and spots on their arms and backs. Eagle feathers decorated their long hair, and fox skins hung from their blue kilts. With every sideways step, the turquoise strings around their necks and the tortoise shell rattles tied to their knees clapped in time.

"There's my jerkwater brother." Cecil Somiviki pointed out a dancer to Youngman. "The one in the wig. So scared he's ready to shit silver dollars."

About five hundred Hopis sat on roofs and ladders, eating piki bread and drinking Cokes, the young men dressed up like dark cowboys, girls in ceremonial trim. A delegation of Navajos, each glittering like a presentation case of silver jewelry, stayed together, but the white tourists, exhausted by their climb from the parking lot a thousand feet down in the squash fields and their foreheads burned pink over dusty sunglasses, spread around the edge of the dirt plaza. Youngman looked for Anne. Walker Chee was there, a velvet sash tied around his razor-cut hair.

"Headpounder's still after your ass," Cecil muttered. "Well, I can't fire you today anyway. Oh oh, lady!" He reached across Youngman and grabbed an Instamatic a white woman had wrapped in her scarf. "No photos, ma'am, you read the signs."

She had swallow wing sunglasses and zinc cream on her nose.

"Signs?"

Her smile turned into an oval as Cecil opened the back of the camera and ground the film cartridge under his boot. He dropped the camera into a sack and gave her a numbered piece of paper.

"Collect it after the dance."

"This is a religious ceremony," Youngman told her.

"Outdoors?" she squawked. "Come on."

"Remember," Cecil said, "no tickee, no camera." He and Youngman moved on along the perimeter of the crowd, keeping their eyes out for more cameras, or tape recorders, or sketch pads. "Damn Bear Strap Clan's supposed to be catching these yoyos down in the parking lot."

The ladder from the Snake Clan kiva flew pennants of feathers and horsehair. Youngman was surprised to see feathers still flying from the Fire Clan kiva, as well.

"Yeah," Cecil answered his question, "those old boys been down there for days. Hey, we got ourselves another amateur anthropologist."

A white teenager clutched a torn airline bag that, under Youngman's hands, revealed a Panasonic recorder and a Glad Bag of grass.

"Far out." Cecil took the recorder. "What's the matter with you today, Youngman? Usually you're the one who finds all the goodies."

In the center of the plaza was a standing bower of green cottonwood branches and a hole covered over by a board. The dancers stamped on the board, warning the spirits below that messengers were on their way requesting rain, singing, "Ho-o-ah, ho-o-ah, ho-o-aha, ho-o-ha!" One of the dancers held up the "messengers," handfuls of snakes.

Youngman and Cecil worked their way to the front of the crowd, while those dancers called "gatherers"

133

fanned out around the edge of the plaza. Their job was simply to gather any loose snakes before they got into the crowd. Antelope priests kept time with pebble rattles. Youngman felt adrenalin hitting him like Scotch. Cecil even was suddenly excited; except for his job, he would have been dancing. The crowd took a step back.

"Sonovabitch, sonovabitch," Cecil kept repeating to himself.

The first dancer bit his snake about ten inches behind the head and supported the rest of the snake's body with his left hand. By the dancer's right shoulder was another dancer with an eagle feather "snake whip." The tail of a six-foot diamondback dragged over the ground. They had to dance a snake four times around the cottonwood bower in the center of the plaza, and then pick up another snake and start again. That's how they got rain.

"They pull the fangs, you know," Youngman heard a white father telling his son.

Crouched, dancing on the balls of his feet, Powell Somiviki went by.

"Shit, he's got the snake on the wrong side," Cecil said.

Powell's eyes rolled nearly out of sight. His knees wobbled. From the left side of his mouth and out of reach of the eagle feather, a blood-colored rattler pushed its snout along Powell's cheek. The snake's gaping mouth displayed two yellowish fangs. Youngman watched the snake wrap its tail around Powell's arm, trying to coil for a strike. Powell danced away while the snake sought its angle.

"Sonovabitch," Cecil said.

"Dad, I saw—"

"They milk them," the father answered.

A black rattler darted away from the dancers and across the plaza, followed casually by a gatherer. Although the gatherer caught up, he didn't stop the snake,

134

a fact that wasn't appreciated by the crowd until the big rattler was escaping between their legs. Shouting, they jumped against the houses or ran towards the road. The gatherer scooped up the snake by the tail and carried it back.

Powell was on his knees on the other side of the plaza. He'd only fainted. The sidewinder still hadn't coiled sufficiently around Powell's arm to strike and the dancer with Powell helped by unwrapping the rattler's tail and reversing the head in Powell's mouth.

"See what a college education does for you," Cecil sweated. "You don't know right from left. Stupid—"

The dance went on. Walker Chee excused himself to visit one of the outhouses along the side of the mesa. When he came out, Youngman was waiting.

"How's the Loloma boy?"

"I gave a report to the elders." Chee tried to slip by.

"How is he?" Youngman blocked the way.

"He's in good hands. By the way, you people are missing a great thing here. You could auction off the Snake Dance to the television networks, you'd pull in a million dollars a year. For doing nothing, just what you always do. This could be the biggest attraction in the country."

Youngman was amazed. Talking to Chee was like trying to catch a lizard by the tail. Even if you pinned him down, he got away.

By the time Youngman returned to the plaza, one of the dancers was bitten. A bullsnake had him by the neck until the shadow of an eagle feather passed over the snake's eyes and it let go, hitting the ground with a thump. Powell danced over the bullsnake, a new rattler in his mouth, the rattler's muzzle resting on Powell's shoulder and its tail swaying almost in time to Powell's steps. Man and snake, two parts of nature, intimately joined and not by chance; the legends spoke of the snake wife. What the whites, what even Navajos would

135

never understand, Abner always said, was that the Snake Dance was a dance of life, not of death.

"That boy, he did okay," Cecil winked at Youngman.

When the last snake was brought back to the cottonwood bower, the head of the Snake Clan made a circle of cornmeal with lines leading east, west, south, north, to the sun and to the underworld. While he prayed, the dancers threw their snakes into the circle where they writhed in a heap. Finally, all the dancers scrambled for snakes, each grabbing as many as he could carry, and ran from the plaza, down the narrow path that hugged the mesa wall, to the desert, where they would run for miles more before releasing the reptiles.

Youngman, Cecil, and a second deputy called Frank gave back confiscated cameras and directed tourist traffic out of the parking lot in the squash field and when the lot was almost empty they had some cold beers on the tailgate of Cecil's station wagon.

Anne hadn't shown. Obviously, Youngman thought, she had better things to do.

"Not the worst Snake Dance I ever seen. Not the best," Cecil directed the spray of his beer away, "but not the worst."

"Your brother looked good," Frank burped.

"A little shaky at the start," Cecil frowned. "Like I told him, though, you can't fight it. You got the belief in you, you'll be okay."

"Who was it got bit?" Youngman tried to get into the spirit.

"What's his name . . . Butterfly. No, Butterfly's brother. Oh, I'm gonna rag him tomorrow," Cecil laughed. "Wasn't it swell to see Powell with those snakes?"

Cecil scratched his crotch with satisfaction. Frank was the deputy from Walpi pueblo; he had enough white blood to give him whiskers and a long nose, and behind his back friends called him Horseface.

"See when they let those snakes get in the crowd?" he nudged Youngman. "That fat blonde. Thought she was gonna stay in the air for a month at least."

"A laugh riot," Youngman said.

"They wanna come and see the dance, they take their chances," Cecil said. "No one asked 'em. This ain't Gallup. They wanta get drunk, see some phony dances and Roy Rogers, they can go to Gallup."

"You know Roy Rogers got Trigger stuffed in his house?" Frank turned serious.

"No!" Cecil was disgusted. "Stuffed with what?"

The few vehicles left in the lot were Hopi panel trucks and Walker Chee's Le Sabre.

"Wonder what Chee's hanging around for?" Youngman accepted a smoke from Frank.

"Business," Cecil said in a small voice.

"Business?"

"That's what I hear. Bastard's got no respect at all." Cecil spat on the ground.

"What kind of business?"

"Oh, some shit about letting the headpounders do all the policing of the joint lands. Doing us a favor, as usual. Hell, it wasn't joint land until the Navajos got to their friends in the Bureau and stole the land from us. By the time the headpounders and the Bureau get finished we're gonna have just enough land to piss in from a squat."

"Speakin' of Chee, I ran into a funny guy a couple weeks back," Frank said. "Big pahan with reddish hair, said he was a doctor. Drove a funny truck."

"I met him," Youngman said. "What made him funny?"

"Nothing, first time I saw him. Second time, I ran into him down at Five House Butte. He asked me about bats. He ask you about bats?"

Cecil and Frank stayed to open some more cans while Youngman walked back to the pueblo. The noise

137

of family get-togethers came out of screen doors, along with aroma of fried rabbit. Through one window he could see Chee and some other Navajos with the old men of the pueblo. Youngman sat alone where the plaza ended in thin air. He let his feet hang off the edge.

The sun burned level with his eyes. He looked down between his boots, where a juniper tree struggling on an outcrop obscured the long drop. With field glasses, he might have been able to see the dancers returning from the desert. Dark spots moving at a lope through shadows that could lie across half a mile of sand. The air was a haze, purple to the east, golden to the west. Beyond the desert, on the other side of the mountains, the towns would just be lighting up. Winslow, Flagstaff, Tucson, Phoenix. Boulevards, palm trees, motel neon, swimming pools, all lit, all powered by water that was bought, stolen, divided, overestimated and disappearing. Ho-ah-ha, everybody wants rain.

Bats, though. Why would the pahan who was after a slice of old Abner want bats? If he did want them, why wasn't he at the Carlsbad Caverns where there were millions? What was so secretive about looking for bats?

Everyone had seemed to be all right at Momoa's ranch, he thought. And wondered why he'd bothered thinking of Momoa until he remembered that was where Anne was heading. Abner and the Loloma boy were both attacked east of Gilboa. She was going west. And she had a radio.

The only problem she had was him. He remembered the first time he and Anne camped together, up on Dinnebito Wash. Camping was a formal word for it. Just catching enough trout to eat. Making love on a blanket.

On the second night, she'd started talking about her family, and on the third night she asked about his.

"No family and no stories," he said.

138

"I saw those sketches you did. That terrible bloody face in all of them. It looked full of symbolism to me."

"Symbolism, hell," he answered. "That's Masaw."

To entertain her, he told her stories about Maski Canyon. The story about how Masaw escaped bloody and burned from a flaming pit that could never be put out. The story about the city of the dead. When she asked him to take her there, he put her off.

"What you mean is, this place doesn't really exist, does it?" she laughed.

"Something like that." He took the easy way out.

"Like 'somewhere over the rainbow?' "

"Let me put it this way. If you're there, you're lost."

One thing bothered her.

"How can you do the drawings if you've never seen Masaw?"

"Abner tells me what to draw."

"He sees Masaw?"

"Abner has connections."

"Abner's going to poison himself with datura someday."

"That, too."

Wrong, as it turned out, Youngman thought.

Abner and Anne, the only two people he cared about. One dead and the other leaving. But only leaving the reservation, not him necessarily. Not unless he insisted on staying, and what for? To end up as shriveled as Stone Man or a pariah like Abner? Chee almost had him out of his job already. Cecil refused to investigate what had happened to Abner's body.

Why not go with Anne? Or, phrased the way most whites would like to put it, why live like an Indian? Why live dirty on scrub land, sweating all day and freezing at night. With some vocational training he could work nine-to-five in an air-conditioned office and own two suits and an economy car and have two weeks vacation. Or, if he had sufficient cunning, become a professional Indian like Chee. Not that Anne would ever put the question that way. For her, it was merely a matter of love. Of "commitment," as she put it. But Youngman was already committed. Being born a reservation Indian was the same as committing a crime and being sentenced to life in isolation. Quarantined with the perverse sickness that made life among whites the same as suffocation. The evidence-symptoms of this crime-disease: self-pity, suspiciousness, stupidity, and pride. Was there an Indian of the twentieth century, Youngman asked, who wasn't schizophrenic? And who didn't use it as an excuse? Did anyone do it as well as him?

Youngman heard steps crossing the plaza and Harold Masito sat beside him, smoking a handrolled cigarette of mesa tobacco, stuff that was three times stronger than store-bought. The Bear Strap priest wore his shirt formally buttoned at the neck. In the sideways angle of the sun, his face was as rough as sandstone.

"No clouds yet." He stared at the mountains.

"Not yet."

"You trying to think 'em up? Can't think 'em up. We do our part and the rains come. Couple of days, maybe more. Not instant. Maybe we get a breeze tonight. Get a real rain, not like yesterday."

"I was thinking of Abner, really," Youngman said. "Abner and bats."

They sat in silence for a minute, watching a mesquite ball roll over the ground far below. It bounced over some soda cans that had been pitched from the mesa. The cans could be used. Cut up and put over corn shoots in the spring.

"I been thinking about Abner, too," Harold said. "We shouldn't never chased him off the mesa."

"You thought he was a witch, remember."

"He was. But he had the power. Only kind of power we got is Masaw, this land. Abner could talk to Masaw

140

and we chased Abner out, and now we keep losing the land. Me, I thought I was a pretty brave fellow. I shouldn't of been scared of Abner. You weren't."

"I didn't think he was a witch."

"And now?"

"No. Someone else seems to, though. They robbed his grave. You wouldn't know anything about that, would you?"

"You mean, he's not in it."

"Yeah. That's not mysterious to me. The only thing I can't figure is what killed him. I never saw wounds like that before. Weren't any tracks."

Harold passed the cigarette.

"Tracks are only there when you see 'em. Abner did things right. I seen him last night, in dreams. That's why I come out here to you now."

"Oh?" Youngman was bitterly amused. "Now that you'll talk to him, what did Abner have to say?"

"He said for me to help you 'cause you don't know how to read."

"Uncle, I can't do much but I can read, thank you."

"Words."

"Yeah."

"You find any words when you found Abner?"

"No."

Harold grunted as if he'd made a point.

"So what was I going to read?" Youngman asked with exasperation. "Some scribbles of sand on the floor? Look, it's a little late for you to come around on Abner's behalf. I didn't chase him off the mesa, you did. With witch stories—"

"He stole the tablet. He told me in my dream."

"What?" Youngman was stopped short.

"He stole the Fire Clan tablet so the Pahana couldn't come back. The real White Brother has a corner of the tablet and when he comes we're supposed to put the tablet back together and everything will be okay. We

141

always had that tablet even before we got to this world so we'd know the Pahana when he got here."

"Before this world?"

"From the Mayan world. Abner could read Mayan."

"Oh." Youngman kept a straight face. "He never mentioned it to me." How about Greek and Latin, he thought to himself.

"We had to leave the Mayans 'cause life was too easy there."

"Sounds like a good reason."

"Here with Masaw we have to tend to the ceremonies to get any rain and corn at all. That's how we stay close to the right way. I know it's hard but we were chosen—"

"Not chosen," Youngman lost his patience. "Fucked. We are the God-fucked of the earth. Look at us! Walking around in rags, eating corn other people wouldn't throw to pigs, sleeping in hovels, and what do we do but spend all our time congratulating ourselves on being the most God-fucked and hopeless people on earth. Because that's what we are and nobody did it to us, we did it to ourselves. And we're so fucking dumb we're proud of it."

As soon as the words were out of his mouth, Youngman was ashamed. Harold regarded him with shock.

"I'm sorry, uncle. That was unfair and stupid. Okay? You were telling me about the tablet Abner stole."

"There is such a tablet."

"I'm sure there is," Youngman tried to mollify Harold.

"We took it to Washington to President Taft, I remember, to see if he was the Pahana."

Let me guess, Youngman thought.

"Was he?" he asked.

"No." Harold stayed downcast.

Youngman found himself disconcerted by the memory of the altar Abner had set up in his shed. Abner had left a place on the altar for the tablet.

"Anyway, it doesn't matter," Harold's face brightened, "now that Abner gave it back to Masaw. The Pahana missed his chance. You aren't going to leave the reservation, are you?" Harold added.

"Why should I?" Youngman was surprised.

"Talk is you're going to get fired. Chee's in there saying he's going to give us a lot of help but he wants you fired."

"The elders wouldn't do that and neither would Cecil."

"Not up to Cecil. And Chee, he's a good talker. And maybe it's 'cause you took up with that white girl. You think there was no bad feelings about that?"

"Just between her and me."

"Well, that's the way it is," Harold shrugged and slapped his palms down on his knees. "Gotta get back. My boy he brought up some ice cream in a ice bucket. You finish this." He gave Youngman the last of his cigarette.

Fired, Youngman thought. He hadn't thought much of his job until now. Except that it wasn't worth a damn and if he couldn't hold a job like that what could he do?

"Abner told me another thing in that dream," Harold said.

"Yeah?"

"He said for you to show me those pictures you took of him."

Youngman sat up and exhaled a stream of pungent smoke that fluttered against the air. The prospect of being fired remained in his mind but it did occur to him that he hadn't told anyone about the pictures he took of Abner dead in the shack. No one else knew about them except Anne and the campers. Maybe they'd talked to Selwyn.

"Okay," he said slowly, "I'll bring them. I don't have them on—"

He touched his shirt pocket and felt something flat,

and brought out the Polaroid snapshots of Abner spread-eagled on the ground. Youngman thought he'd filed them away with the death report; he'd been sure he hadn't put them in his pocket.

"I guess I was wrong. What do you want them for?"

"To read for you." Harold took the pictures.

He'd forgotten to file the snapshots, that was all, Youngman told himself.

The old Bear Strap Clan priest studied the photos slowly, one by one.

"Coyote is you. Shrike is Masaw's bird, brings him messages. Fire is . . . ," Harold frowned, "fire is broken. Spirals and swastikas are backwards. They're backwards. He did it."

Harold's face fell like a wall crumbling. His eyes were first surprised and then furious.

"We shouldn't of chased him, we should of killed him."

"Read the rest for me," Youngman asked.

Harold ripped the photos in half and threw them into the wind that rose up the mesa wall. Youngman tried to snatch some out of the air, but the shredded pictures skipped away, over the drop to the desert.

"Not going to read any more." Harold stood. "Not going to help you. So long."

Youngman stared at the bits of paper fluttering higher into the sky. Now, he'd never know what Abner did.

"Maybe the Fire Clan priests can help," he turned to say, but Harold was already slipping into his house.

The last light of the day was fading. The square stone-and-mud houses of the pueblo were turning to smaller squares of light, the off-white of gas lamps. Voices and the sounds of meals echoed through the alleys. Cottonwood leaves drifted over the plaza.

Youngman stirred himself, stretched, and headed for the road to the parking lot. Cecil had invited him for
144

dinner. Near the end of the plaza, though, Youngman found himself standing by the third kiva, where the totem of the Fire Clan hung from the top rung of the ladder that led down to the underground chamber. It was very unusual, practically sacrilegious, for the priests to stay in the kiva during a Snake Dance. It was definitely worse for anyone to disturb them, though.

He stood by the ladder, listening for a word, the shake of a rattle, a murmur of movement below. He blocked from his mind the sounds of the houses, the shuffle of wind. The kiva was totally silent. Juniper branches tied to the ladder below the entrance hole blocked any view of the chamber, but Youngman caught the odor of spoiled food.

He shook the ladder tentatively. There was no response. Stone Man had said eight priests were in the kiva; one of them should have noticed the ladder. Although they could have left last night or the night before without anyone noticing. The kiva could be empty. He watched a black beetle with wings marked scarlet climb from the entrance up the ladder. A carrion beetle.

A laugh reverberated in an alley. The plaza was still empty except for Youngman. A second beetle came after the first.

Youngman started down the ladder. As his boots pushed through the juniper branches he was sure he'd be greeted by angry challenges. There were no challenges, not a sound but the creaking of the ladder rungs. He shook another insect from his hand. The kiva was cold. Not cool. Cold that made his shirt cling to his back. And dark. The pale shaft of light that came through the entrance hole faded before it touched the floor. When Youngman reached bottom, the light died on his face. He could see nothing but the gray dome of the kiva ceiling curving into black space. The air was thick, hard to breathe, and slightly sweet.

He lit a match.

He was surrounded by a circle of men sitting against the walls of the kiva. All the men were stripped to the waist. Some held prayer sticks. One who stared at Youngman had his lap covered by cornmeal and colored sand. There wasn't a mark on them, except that their skin had turned black as if singed and foam had dried to a crust on their mouths and chests, and they were dead.

The Navajo helicopter sat in the floodlights set up around the plaza. A rack of germ-killing ultraviolet lights was aimed at the kiva, from which climbed, clumsy as a moonwalker, a figure in airtight vinyl coveralls. The cloth of the suit was impregnated with diethyltoluamide rat repellent. The face plate showed eyes and an oxygen mask. A similar figure followed and, together, the two men carried a sagging cocoon of the same shiny material to the helicopter. It was the fourth sealed bag they'd carried to the helicopter from the kiva. They went back for more.

"Ten o'clock." Walker Chee looked at his watch. He, Youngman and Cecil, and the village elders watched from Stone Man's roof, a hundred feet away. The entire village, many of them wrapped in blankets against the night chill, were on the roofs and silently watching the floodlit scene. "Lucky this didn't happen this afternoon."

"Yeah," Youngman agreed. "All we'd need is a few hundred whites racing out of here saying there's an epidemic."

"Wait a second, you don't know what you're talking about."

"I want to know what you're both talking about," Cecil interrupted. "Epidemic of what?"

"He doesn't know what he's talking about," Chee answered. "They could've died of anything. He said they looked burned."

146

"I said they *looked* burned. They weren't burned," Youngman corrected him.

"Anyway, another copter is on its way. All I meant before was that it's lucky we don't have to inoculate that crowd you had this afternoon. That's," Chee glared at Youngman, "how wild rumors get started."

"And just what the hell are you going to inoculate them against?" Youngman demanded.

"We'll use general antibiotics like streptomycin." Chee turned to the elder. "I'm just trying to help you people. Sheriff, are you going to get your deputy off my back?"

A sixth silvery cocoon was being carried from the kiva. The same pueblo elders who had been buying the most important sales pitch of Walker Chee's life just hours before studied the Navajo chairman now with open suspicion.

"A lot of people here don't take to needles of no kind," Cecil said. "Matter of fact, seeing's how this fucks up the Rain Dance, not a good idea for you to be giving orders here."

"This is a lot more serious than any Rain Dance!" Chee lost his temper.

"Tell us," Youngman suggested. "Start with how you're going to want this whole village quarantined."

"Look," Chee told Cecil, "you want a jailbird for a deputy, that's your business. I don't have to deal—"

"You gonna want this place quarantined?" Cecil asked.

"As a precautionary measure—" Chee found faces watching him from all the near roofs. "It's a normal measure."

The seventh cocoon was laid out in the helicopter. One of the two figures in overalls waved to Chee. The second figure returned to the kiva with a flame thrower. A stream of fire spewed into the underground chamber.

Stone Man recoiled. "I saw eight priests go down there."

Chee took a hand radio from his belt and spoke into it.

"Doctor, you got all the bodies out of there, didn't you?"

The radio answered in the affirmative, although Youngman hadn't seen either of the men in airtight coveralls use a radio of their own. Which meant they had collar mikes and earphones.

"Good," Chee said. "There weren't any more bodies, just seven," he told Stone Man.

"Did they see a small stone tablet?" Stone Man asked.

Chee shrugged, but passed on the question.

"Every item was accounted for. There was nothing like you describe," the radio answered.

"Give me the radio," Youngman said.

"You're out of the picture." Chee shook his head. "Your people fired you tonight."

"Give him what he asks for." Stone Man stared at the desecrated kiva. Tears stood in his eyes. "Do it."

Youngman put his hand out.

"Duran," Chee lowered his voice, "you saw those bodies. There weren't any wounds on them. No swelling, buboes, nothing. Don't try to make something out of nothing. Don't start a panic."

"Thank you." Youngman took the radio. "Doctor, which one are you? Raise your hand."

The figure without the flame thrower raised his right hand.

"Doctor, what killed the men in the kiva?"

The voice that answered was nasal and clipped, a white voice. The doctor who had come to Gilboa for Isa Loloma, Youngman guessed.

"There are no clear indicators. The evidence of froth
148

does lead us to believe there were pulmonary complications."

"A disease, then."

"Or toxic agents. Maybe a disease."

"A highly contagious disease."

"Not necessarily. The situation of the chamber is highly abnormal. Close quarters, shared food, lack of hygiene, etc. A disease that isn't normally contagious at all could become so."

"Did you see any fleas or flea bites?"

"Not so far."

"Swollen places?"

"No swellings at all. I can assure you there was no indication of bubonic plague, if that's what you're getting at. These precautions we're taking are normal prophylactic methods in dealing with a possibly contagious and undetermined disease. Again, I must mention toxic agents. What they ate or breathed. The public hygiene of the pueblo itself leaves a great deal to be desired."

"Okay, Doctor, let's cut the shit for a start. We had a nurse up here who spent two years teaching me about your goddamn indicators. The indicators of those priests were, one, froth, which means their lungs were infected. Two, cyanosis, black skin, which means their lungs were so congested there was no oxygen in their blood. Three, seven men died in two days. In other words, they were killed by pneumonic plague, which is a hell of a lot more infectious than bubonic plague."

"What's the difference?" Cecil asked.

"You don't need any fleas. Just one man with plague and a cold in his lungs so he can kill his friends with a cough. It's about a hundred percent fatal. Right, Doctor?" Youngman added to the radio.

The figure in coveralls took a long time answering.

"As long as the men were dead, had stopped breathing out any bacilli, and they weren't handled improperly, the chances of further infection are practically nil."

149

"Then it was pneumonic plague."

"That's premature speculation. We'll do autopsies, the same as we did on the boy——"

Chee's signal to the doctor was too late.

"So," Youngman glared at the Navajo, "you son of a bitch."

"The main thing is to avoid a panic," Chee said.

". . . pathogenic signs on the boy's body would indicate the possibility of bubonic plague," the radio went on. "There were flea bites we suspect were vectors, points of entry for the bacilli. I must stress, he was an isolated case."

"Until tonight."

"Perhaps," the voice conceded, "until tonight."

"Even eight cases don't make an epidemic," Chee said.

Youngman looked at the two figures in bright coveralls, the flame thrower, the bank of floodlights and rack of ultraviolet lights, the helicopter stuffed with man-size sacks. An invasion of twentieth century apparatus such as Shongopovi had never seen before.

"But if it is," Youngman said, "if it is an epidemic, Chee, you're ready, aren't you? That's what interests me. You're so goddamn ready."

"So? You're lucky I'm here."

"Maybe." Youngman gave the radio back. "Cecil, Joe Momoa usually makes it to the Rain Dance, doesn't he?"

"Never misses it. And Joe Jr. and Ben, they come in on their bikes."

"See them today?"

"Nope."

"Neither did I."

"If you had any phones here——" Chee said.

"You do," Youngman said, "in your car."

Youngman, Chee, the white doctor, and the Navajo patrolman called Begay flew out to Dinnebito Wash in the second helicopter. Headlights probed the dark at 150 mph because the last radio report was there was still no answer on the Momoa phone.

"So I'm a son of a bitch, am I?" Chee asked Youngman. "If that's true why am I helping you?"

"Because you're in a corner, because you're hiding something. Because you're scared."

In the twin beams, the desert slid by as two pale tracks spotted with brush, undulating as the copter flew over a dune. Youngman tapped the pilot on the shoulder.

"Stone chimneys coming up, better climb a little."

"I don't see anything."

"Climb anyway."

The copter rose fifty feet. A slight tilt to the aircraft swung the beam and picked up a red column of sandstone reaching to the skids. The copter hopped another fifty feet.

Youngman had no good memories of riding in helicopters; he had no good memories of the Army. Like the Army, copters were too complicated and illogical, loud and wasteful. Sitting beside Youngman, the doctor he'd spoken to over the radio on the plaza was distributing vinyl coveralls from a box stencilled, "Center for Disease Control—Sterile Until Opened or Damaged."

"I don't mind lying to you," Chee said, "and I don't mind being a son of a bitch. That's what it takes. You hear me?"

"For what?" Youngman stretched his legs as best he could.

"To be like them. Like the whites. You're not so dumb you haven't figured it out yet. You don't like it but don't try to lie to me. You know."

"I don't know what the hell you're talking about."

"Yeah? I'm saying we're on the same side. It's you

151

and me, Duran, you and me on the same side against the whites."

"You're prejudiced?"

"You're not? Is anyone not? Whites aren't? I'm in Houston, Phoenix, Dallas every other week and I got loads of wonderful white bankers who stand up when I come in an office. And I know that each and every one of them would rather deal with a sharp stick up the ass than me. They take me to lunch—not at their private clubs, hear—and feed me steak and lobster and when I'm gone they spit it out. They hate me to begin with and they hate me more because I make them pay. I make them pay millions. Nothing's changed, Duran. They still want to steal it all. They want to starve us out, but they can't do that now, Duran, and you can thank the Arabs for that. They're running out of coal and gas and oil, and they're running out of time. Not enough time to starve us and so they have to buy. You know what else I found out? They're no smarter than us. But they have money and they have Washington and they keep one thing in mind: it's them against us. If we don't stick together, Duran, we're dead."

While Chee talked, the doctor pantomimed how to get into the coveralls. Feet first. Ankles snapped tight. Air tank slung over the back. Air hose attached and hung down over the collarbone. Collar mike and ear phone wired to breast pocket radio. The suit zippered from the thigh to the collar. Tape over zipper. Youngman had expected some precautions to be taken on the night flight. Nothing like this, though.

"They know they can't fool me. So," Chee said, "all they can do now is go around my back. Get some opposition against me in the tribal council. Just as good, get around me to the Hopis. They're counting on you to stab me in the back."

Two helicopters, that interested Youngman. One copter as a gift, that was possible. Two? Hueys were a quarter of a million dollars new. Used, they still weren't cheap. No one gave away two Hueys, not even to Walker Chee.

"We're on the same team, Duran. That crap about different tribes is out. You don't like me and I don't like you. Tough, we're going to have to live with it. There's something else you have to live with. I'm the only Indian in four states, maybe the only one in the country, who can save us. Not Rain Dances, not witch doctors, not bleeding heart liberals. Me! Because I know bank statements and interest rates and bribing the right bureaucrat and because I'm a son of a bitch. The best one we have."

"That's why you didn't take me into quarantine at Ship Rock? You didn't want me talking about an epidemic and 'stabbing you in the back?' "

"Now you're being dumb again." Chee pulled his suit on. "You can see I'm doing everything I can to stop an . . . any more cases."

"And getting me fired, that was the good report you were going to put in for me?"

"That can change, Deputy. If you get on the team, there shouldn't be any problem."

The ground had swelled into foothills and the copter lights cut through piñon groves and sloping meadows.

"Time for the masks," the doctor said.

"Wait until Joe Momoa gets a look at us," Chee joked. "We'll scare him to death."

The rows of a piñon plantation rolled under the bay door. Then a rocky field, a stream with stones pale as eyes. Another piñon grove. A road, more piñons, an empty corral, and the Momoa house, all its lights blazing. The copter passed over the house twice before settling in a landscaped yard.

A bat hovered over a cactus. In the moonlight, the flowers of the cactus were white and fleshy and almost

153

fluorescent, and gave off an odor of musk. The bat thrust its nose through a soft bush of anthers to lick up nectar on its long tongue.

"They're back!"

"No," Anne fed more brush to the fire. "He's a cactus bat. He pollinates them."

"Like a butterfly," Franklin laughed and coughed. "A desert butterfly."

On all fours, she blew an ember into a flame. Startled, the bat wheeled away from the cactus and into the dark.

"How's Henry?" Franklin pushed himself up on his elbows. "Where is he?"

Anne had kept the fire going all day, sending a futile smoke signal into the sky. Now she wanted light. The flaring brush lit up a pile of stones about twenty yards from the van.

"There. I buried him this afternoon while you were asleep. You've been asleep all day."

She'd noosed a gila monster earlier. She cut off the fatty tail, stuck a stake through it, and laid it in the fire. Her broken fingers were swollen and purple. Chopped cactus filled the sack she'd made from her shirt. Franklin rubbed the bristle on his chin; any other time, being alone with a young woman would have roused him like a goat. Any other time.

"God, those stars are bright." He let his head sink back.

"They're always bright. Here they're clear."

"Blinding, those stars."

Anne picked up the last of the raw snake meat.

"You have to eat."

"No."

"Suck on it, at least."

He waved her away.

"You're going to survive this, aren't you, Miss Dillon? You can actually live out here."

154

"Someone spent a lot of time showing me how to."

"And you think someone's going to rescue you. That Indian deputy, right?"

She was about to tell him to shut up when she decided there was no point in lying.

"Yes, I think he will. Maybe he'll rescue both of us."

"No, this is fine with me. Funny, I was fast enough to shut the door on Claire, and now I really don't care."

"You have to try."

"Tell me," he twisted his face towards her, "do you forgive me for leaving my own wife to die? Do you?" He waited a moment. "No, and I don't think anyone else would. If I die here I'm lucky."

Anne turned over the lizard tail. The beady skin peeled off in the fire, revealing a waxy fat lightly veined.

Franklin pushed himself up on one elbow.

"I saw God, you know, while I was sleeping. Well, it was a lot like this. I was out in the desert, lost, alone, and I saw a campfire. As I went towards it I could make out a man squatting, his face to the fire. He was a big man and he had a blanket or something over his shoulders. I called out and, without looking back at me, he waved me to come closer to the fire. He was cooking supper and I was hungry, so I ran to the fire. In fact, I was reaching for the food when I really saw him. He was twice as big as a man but what was most remarkable about him was his face. It was huge and covered with blood. His nose was broken, I could see that, but that couldn't account for all that blood. Yet, he was friendly. He said I could stay. He seemed to know who I was. I asked who he was, and he said he was God. That's all."

"That's Masaw, the Hopi god. You just read about him before you came camping, that's why you had the dream."

"I never did get to those books," Franklin shook his head slowly. "Thanks, I feel better now."

155

Franklin was dying from dehydration. Anne couldn't understand why he wouldn't drink. The bat bites were superficial, the broken legs accounted only for pain, and she'd seen no signs of internal injuries or hemorrhaging. Still, he couldn't keep even cactus juice down and he didn't seem to be in agony. He was simply, deliberately, drifting away.

For that matter, she didn't understand why Henry had died.

She did realize her own survival had a time limit. Her pants were hanging loosely around her hips. She no longer had the strength to walk back to Gilboa even if she spaced the journey over three nights. So she'd hold out. Youngman would come. In fact, she was positive, Youngman was searching for her already.

"Someone's going to find us," she said.

Franklin didn't answer. He was stretched out on his back, almost relaxed, staring at the sky. Anne knelt beside him and wrung her shirt so that cactus juice dripped.

"Suck this. Just get your mouth wet."

His eyes were open but light years away.

"You don't have to swall—"

As her elbow touched his chest, she jumped away. She'd thought the shirt was only puffed from the position of his body; it wasn't. She put her fingers on the center of his shirt and felt soft, spongy flesh. Anne undid the buttons and pulled the shirt open. Franklin's sternum was swollen into a round, pink bubo. She pulled the shirt all the way open. There were even larger buboes under his armpits.

"So bright," he muttered.

The front door was open. The head of an eight-point buck decorated the hall. In the living room, a chandelier with crystal pendants lit more heads, a rifle rack, oils

156

of sporting scenes, religious samplers, Navajo rugs, and a glass case of silver jewelry.

There was no point in calling out to the Momoas through the air masks; the men could communicate by radio only among themselves. In the airtight suit, Youngman felt clammy and warm. The men looked like visitors from another planet; Youngman felt like one. He picked up the phone.

"It's dead."

"There's our answer," Chee said. "Have any bad storms up here lately?"

"Couple days ago."

"There's a pole down. End of mystery."

"Probably." Putting the phone down, Youngman's foot nudged an open bottle of Pepsi from under the sofa. There was still some soda in the bottle and some had dried on the carpet. "Let's go on."

The downstairs bathroom was empty and neat. In Joe Momoa's den, on his desk, was a pile of first-of-the-month bill payments ready to be mailed. Youngman looked in an aquarium tank. The big fish looked healthy. Two small fish, half-eaten, floated on the surface. The aerator bubbled. He tapped fish food into the water.

No one was in the kitchen. The doctor opened the copper-tinted refrigerator.

"Food's fresh. Not even the milk is separated."

The copper-tinted cabinets were polished, butcher block tables wiped free of the smallest crumb.

"Bear meat." Begay looked in the freezer. "That's the way to live."

"Look at this." Youngman pulled a blood-stained rag out of a trash can.

"So?" Chee said. "That could be from anything. Maybe the bear."

By then, Youngman was already through the louvered doors of the laundry alcove. He opened the top of the dryer and started flinging clothes onto the kitchen floor.

"What the hell are you up to?" Chee asked.

"We'll see."

Youngman spread the clothes over the tiled floor. Two shirts and a dress were discolored brown.

"That could be anything, could be rust marks," Chee said. "Right, doctor?"

"Possible." The doctor put the stained clothes in a sack.

"Damn right," Chee said. "If Joe comes in and sees this mess, he's going to have your hide, Duran. Of course, he'll have to stand in line."

They turned to a sound at the kitchen's outside door. Youngman heard a sigh of relief over his radio, he couldn't tell who from. Begay opened the door. A collie entered, its tail low and wagging, shuffled to an empty food bowl, and returned to the men.

"Momoa's?"

"His wife's," Youngman said. "Joe wouldn't let a work dog in the house any more than he'd let a horse."

The collie sniffed the clothes on the floor. As if it were reminded of something, the dog started whining and backing into the hall. Three or four times, the dog went back and forth between the kitchen and the hall.

"Oh, shit," Begay said. "What a bitch. Oh, Christ."

For the first time, Youngman felt a bond with the Navajo patrolman. A feeling, a certainty, that the house wasn't empty.

The dog led them to the second floor and along a carpeted hall to a master bedroom, where Mrs. Momoa lay peacefully dead on a king size bed. Her dress was puffed into strange shapes from the buboes around her neck and under her arms. A jar of aspirin and a thermometer were on the night table.

In another bedroom decorated with quarterhorse trophies they found Joe Jr. Because he was naked, they saw immediately the buboes around his groin. His forearms and the back of his neck were bandaged. The doctor turned him over and removed the bandages. There was no skin on the flesh underneath.

"Like the Hopi boy—"

"Shut up," the doctor told Begay. "Bring the lamp closer."

"Those are like the wounds on the boy," Youngman said.

"I know," the doctor snapped. "I did the autopsy. Let me . . . Very unusual. Unique. These are actually a great many crater-like wounds. Damn! They cleaned them, otherwise we'd get a little of the saliva to go by. Deputy, you're such a hotshot, maybe you can tell me what kind of animal makes a bite like this."

"Bats."

The doctor gaped up through his visor.

"What the hell are you talking about?" Chee pushed Youngman away from the bed.

"Whatever bit Joe Jr., the horses here, and Isa Loloma attacked them in the dark and didn't leave any tracks on the ground. The only animal I know that flies and has teeth is bats."

"You ever seen a bat bite like that, ever?" Chee demanded.

"No," Youngman admitted.

"Then you don't know what you're talking about. Do you?"

"I don't know, but I'm sure."

"You're sure about an impossibility," the doctor interrupted. "The immediate concern here is how long ago you saw these people, Deputy."

"Four days."

"This is the most virulent form of plague I've ever seen, if you're correct. If he is correct, Mr. Chee, you've got problems."

After searching through the rest of the house, they

carried the two bodies in sacks to the helicopter and went on to the renovated barn. The upper section had been redone as a paneled rec room with ping pong and billard tables. In a place of honor was a framed photo of Joe with Senator Goldwater. Joe himself was in the bathroom beside a toilet full of vomit. His limbs were limp, but his torso was still stiff from rigor mortis. Chee commented optimistically on the lack of buboes, and the doctor pointed out black spots on Momoa's face. Capillary hemorrhage, another sign of plague.

"The young man, the one with the wounds, died first. I'd guess that he transmitted fleas to the others," the doctor said as they dragged Joe into the rec room to stuff him in a bag. "As long as they didn't have any visitors, we may get by."

"Of course, we'll get by," Chee agreed.

"Like hell," Youngman said.

He stood in front of the maps on the rec room walls. Most of the maps were Joe's Mormon items: Biblical Israel, the diaspora of the Jews, and the travels of Brigham Young. On another wall was a large topological map of the reservation. The Painted Desert was in the middle, the Black Mesa at the top, Dinnebito Wash to the northwest, Antelope Mesa to the east.

"You've got three stiffs here," he marked Dinnebito Wash with the pool chalk, "seven here," he marked Shongopovi on the Black Mesa, "one here," he marked the desert east of Gilboa where the boy had been attacked. "And one more here you don't even know about," he added a mark for Abner southeast of Gilboa, "because he died from loss of blood before he got a chance to develop any disease."

Youngman connected the marks, drawing a rough equilateral triangle about thirty-five miles to a side.

"In other words, in an area around five hundred square miles something you can't even identify has killed or fatally infected twelve people and you two are still doing charades. Have you contacted Phoenix yet? Washington? Anyone?"

"No," the doctor admitted unhappily.

"There's no cause for alarm," Chee said.

"Then take your space suit off. Go ahead."

"Don't be childish. What I meant was, there's no reason to start a scare. We have a few deaths here, not anything else."

"You have an epidemic. Just the start of one, but that's what you've got. Not 'a problem,' doctor. Not just a few deaths, because there'll be more rolling in. Damn it, look at that map. You tell me there hasn't been any plague activity among animals and the truth is you don't know what animals are spreading plague. Spreading it already over half my reservation. Yours'll be next. Quarantine the whole Hopi Nation, is that your answer? Quarantine the Navajo Nation? Arizona and New Mexico, too?"

"You're a panic starter, that's what you are."

"Yes. That's exactly what I'm going to do, unless we make a deal."

"Ah. You want us to fly you out to Albuquerque, put a little money your way?"

"No. You assume only the family here was infected, and I think you're right. But someone was supposed to be here. Whites, in fact, a group of campers who were going to bunk here and fish Joe's stream. They didn't make it, or one of those campers, a nurse, would have tended the family."

"She couldn't have helped them," the doctor said.

"Well, she would have given them more than aspirin. Anyway, she isn't here and she hasn't checked in anyplace else, and that puts her," he pointed to the middle of the triangle, "there. There are seven people in that van. I want both your copters in the desert tomorrow looking for them. From then on I shut up, that's the deal."

"You're crazy. We had two cases of plague of our own up towards Moenkopi yesterday—"

"Oh, you did? You didn't tell me. So that makes it fourteen cases and, what, about six hundred square miles. And you were keeping that a secret?"

"Those copters have to be on hand for emergencies. Not running errands for you."

"But that's the deal. Otherwise, I'll call every health department official in the state tomorrow. By the way, why do you want to keep this such a secret?"

"Begay," Chee stepped back, and the patrolman stepped towards Youngman.

"Begay," Youngman said, "come any closer and I'll rip that cute cloth helmet right off your head. Want to take a chance on plague just for Chairman Chee?" While Begay hesitated, Youngman drew a revolver from the deep pocket of his coveralls. "Joe always kept a loaded Colt .44 behind the dryer in his laundry room. He believed in safety."

"Okay," Chee shrugged, "it looks like we have a Mexican standoff."

"No, it looks like you give me two copters."

"A compromise. One copter, up until an emergency."

"Both, until we find them. Look, Chee, I know when I've hit a nerve and right now your nerves are singing. What are you trying to hide? You can tell me, we're on the same team, right?"

"Okay," Chee put a glove up, "just to shut you up. And I mean about everything. About tonight or anything else, you know nothing and you say nothing."

"Two copters at dawn at Gilboa. Only pilots and doctors."

"Excuse me," the doctor interrupted, "we have ten minutes of air left in our tanks, and you did say there were four members of this family. We've only found three."

162

"We'll check the garage downstairs," Youngman said. "After you."

The garage was empty, but lit. The end wall was padded for handgun practice; a fresh paper target hung from a clothesline. Tire chains, fan belts, and wrenches arranged by size filled up the side walls. Joe's lovingly polished pick-up sat in the middle of the floor, along with a BMW cycle.

"Ben's Harley is gone," Youngman noticed.

"Then he left before the others got sick."

"No, someone had to go for help with the phone wires down."

"You were the only one to say there might be sick folks up here."

"He didn't make it." Youngman was still thinking. He stayed slightly apart from the others, with his hand on the gun. "Ben used to work for the telephone company. He stopped to fix the wires."

He didn't bother adding that the phone was dead. Their air tanks were running out. After one circuit around the house, they returned to the copter on the lawn and dumped Joe's body inside with his wife and son.

"We forgot to turn the lights out." Begay looked back at the house. "Weird. We should of turned the lights out."

Begay was right. The lights in the garage, the rec room, kitchen, every bedroom and hallway had been left on by the Momons. The house blazed against the dark hills.

The collie had followed the bodies to the copter and sat forlornly by the skids.

"Everything's under control here, doc, wouldn't you say?" Chee remarked.

The question was an order. Youngman, his gun on his lap, was fascinated by Chee's desperation.

"Fourteen deaths in two days is not 'under control,' " the doctor said softly.

"With cooperation, though, we can handle it."

Through his visor, Youngman watched the doctor's eyes move from Chee to him and to the dog.

"You better put that dog in a sack," he said.

"The sack's airtight," Begay protested. "He'll suffocate."

"That's the idea. Dogs have fleas."

By flying over the hill road on the way back, they found Ben Momoa. His Harley Davidson 750 was leaning against a telephone pole. Ben hung by a repairman's belt from the top of the pole. In the helicopter's lights, his clothes shredded and black with blood, he might have been the sacrifice of a gruesome rite.

Chee himself went down in a sling to hoist Ben up.

"Maybe I can do the same thing for you sometime, Duran," he shouted up.

The moths heard them coming, heard the net of whispers cast before their coming. Some of the insects dropped to the ground and others began desperate evasive maneuvers. But the bats passed by them, ignoring the moths, listening for the echo of a different prey altogether.

The inner ear of the bats contained, in fact, two separate organs of sense: one for mid-air orientation, another for hearing. The one for hearing, the spiraled cochlea, was proportionately about a thousand times longer than a human's and rich in "trigger" hairs. The hairs stirred to the slightest echo, which was simultaneously interpreted as an insect or an obstacle or another bat, opposite from a human system which heard a voice clearer than its shadow. And when the echoes were reflected from something large and warm and alive, from the Food, the cries and the echoes increased to machine gun rapidity.

164

Mixed with the echoes was the bleat of a goat.

There were four goats tethered to a tamarisk tree, three of them asleep. The fourth shifted its hooves nervously, ears pricked to the rustle of the wind. As the rustle settled down, so did the goat and nibbled at the tree's bark. Some grass even grew around the tree; wherever a tamarisk stood there was bound to be water. Then the goat backed up as something hopped towards it. Curious, the goat thrust its nose forward and the thing hopped into the air and flew.

By now, more than a hundred bats were on the ground. Membranes folded, resting their weight on their hind legs and the wrists of their wings, they hopped or ran rapidly around the tree. There was a feeding order and there were preferences. Better young and tender Food than old, better pregnant and blood-gorged Food than male, best the oestrous Food with an overflowing scent that turned hunger into a frenzy. The big bats, the females, surged forward. The Food thrust its nose out again, slit eyes bulging, and the nearest bat stared back in return first at the eyes and then at a dark patch on the Food's shoulder before leaping, stroking the air twice and landing on the patch. Two incisors scooped away hair and skin, and the bat's long red tongue darted to meet the blood filling the crater and tinging the air with warm sweetness. The outer edges of the tongue curled down around two grooves on the underside of the tongue, forming the sucking channels. A second bat landed, lighter than a touch, on the other shoulder. The Food ran back and forth on the end of its rope. The other Food remained sleeping as blankets gathered over them. More incisors bit. Ground and air seemed to close in on the goats and envelop them. The first bat was already releasing a black, pitchy urine, and the rest of the bats swarmed to tap the Food. Filling themselves, they paid no notice to the tamarisk tree and the hanging bulbs that bathed them in ultraviolet light, or to the

165

Land Rover sitting thirty yards away, where Paine opened a window vent just enough to insert the barrel of an air gun. Running the length of the barrel was an ultraviolet-sensitive sniper scope. The crosshairs rested first on one bat and then on another, leisurely choosing the right specimens for dissection. From their activity, the bats didn't seem to be affected by plague, but only the scalpel and microscope would tell.

It would take hours for all the bats to feed. He could pick his shots.

CHAPTER SIX

Youngman kept seeing the bright lights of the Momoa house through his sleep. He woke in the dark remembering the red-haired man who wanted part of Abner. Who asked Frank about bats.

Paine was from Chee. Chee knew all along.

By sunrise, Youngman had covered his jeep with brush on a hill about a mile out of Gilboa. He lay on his stomach under a mesquite tree and watched through field glasses.

The helicopters came straight out of the sun, making Youngman's eyes water. They landed in tandem on the street in front of the hogan and two figures emerged from each copter, wearing white and carrying medical bags. They came out of the shed ten seconds later holding handguns. Four uniformed Navajo patrolmen joined them from the copters; Youngman recognized Begay. They ran to the trading post, where they stayed five minutes. Then they returned to the copters, climbed on, and took off. The copters circled low around Gilboa, trying to pick up tire tracks and not finding any because Youngman had covered them. After a while, they quit and headed north towards the mesa in case he'd gone that way.

Youngman drove back to his hogan. He wasn't feeling clever. He should have extracted Chee's promise in public, or set the meeting place at a pueblo, or told Cecil what was up. Instead, he'd stupidly isolated himself in the middle of the desert.

The first thing he did was try to radio Cecil, only the Navajos had pocketed half the tubes from the radio, so he threw his rifle and bedroll into the jeep and drove on to the trading post. Selwyn was in his bathrobe at the counter. He lifted his hand proudly and showed off a dead fly.

"Where's your radio transmitter, Selwyn?"

"Broken. I showed it to those Navajos and they tried to fix it, but they couldn't. It's broken for good, I guess. You just missed them. They're looking for you."

"Give me some rifle shells and some .44's, too." Youngman still had Joe's Colt. "And Spam, a six-pack, and salt tablets."

Selwyn swept the fly away and started filling the counter.

"Regular radio's working. I heard about that fire at Momoa's place."

"What fire?"

"Whole family burned up," Selwyn dusted off the beer cans. "Last night. You didn't hear about that? Well, you wouldn't care, you hated that bastard as much as me."

Youngman wiped a display case and squinted through the glass.

"You still got those transistor radios. I'll take one and some batteries. Put it on my account."

"Sure, what else? You know, Youngman, I hope someone invents cash soon."

Youngman took the goods and went out to the porch.

"Been up since five," Selwyn followed him, bathrobe flopping around bare feet. "One of the first signs of growing old, insomnia. You in trouble, Youngman?"

The deputy was searching the sky in case one of the copters doubled back. The shadows of dawn were already drying up.

168

"You in trouble, huh?"

"Yeah, but no more than anyone else. Take care of yourself, old boy." Youngman stuffed his purchases except for the transistor radio into his bedroll and slid behind the wheel. "I always meant to tell you, nothing wrong with your daughters. Keep their windows shut tonight."

"What?"

But the Indian's jeep was gathering speed, headed on the road west.

Anne listened to the van radio through the shattered windshield.

She'd buried Franklin in the hour before dawn and spent a day's worth of strength. She'd spent the next day's strength simply washing herself with gasoline siphoned from the fuel tank. By now, they had to be searching for her, though. By now, Youngman was coming.

The radio accompanied her reverie.

. . . As you all know, yesterday's Rain Dance at Shongopovi was marred by the tragic death of seven elders at the pueblo. At first it was feared that the deceased were victims of swine flu, which is particularly dangerous to persons of advanced age. Autopsies showed, however, that the seven died of food poisoning from spoiled foods left in their ceremonial chamber. Other tragic news comes from Dinnebito Wash, where the popular family of Joe Momoa died in a fire at their ranch home. The fire started in the basement, according to official spokesmen of the Tuba City Fire Department, and then spread rapidly through the ventilating system. Four persons died. And now here's a message from Hubbell's Trading Post, where you'll always find . . .

Heat waves began percolating from the sand. Anne's knees were cut up from scrambling after lizards. Tentatively, she felt her armpits and groin for swelling. Nothing yet. It was funny, she thought. She'd always been aware of the endemic plague in the desert and not once had she seen a real case. Then a week before she leaves the desert, a man dies of plague before her eyes and she doesn't even recognize the signs. The lassitude. Fever. Buboes. The word "bubo" was funny. Like bauble. An adornment.

Motionless, she again experienced the sense that she was vanishing into the desert. Part of her found this disorienting but comforting. This "oneness" was the Hopi Way, and she was amused that she'd only felt it on the point of death, and she considered that this might be the secret of the Hopis' super-religiosity, because they were always on the point of extinction.

Another part of her continued to calculate survival. Usually, there was rain within two or three days after a Snake Dance. It was the time of year, of course. With enough water to drink and cloud cover, she might be able to walk the desert. On the other hand, it might be wiser to collect as much rain water as she could and stay by the van since that was what Youngman would be looking for. He'd be coming from Dinnebito Wash if he'd gone there to meet her at Momoa's. Only, the radio said Momoa was dead.

The sand rippled. A small mirage lapped at the two new graves. By noon, she knew, the whole desert would look like an ocean, like the ocean it once was a million years ago. Momoa was dead, she repeated to herself. Burned. So if she and Franklin and the others had reached the ranch and bunked over, they would have died in a fire anyway.

The radio went on, draining the last of the van's battery.

. . . That was Johnny Cash's latest. Johnny's going to be at the All Indian Powwow in Flagstaff, by the way, and you're not going to want to miss that. A time to get together with old friends and make new ones. Hey, who says you can't get a good recapped tire for half the price you'd pay for a new one . . .

A skink twisted its head to study Anne. She didn't have the energy to reach for her fishing pole. If Momoa was dead, how would Youngman know she didn't get out of the desert? She tried to concentrate, but half her mind was wandering on its own. Answers slipped away from her grasp.

. . . A health advisory note I want to pass along. Officials say they haven't determined the source of the food poisoning incident on the mesa. There may be more cases. This is serious. Signs to look out for, they say, are stomach pains, dizziness, fever, or any suspicious marks or swellings, or throwing up or diarrhea. If you have or you know anyone who has these symptoms, contact the medical clinics in Ship Rock or Window Rock or here in Tuba City at once. Say, wouldn't you like to get in on the CB radio fun . . .

No mention of a missing camping party. No mention of rain. It occurred to her it was important for her to be rescued, not only for her own sake but to warn about the plague. About the bats. Bats didn't carry rodent fleas so the bats and the plague were unrelated, but . . . The effort of thought was tiring her out. It was so much easier to watch the growing mirage, to lose herself in it, to let her mind float. Hallucination was a sign of dehydration; a lack of water changed the whole chemical balance of the body, but it was so seductive. She

171

enjoyed thinking she might see Youngman coming, wading towards her through a dusty surf.

Her mind went on in a crueler direction. There was a story Youngman once told her about a young man who went to the Maski Canyon, arriving at night at a fine, big pueblo built underneath the ground. Smoke rose from chimneys, children ran up and down ladders and beacon fires burned on the roofs. The young man was not only welcomed in this strange pueblo beneath the earth, he was washed and fed and taken to a great dance hall where festivities were just beginning. He'd never seen such laughing and dancing, and beautiful girls who ran around singing and joking, pointing to each other and shouting, "Hapa! Hapa! Is! Is!" "Dead! Dead! This! This!" The fun went on for most of the night, and when he was tired he was led to bed by the two most beautiful girls. They removed his clothes and theirs. He kissed their lips and breasts and spread their legs, making love to each girl in turn until they all fell asleep, the girls lying on top of him. He woke, shielding his eyes because the daylight was much brighter than he expected, and he saw that the reason was there was no ceiling. The room which was so fine at night was now filled with sand. Parts of the wall were collapsed and the windows were broken, and bits of the rafters that were left were falling down in the wind onto the floor. He sat up, and bones fell from his chest. The entire room was full of skeletons, two of them embracing him in their arms. In fear and disgust, he broke their clutch and ran. . . .

Youngman wasn't coming, she told herself. No one was, not in time. Not until she was something to be shoveled instead of loved. Her head rocked back and forth and she heard the clicking of lizard claws running over the van. She didn't hear the fading voice of the radio.

. . . Another health advisory to pass along. A jack rabbit turned in to health authorities has proven to have an animal form of plague. Hopi Deputy Youngman Duran turned in the rabbit and he is now being sought by authorities so they can administer necessary injections of vaccine. This is an infectious disease and people are advised not to approach the deputy, only to inform authorities of his whereabouts . . .

Instead of staying on flat ground, Youngman deflated his tires and crossed as many dunes as he could on the chance he might be able to spot the van. Or smoke signals or the glint of a mirror. Or vultures. From time to time, he turned on the transistor radio to monitor what Chee was doing, and also because he knew if the campers came out of the desert Chee would broadcast their arrival. The jeep whined, sliding sideways down through mesquite, chewing the brush in its wheels.

Youngman felt no bitterness towards Chee for lies and betrayal; it was as pointless as the desert being bitter at the sun. Survival was not a matter of morals. A snake didn't debate the ethics of eating a ground squirrel; it was eat or die. The Navajos, 135,000 of them, were surviving. The Hopis, 6,000 of them, were not. They could blame the Navajos, blame the pahans, blame witches. It was the desert, their own home, that was killing them. It was a changing desert, drier since the Navajos and whites stole the rivers, seized water the same way a snake bit.

Staying alive supplied its own morality. By that standard, Chee was a hero and Youngman was, perhaps, a coward. That's what they called him in the Army. Heap big coward.

The jeep would only do 50. Youngman kept his foot down, relying on his steering. Running away, it could be

173

termed, he thought. Avoiding the responsibility of falling into lockstep once again. That's why he'd come
back to the desert in the first place, to escape a world
he didn't fit into. Probably, he admitted to himself, that
was why he'd fought quarantine. Not from courage but
because the threat of confinement, any kind of confinement after the years in the stockade, was enough to
make him shake like a boy. He wasn't even brave
enough to face quarantine knowing that he had the answer. The answer to the bites, the running blood, the
lack of tracks, the lights at Momoa's, the night Abner
died. He had it, and his only solace for not turning back
was that no one would believe him because it was impossible. An impossible nightmare.

At midday, the sun seemed to pulse yellow and huge.
Not only shadows, objects themselves shrank. It was a
time when even lizards crouched under rocks. Prairie
dogs and sand boas dug deep away from the heat.

Youngman was crossing a dry alkali hole when he
heard the jeep's engine block crack, and he shifted to
neutral and rolled an extra hundred yards. The hood
was too hot to touch so he kicked it open. The block
was close to red hot, and crawling under the jeep on his
back he found a hole in the radiator that a rock had
punched and drained the radiator dry.

He rolled away and closed his eyes. Gilboa was thirty
miles to the east, and the mesa forty miles north. There
was a federal highway forty miles west.

"Damn."

He'd done it. He'd finally reached nowhere, with no
way out but to follow his own tracks.

Was it worth it?

Hayden Paine stood on the roof of his Land Rover.
Field glasses accentuated heat waves. Saguaro cactus
seemed to undulate and dance, mesquite and yucca became floating islands, a canyon twenty miles off turned
174

into a stately sailing ship standing above its own reflection. Occasionally, he thought he caught true movement out of the corner of his eye. He'd turn the glasses and the movement would fade, a chimera. Besides, his interest was the canyons. He hadn't come to them as much as he'd been drawn. Each sunset, he'd tracked the path of the bats on his oscilloscope. Each sunrise, he'd driven another ten miles on a predicated path and tracked the bats again on the flight homeward. Studying the black and brick-red escarpments of the canyons, his excitement grew.

He climbed down to the table and isolation box he'd set up on the ground. His trap of the night before was successful. Four goats, bought from a Navajo near Tuba City, were dead, drained until their blood pressure failed. Paine, in return, had killed four bats.

The isolation box was a simple one without air filters, good only for pathology. Two latex gloves with accordion wrists reached through a lucite panel to syringes and dissecting tools. Pins spread the dead bat's wings. Fleas hopped against the walls, because a dead host was no host at all. A colorful sun umbrella shaded Paine while he worked.

For an hour, he painstakingly examined the bat, shaving the fur in search of swellings and extracting blood specimens for analysis. Human plague normally began when the usual rodent population host died from animal plague. The fleas sought new hosts. But the bats weren't dying off; if anything, they seemed to be flourishing. Despite the imprisoned fleas and other bat parasites hopping around it, the bat in the glove box showed no signs of illness. Was it possible for an animal to play the role of a plague bacillus host and itself remain healthy? Was it conceivable that the vampires, drawing blood from different human populations, had picked up plague antibodies in a natural system of inoculation? One answer was that the same bats that had

175

spread fatal *derriengue* in Venezuela were themselves vigorous and thriving.

The desert canyons drew his attention again. He'd always hunted vampires before in the semi-tropics among lush vegetation. Paine assembled his maps and carried them onto the Land Rover, where the heat of the truck burned through the soles of his boots. The temperature was 120°F in the shade. Bats could survive a cave temperature of close to 100°F, but there had to be enough moisture to keep the membranes of their wings from drying out. The Geological Survey's topological map showed only a labyrinth of rugged, apparently barren canyons that, according to one map supplied by Chee, were called Cañon de Maski. He swung around slowly, taking in the Painted Desert through his field glasses.

Heat waves had settled into a steady simmer as if the sand was on the point of bursting into flame. Straight cacti were twisted into corkscrews. To the northeast, the Black Mesa was a thin black line drawn in a blue sky over the horizon. Directly to the east, something was running. It was the same moving object Paine had seen before he examined the bat. He played with the focus. Sometimes the object would dissolve altogether into thin air, then it would coalesce for a second and be almost distinct. It was definitely coming closer and it was doing so on two legs. Paine understood the mechanics of the desert. A man could run in desert heat without water for one hour before prostration dropped him. In the high altitude of Arizona, maybe forty minutes. So the man wasn't there, Paine was seeing a mirage. Even as he decided so, the figure broke into floating spots and disappeared. Paine stared through the glasses for another five minutes. The man was gone.

The heat on the Rover was unbearable. Paine retreated to swallow two salt tablets with a pint of water and to study his other maps, which were in a plastic binder inscribed *Earth Resources Observation Sys-*
176

tems—Landsat II, III. The maps themselves were splotches of color on acetate, undecipherable unless laid over a second map of manmade boundaries. They were among the most expensive maps ever charted. The power companies had paid more for them than Chee was paying Paine and the truth was that, by the maps, an investment of millions could rest on Paine. Another truth was that he would have done the work for nothing.

Paine had put the maps away when he found himself unconsciously raising his field glasses to the east. The running man was a mile off. He was covering ground in long, easy strides, a pack of some kind strapped to his back, a wide brimmed hat shading his face. From time to time, heat waves or terrain would rise to his chest but he kept coming, his arms swinging loosely. Once, he dissolved into blue, only to reappear closer than before. Paine could see him without glasses. A dark, lean man. The pack, a bedroll wrapped around a rifle. He kept coming, shifting against the distorted background, legs rhythmically pumping. Following the Land Rover's tracks, Paine realized. Skirting a dune, past a withered barrel cactus. Paine recognized the face.

The Indian only slowed down the last twenty yards, looking at Paine silently enough to remind Paine that they were enemies, before he slumped in the shade of the Rover.

Paine had waited too long. If he'd seen a vehicle approaching over the desert, he would have driven off; a man on foot he simply hadn't believed. And this was the last man Paine wanted to see. The Indian closed his eyes and luxuriantly breathed the relatively cool air of the shade through his mouth. The soles of his boots were punctured by thorns and stained with blood.

Paine was nervous. The damn Indian had used the silent treatment before. At last, the Indian sat up to remove his boots.

"What do you want?" Paine was brusque. "What are you following me for?"

"You have a cold beer?" Youngman asked.

He washed his feet with one beer and drank two other cans. Despite the six-pack he'd drunk up on the run, he was still thirsty.

"Paine, you look like you're seeing a ghost."

"You should be one. I saw you out there two hours ago."

"And you didn't come after me?"

"I thought you were a mirage."

"You hoped I was one. Well, don't get uptight. I'm happy enough to see you."

Youngman's laugh was at himself. It reinforced Paine's suspicion that he was constantly underestimating the deputy. Obviously, Chee had too, because Duran was scheduled to be locked up this morning. The idea of a man escaping on foot across the Painted Desert intrigued Paine.

"How long could you have run?"

"Maybe five more steps. How far is it to that table?"

"I was just doing a wildlife study—"

Youngman got to his feet and walked to the shaded table. Paine followed him anxiously. Chee said Duran knew nothing, but Chee also said Duran was an ignorant drunkard, a typical reservation Indian.

The bat was still spread out in the glove box. Its wings had dried into dark parchment around which were laid the organs of a gutted stomach cavity. The stomach itself looked like a worm.

"Mind?" Youngman asked.

Paine shrugged.

Youngman inserted his hands into the gloves and picked up the scalpels in the box. He peeled back the bat's lips, exposing two broad incisors that filled half the upper jaw. The rest of the jaws were taken up by heavy, dagger-shaped canine teeth; the bottom incisors

178

and back molars were practically nonexistent. Youngman skewered the stomach on a scalpel and ran it across the dead bat's teeth, which sliced the stomach in two.

"It was the teeth." Youngman smiled. "It was the teeth I couldn't figure out."

The Indian knew. How, Paine couldn't start to guess. He didn't understand his own reactions because he thought he would have killed anyone who interfered and instead he felt as much relief as anger. He balanced between the two emotions.

"Why did you follow me, Duran?"

"I'll tell you while I drive."

Anne was poised on the end of the three-meter board, from which she could see all the swimming pools in Phoenix so that the entire city seemed to be set in turquoise, and she remembered a story by John Cheever called *The Swimmer* in which a man set out to swim a Connecticut county by following a line of swimming pools.

"Jump!" her father called from the outdoor bar. "Come on, honey!"

Tables were set out beside the pool for guests and a mariachi band played in the garden. Anne noticed that her mother had switched from roses to a rock garden of cactus and succulents. Water lilies floated on the pool, the same as they'd done for her graduation party. This was her graduation party, she remembered.

"You have to jump, dear," her mother called.

Of course, her parents wanted her to take that job at the Heard Museum downtown. There were wonderful kachina dolls at the Heard. Anne considered using her medical training on one of the reservations, though. Indians were fascinating.

She dived, flying on widespread arms until she plunged into a brilliant blue pool, tasting the pure wa-

ter, watching the lily pads float overhead like spots before the eyes. Leisurely, she came to the surface and
pulled herself out of the pool. The top of her bathing
suit had come off, but no one seemed to notice, which
struck her as odd. She pushed her wet hair away from
her eyes and saw Youngman at a table with a big, red-
haired guy. They had a tall drink waiting for her so she
joined them.

"I love you," Youngman said. "I'm taking you out of
here, anyplace you want to go."

This was flattering but the party had only begun. The
other man put a wet towel around her.

"Haven't you got a dry one?" she asked.

"You need a wet one."

Ridiculous, she was soaked. Still, she didn't want to
make a scene, and Youngman seemed so pleased. He
smiled so seldom and now he was gushing like a boy.

"Drink a little bit more, just sip it. You're going to be
all right and as soon as you can go, we're heading out.
Just you and me, okay? Right now, we have to get your
temperature down."

"How did you get here?" Anne asked. It wasn't like
her father to invite Indians to social occasions.

"The smoke from the fire. You led us here. You did
a great job."

Chatter mixed with the tinkling of glasses while the
mariachis strolled between the tables. Anne was afraid
someone would request "Guadalajara." The song always made her dizzy.

"Turn off the radio," Youngman said, and the other
man went into the rock garden, where one of the guests
had inappropriately parked a van. Her mother would be
furious. "His name is Paine."

"I don't see any signs of infection. Besides the broken
fingers and heat prostration, she's okay. If we can just
get her fever down. Lucky she didn't get more sunburn
or she couldn't have made it," Paine said.

180

"She's lost about twelve pounds in body fluid too. I've seen her looking better," Youngman tried to joke.

"Thank you." She covered her breasts.

"No." Youngman took the towel away and replaced it with a fresh, wet one.

"The others." Anne looked, embarrassed, at the guests.

"Dead. You buried them. We found the camp. You're the only one left. Thank God, we found you when we did."

"I didn't think you were coming." Anne knew how sensitive Youngman could be about mixing with whites.

"I should have come sooner."

Anne was concerned because Youngman seemed so worried. His face was dusty and haggard, and the whites of his eyes were red.

"Are you all right?" she asked.

"So far, I haven't caught it. That's another reason we have to get out of here."

Paine tried to ask her a question but there was a commotion as all the other guests left, taking their chairs and tables away. She was confused, trying to find her father. No one was even saying goodbye. She didn't want to be left alone.

"Can you hear me, Anne?" Youngman asked her. "Can you answer us?"

She nodded. Anything to keep him from going.

"Was it bats?"

One of the departing women turned and started screaming. It was the reverend's wife, screaming so loudly that Anne put her hands over her ears but the scream filled her brain, overflowed it, and came out her own mouth.

The late afternoon was strangely cool and quiet. A breeze filtered through the mesh walls of Paine's field tent. He called it a "cocoon." Growing out of the back

181

of the Land Rover the way it did, Anne thought the resemblance was more to a queen bee. She lay on a bed-roll, sipping weak tea, her head propped on a specimen case. Paine was scrambling powdered eggs on a Coleman stove. Youngman stayed beside her.

"Tomorrow you'll be in good enough shape to get out of here." He took her hand. "And that's just what we're going to do. Far away. Paine's driving us to the highway tomorrow."

"You changed your mind."

"Yeah, and all it took was you almost getting killed. If you still want me to go with you."

Against her drawn face, Anne's eyes were larger than ever. Almost lost in one of Paine's shirts, she looked more like a child than ever. Youngman thought a hug would break her.

"You're sure?" she asked.

"My reservation days are over and I'm going to join the living. I finally figured it out. You're my ticket from here because I love you enough to be where you are, wherever that is. Look what happens when I let you out of my sight."

"I knew you'd come for me, Youngman, really I did." She took his hand.

"Just relax. Tomorrow, we'll make a fresh start out of here, to begin with."

Paine joined them with two plates of curdled looking eggs. He hadn't wanted any company. On the other hand, the presence of the deputy and the girl made Paine aware of the loneliness he'd lived in so long. He was drawn to them the way a permanently cold person might idly be drawn to a fire, realizing he could see the glow without feeling the warmth.

"How did you guess?" He handed Youngman a plate.

"The answer wasn't hard. It was just impossible. The attacks were made by a night animal that didn't leave tracks, an animal that could fly to the top of a telephone pole and had teeth. But that kind of animal doesn't kill people, not with teeth like that. Never saw any animal with teeth like that. But I thought about a family of people dying and huddling inside a house with all the lights on and I remembered about a Mr. Paine asking a deputy down at Five House Butte if he'd seen any bats. From then on I knew I was right even if I couldn't prove it. You proved it for me."

"We have a lot to thank you for," Anne told Paine.

"Like hell," Youngman interrupted. "He's just involved in one of Walker Chee's rip-offs. You think he's doing this for the poor Indians? To clean up a reservation? No, but to tidy things up for a new stripmine or keep the tourists rolling in, now that's worth Mr. Paine's hire. That's all he is. A hired man. You tell me if I'm wrong, Paine."

Before Paine answered, his radio came alive with call numbers. When he tried to ignore the signal the radio called him by name even more insistently. He glanced at the Indian before moving to the table where the radio sat. Although the signal was ragged with static, Youngman already recognized Walker Chee's voice.

"Get back here to Window Rock," Chee said.

"You called me at the wrong time."

"That's an order. We'll set up some defense systems. I've explained everything to my friend Mr. Piggot and he'll get us all the equipment we need."

Paine turned with the mike so that he could watch the deputy and the girl. The girl listened intensely, the deputy smiled in a different direction.

"Like what?" Paine asked.

"Anything. Piggot has connections."

"Like what?" Paine repeated.

"We'll set up a defense perimeter . . ."

"Around the desert?"

"At special points. We'll get nets . . ."

"How high? How wide?"

"And arc lamps, floodlights . . ."

"Lights are where people are, they don't mind lights."

"Let me finish," Chee said. "The big thing is we'll have small planes with DDT. As soon as radar picks up the bats . . ."

"It won't. Vampires fly under radar."

"God damn it, we wouldn't be in this fix if you'd finished the fucking bats like you said you would."

"I will."

"You say that every day and every night is worse."

"I've been tracking them. I'm getting close."

There was a pause before Chee came on again.

"Where are you right now?"

"I can't say exactly."

"But you're close to the bats, you said. Where do you think they are?"

"I can't be positive about that, either. But, I'd guess," Paine watched Youngman's eyes slide towards him, "Mansion Mesa."

"Mansion Mesa. Okay, Paine, I'm ordering you to start for Window Rock now."

"No."

"You haven't been paid yet, Paine."

"I haven't killed the bats yet. Signing off."

"Paine—"

Paine flicked the receiver off and wrapped the mike cord around his hand.

"We're nowhere near Mansion Mesa," Youngman said. "That's forty miles southeast of here."

"That's right."

Paine ripped the mike cord from the radio.

"But now you can't tell them where the bats really are," Anne said.

"Now no one can tell them." Paine threw the mike as far as he could.

184

"That's all right." Youngman poured himself some coffee. "He can't tell them where to find me."

"Youngman was right about you," Anne told Paine. "You're here for the companies. Well, I'd like to know just what company I should be grateful to for saving my life."

"What does it matter?" Youngman shrugged. "I don't care. I'm finished here. As soon as we get to the highway that'll be the end for us." He lifted his mug. "Cheers."

Anne removed her hand from Youngman's. Momentarily, she felt as distant from him as she did from Paine. She was not distant, she thought. They were. Paine, large, a tan that was ghostly pale in contrast to Youngman's skin, hulking but somehow absent. Youngman, dark and lean, and encased in so much cynicism that he seemed almost untouchable. Together they'd rescued her and now she felt almost superfluous to either of them.

Youngman pulled his rifle close to his knee while Paine slipped a CO_2 cartridge into an air gun.

"You kill bats, that's what you do for a living?" Anne asked.

"Uh huh."

"There's a good living in that? Bat killing?" Youngman asked.

"From Mexico south, pretty good."

"And you kill them with that?" Youngman looked at the air gun.

"No. With that." Paine pointed the gun at a red canister marked DANGER in English, French, and Spanish that leaned against the rear door of the Rover. "Cyanogas. That's if you have to go into the cave. You never go into the cave if you can help it. If you can help it, you get them through an old food source."

"Like?"

"Cattle, usually. Bats will return to a herd they've already fed off. They sort of 'own' different herds in a territorial way. You smear 'Vampirol' on an old wound."

"I like it." Youngman lit a cigarette. "Vampirol. Sounds like something for unwanted body hair."

"It's honey and strychnine. It works, but it's a slow way of killing them."

"Do you hate bats?" Anne asked.

Paine laid the gun down and went into the Rover. He returned with a bottle of Napoleon brandy and three paper cups.

"We're out of their usual flight path." He filled the cups and gave one to Anne. "Let's—"

"This is a party?" Youngman was amazed. "What the hell makes you think I want to drink with you?"

"Sorry, Chee told me you were a wino."

"What else?"

"A shiftless, ignorant reservation bum." Paine held the cup out.

"You know what a piñon is? A white nut."

"So?"

Paine kept the cup steady. Anne expected Youngman to push Paine's hand away, but instead he took the cup.

"Honey and strychnine, huh?"

"That's the easy way of doing it."

Paine threw back his brandy in a swallow.

"Crazy, fucking pahan," Youngman muttered and downed half of his cup.

"What's that?" Paine refilled his cup.

"I was just saying we get all kinds of white nuts around here. Usually, they want to bag a mountain lion or a wolf. First time I ever met one who was after bats."

"You don't think much of them."

"Never thought about them at all, Paine."

"Think about them. Think about an animal that aerodynamically is more maneuverable than a fly. That possesses a system of echolocation more sophisticated

186

than the navigational technology of a military bomber. That sees in the dark as well as a cat. That, unique in nature, has made the leap of efficiently converting the blood of other vertebrates into its own blood."

"A hell of a salesman, isn't he?" Youngman made an aside to Anne.

"I'm not talking about just a drop of blood," Paine said. "When a wild vampire bat feeds, it can drink one and a half times its own weight in blood. Because of the anticoagulant in the vampire's saliva, its victim loses as much blood again in excess of what the bat drinks. Over a year, a single vampire can drain twenty-eight quarts of blood, the entire blood volume of a good cow, or of about six humans."

"Is that so? How can any animal drink 150 percent of its own weight and get off the ground?"

"They piss. They piss while they're drinking. The blood meal is absorbed by the cardiac region of the stomach and the blood fluid goes right on through."

"There were these tarry stains around Abner and the horses that were attacked."

"Piss."

"Yeah, that's efficient," Youngman laughed. "I'll give the little fangers some credit. A little smelly."

Paine smiled agreeably.

"You ought to go into a cave of vampires sometime. One year in Mexico, I gassed a hundred caves. I killed over 50,000 vampires. Interesting killings."

Anne studied the dark red of her brandy. It was Youngman who finally filled the silence.

"So what is it? You have a high boredom level or you're totally insane? A white man of your talents could make a million selling insurance. Why vampires?"

"The study of vampire bats—"

"You didn't say 'study,' you said 'killing.' Anne asked you before. You hate bats?"

Paine refilled Youngman's cup.

"It's a job. I'm a professional, a man for hire, you said so yourself."

"What if Chee doesn't pay you? Doesn't that worry you?"

"He'll pay me. Pay me double when I'm through." Paine threw down another cup of brandy.

"Idiot Chee, trying to keep this secret," Youngman remarked.

"No, no, he was just acting normally."

"That's normal?"

"Seventy years ago there was an outbreak of plague in San Francisco. State officials refused to believe it. A federal investigator arrived and was beaten up by a mob. California only accepted help after Washington threatened to quarantine the whole state. That's normal."

"But it's not normal for vampire bats to be here. Why are they?"

"Most bats around here migrate over the border by the seasons. Vampires were just south," Paine answered evasively, "and I suppose they finally joined in. Arizona, Texas, New Mexico have caves with millions of bats in each. It's a regular paradise for them."

"For you, too, then. Funny how the bats and you showed up at the same time. And then the bats start spreading plague? That's one hell of a lot of coincidence. I mean, you're not exactly good luck, are you?"

"There's something I don't understand," Anne said. "I thought it was a fact that only rodent fleas could transmit plague."

"It's a commonly known fact," Paine said. "Like only dogs carry rabies."

"What's rabies got to do with plague?"

"Bats. Every year, hundreds of thousands of cattle die from a paralysis like hydrophobia, rabies. In 1950, the disease spread to Trinidad and it spread to people. They killed all the dogs on the island, but people still

188

got it. In fact, it wasn't until vampire bats started attacking them in the daytime that people realized what the real source was, a little late for the eighty-nine victims already dead."

"How did bats pick up rabies?" she asked.

"A wild animal they fed off. The interesting part was that the rabies changed in the bats to a slightly different variant of the disease. And that the majority of the rabid vampires were immune to the disease themselves."

"I thought any animal with rabies died."

"Then you see my point. Any other animal would. At any rate, you said that only rodent fleas carry plague. The truth is that dozens of different fleas are capable of carrying plague and those fleas can be found on man, monkeys, cats, dogs, camels, sheep, even birds. And bats. How could the vampires avoid becoming plague hosts here? Every warmblooded animal is their food and plague is endemic to the animals of this area. When you consider the method of feeding, the oral contact, the profusion of blood and the attraction of blood for fleas—"

"Save it," Youngman said. "Save it for Chee and his friend Piggot, or the Army, or whoever has enough money to be worth scaring. You're wasting it on us."

"But someone should be told," Anne said. "What about the Center for Disease Control?"

"Yeah," Youngman laughed, "they did a bang-up job on swine flu."

"Chee is handling that kind of information flow," Paine answered Anne. "Anyway, even if they did get a team here from the CDC in Atlanta, they don't know how to handle vampires, and they'd end up trying to reach me in Mexico. I'm here already and I know where the bats are."

"Well, I don't understand you! You talk about an

epidemic of plague but we heard you send Chee the wrong way. Are you that crazy?" Anne asked.

Paine was dismayed. The convivial, nearly party air he thought they'd all been enjoying was fading all too suddenly under the force of the girl's outburst. He lifted his paper cup. There was nothing in it. When he set it down he did so clumsily because he was trying to avoid her angry stare and the cup fell over and rolled towards her.

"That's all right." Youngman picked up the cup and poured some more brandy in it for Paine. "I understand you. You're the bat killer. You want to do it yourself."

Two helicopters moved one behind the other towards the sun. In each ship were four men dressed in airtight vinyl suits, and four bombs and DDT. Paine was right about one thing, Chee realized. As soon as the oil companies heard the words "vampire bat" they'd panicked.

"This is the way we stop a fire in an oil field," Piggot said. "We blow it up."

"I don't know. Maybe we should have waited so we could bring Paine."

"Look, we had troubles with fruit bat swarms at our Indonesian wells. We just blasted their roosts. You don't wait for any so-called expert to do it for you. Or any goddamn ecology study. This is where the vampires are so this is where we're going to start, and we're going to keep on until we blow up every goddamn bat cave around here if we have to. That is, if you want any oil revenues. I take it you do."

"You're talking about millions of bats. The Hopis aren't going to stand for that kind of slaughter, not on their land."

"You want to pull out, Chee, just say the word and we'll turn around."

Chee couldn't pull out, as both men knew. Tribal funds
190

were sunk in low-cost housing, Nevada mortgage speculation, land reclamation, and banking. The operating budget for the next year had a projected deficit of $2 million, a deficit that would bring Indian Bureau investigations of misuse of federal money. In his own mind, Chee'd done nothing wrong. He hadn't started worldwide inflation, or caused the Nevada mortgages to be forced. But he knew investigations would scare off private investors he'd courted all around the country. On the other hand, the consortium of oil companies Piggot represented was willing to hand over $2 million for a twenty-year lease on the Maski Canyon and a 10 percent royalty on any oil produced. To begin with, Chee thought his only problem was that the canyon was in joint Navajo-Hopi territory. Then the bats came, and the plague.

A red sun was poised over the horizon. Sgt. Begay rode in the lead copter with the white doctor who'd been at the Momoa ranch, and after Youngman's "impossible" suggestion had made telephone queries from San Diego to Mexico City until he'd found a zoologist who recognized the wounds, and then gone straight to Piggot. Chee fired him. It didn't matter. As the doctor expected, Piggot paid well enough for the information.

"All I'm saying," Chee rephrased his protest, "is maybe we should wait and coordinate with Paine. In case some bats get away."

"Chee, you know how many geologists know more about oil than me? Maybe a thousand and they're all piss-poor and a lot of them work for me and the reason is that I have nerve. That's all the oil business is. Nerve and faith. That's why I'm taking a chance on you. You thought some bats were going to scare me off a strike? See how you wasted time on your expert? You should have come to me at the start."

"But he knows these bats."

"And I know dynamite."

"It's almost sunset. The bats are going to be coming out."

"Good. We blow up the ones coming out and seal the rest in for the DDT to finish off."

"There are a lot of bats."

"That's why we're going to this one first. Look, Chee, you want to be an important man, a hero, and you want to be rich. You go along with us and that's what you'll be, and you know it."

Chee shut his mouth. Piggot was using almost the same argument Chee had used on Duran, only Chee's argument was a fraud and Piggot's was the bottom line. It was always the same bottom line on a white man's contract. The helicopters were Piggot's, not given to Chee, only loaned for geological surveying.

"Two miles at ten degrees south. We have visual contact," the lead copter reported.

"Let's coast." Piggot took the mike.

Both copters swayed slightly sideways to get a better look at Mansion Mesa, a relatively small mesa with an irregular top and crumbling talus walls that did suggest a dilapidated, oversized mansion set down in the middle of the desert. In the full furnace gaze of the setting sun, the mesa glowed orange-hot. A layer of volcanic rock made the mesa top uninhabitable for humans, but the center of the mesa was hollow, a vast cavern occupied by blind salamanders, beetles, cockroaches, coral snakes, pseudoscorpions, and hundreds of colonies of different bats.

"You're sure anything lives in that?" Piggot asked Chee.

"Yes."

"We better swing by first," Piggot ordered over the radio.

The two copters made a circuit around the walls of the mile-wide mesa, watching their silhouettes swim over the walls. The sound of turboprop engines boomed off the rocks.

"Bats!" the first copter called.

On the south wall, about twenty feet from the mesa lip, perhaps a dozen bats straggled into the daylight and dived to the shadow line rising from the desert floor.

"We're going around again," Piggot ordered.

"That's the main entrance," Chee disagreed. "You don't know how fast the sun drops. We have to do it now."

The copters made a second circuit, closer this time, their rotors almost grazing the mesa walls. As they came around to the south, without spotting another entrance, Chee saw that the sun had dropped to its waist. A shadow line of misty blue was directly under the cave entrance and a thin but solid string of bats fluttered out.

"Okay, this is going to be harder than we hoped," Piggot spoke into the mike. "We can't just drop the bombs. We're going to have to fly by and sling them in. The dynamite has a ten-second delayed contact fuse, so you don't have to worry as long as you don't go into a stop hover. We'll stand off and, in case you miss, we'll go in with our load. Let's do it right the first time, though. And don't forget your helmets. There's a chance some of these bats are infected and we don't want to take any chances."

Piggot was already taking chances, Chee thought.

"Tell them to go."

"Hold on, chief. I said we were going to do it right. Look, the bats aren't even coming out now."

The shadow line was halfway up the cavern mouth and rising even as Chee watched. The lead copter backed off a hundred yards while the one carrying Chee and Piggot drifted fifty yards alongside. There was a pause as the men in each aircraft fastened the helmets of their coveralls. They wouldn't be in them long enough to require air tanks. Chee started sweating immediately as more bats

193

emerged. The shadow line touched the top of the cavern entrance. Most of the desert was now a blue pool.

"Ready," the radio announced.

"A $100 bonus for every man who bowls a strike," Piggot told them.

Chee watched Begay get strapped to each side of the Huey's open bay. A satchel charge was handed to Begay. The two copters seesawed in the air. More bats were coming out of the cavern, speckling the air.

"What are they waiting for?"

"Relax," Piggot told Chee.

Begay gave a thumbs up. The lead copter dipped its nose and advanced towards the mesa.

"Keep it at five knots until he throws it and then scram. Good hunting!" Piggot called.

The copter aimed towards the cavern at a 20 degree angle. Begay and the charge were obscured from the second copter's view. A small cloud of about a hundred bats slipped from the cave. Steadily, resolutely, the copter swung towards the mesa wall.

The next seconds were confused in Chee's mind and always would be. The cavern erupted not with hundreds of bats or thousands but with tens of thousands of guano bats, cave bats, red bats, canyon bats, fringed bats, in all close to 500,000 bats as Mansion Mesa spilled out its colonies, the way the mesa always released its bats at sunset, until the helicopter, the mesa, and half the sky were erased by a moving, screaming cloud and Chee's copter almost spun to the ground as it listened to a radio shouting, "Bats! The bats . . ." The sound of their wings overpowered even the howling of the copter's jet engine. Chee never heard the crash of the lead copter into the mesa wall, only that pounding like heavy rain until the charge went off at the base of the mesa, scattering what was left of Begay and the copter over the sands.

CHAPTER SEVEN

The day began hot and windless. There was no movement or shade, or even dimension to be seen. Only the searing white light that evaporated life.

At 6 AM, a general plague alert had come over the Rover's AM radio, followed an hour later by evacuation orders for everyone between the Black Mesa to the north and Castle Butte to the south, and Dinnebito Wash to the west and Route 87 to the east. By 8 AM, the orders from Window Rock were reversed and occupants of the previously mentioned area were instructed to stay where they were, to avoid public gatherings, fumigate their homes and themselves, not to approach any wild animals or any sick domestic animals, to report any unusual wounds or boils or fever. Also, to burn their dead and to stay in, doors and windows shut, at night. In effect, a quarantine of approximately 2500 square miles. And at night, a siege.

"Just the start." Paine spread a map. Circles and dates marked every incident concerning the vampires or plague. "Winslow and Flagstaff are only thirty miles outside the area. Wait and see what happens when the plague reaches there."

"What are these other marks?" Anne asked.

"The X's are sound trackings of the vampires. The triangles are major bat colonies. Mansion Mesa south, Stephen Butte east, San Francisco Mountain caves west.

195

There are millions of bats in the mountain caves. If the vampires move in there and the fleas spread?"

"What then?"

"You can drop Arizona, Utah, and New Mexico off the map of the United States for a start."

"We're dropping them now, we're getting out." Youngman returned from pouring the last jerry can of gasoline into the Land Rover. "Once we get past Route 89, there's a dirt road I know that'll get us up to the Grand Canyon paths. No one will know we came out of the quarantine."

"I only promised to take you to the highway," Paine said.

"You heard the radio. We'd be picked up in a minute on the highway now and stuffed into a ward full of people with plague. That's no escape. We're going to the Grand Canyon, all of us."

"I'm not leaving the desert," Paine said.

"That's up to you. We are, and so's the truck."

"I need the Rover."

"Not like we do."

While the two men argued, Anne walked off by herself and sat beside a withered saguaro. The pulp of the cactus was eaten away, leaving the ribs as open as a cage. Further on, the iterated S's of a sidewinder's track decorated the sand. Beyond was flatness extending to the horizon, which was clear and extraordinarily fine even through the vibration of heat waves. A line so long and unbroken and without any margin, the same line she had concentrated on when she was dying. Dying, she had decided this was the place to die. And the way to die, because she'd lied to Youngman, she'd given up hope of any rescue and being free of that hope, and knowing she'd survived as well and as long as she could alone and without help, she'd reached an unexpected clarity of thought. A clarity of life. Franklin had reached it before his death. It was a sudden gift of the

196

desert, not so much a conscious understanding as an extension of the senses so that she could feel the dry breeze cool within her, see the distant mesas sitting like brown women, be a very part of the desert. It was an absolution from her executioner, this awareness. Perhaps it never was the Indians or the petty ego-satisfaction of volunteerism that had brought her into the desert and to this point. Perhaps it was a lifelong drift towards reality. Because Phoenix was a dream, a false oasis. Youngman wasn't false, only his aspirations of leaving the desert were. Her visions had been real, seeing him run over the sand, because he was a desert animal and he'd never leave it without killing more than half of himself. If she wanted him, she would have to take him whole. Why had he and she been spared the bats and the plague? Why had the desert done that for them? She scooped up sand and let it run like water over her broken fingers.

Youngman lifted his rifle, levered a bullet into the breech, and aimed at Paine's head.

"Give me the keys."

"You'll have to kill me."

"To save us, I'd do it. Throw the keys."

"There are more lives at stake. Your people, the Navajos, everyone in the desert. And that's just the start."

"It's not the end of the world," Youngman said. He would have fired at that point, but he was suddenly looking at a memory of Abner. Then Anne interrupted.

"Beside you," she asked Paine, "who else can stop the bats?"

"No one. There are experts in vampire control in Mexico City, but it would take them a week to organize a team. By then the bats will move to a new cave and the plague will be out of control. It may be out of control now."

"How?"

"A bullet," Paine looked at Youngman's gun, "only

kills the person it hits. Every victim, man or animal, bitten by the bats becomes a vector, a spreader of the plague. Ask your friend how fast the plague has spread in a couple of days. From a few square miles to a few hundred square miles. Geometrically. The more area it covers, the more the rate of spread accelerates. You can probably imagine what will happen if one human vector reaches a major city or an airport. Or even a motel near the Grand Canyon."

"Is it possible Youngman or I do have the plague?"

Paine took longer to answer.

"It's possible."

"And you know where the bats are."

"Almost exactly. I've been tracking their flight paths for five nights. I know the area of their cave. Of course, they could move to a different cave any time, unless I stop them now."

"Don't listen to him," Youngman said. "You don't have plague now. We can get to California. We'll never have to hear about the reservation again. Remember what you told me? We could go anyplace in the world together."

Anne shook her head.

"I'm staying."

"You're going. You don't know what you're talking about."

"I know what I'm talking about. For two years I've gone around this reservation doing nothing but handing out band aids and eye salves. That's next to doing nothing, Youngman, and that was two years of my life. Maybe I did something good for the people, I hope I did. Now you want me to be responsible for letting those people die? To throw away those years? To run away the first time I can really matter? If you want to run, go ahead. But I'm not going with you."

"I can make you go." Youngman swung the rifle towards her.

"No. That you can't do."

"Paine is crazy."

"He can stop the bats."

"Get in the truck."

Anne said nothing but held his eyes on hers, not fighting his stare because she didn't have the strength for that. Instead, yielding, letting his eyes go as deep as they dared, until the rifle dropped.

Youngman made a final attempt.

"I'll trade you. I'll stay here and wait while he drives you out past the quarantine. Then I'll help him when he comes back. He may have maps. He doesn't know the desert."

"Then that settles it," Anne said. "We're all needed. We'll do it together as a team. If," she asked Paine, "that's all right with you?"

"A team?" Paine took the rifle from Youngman. "A team is perfect."

Maski Canyon was a maze of many canyons, some of eroded Kaibob sandstone with walls gouged and pitted by sand-bearing wind, others of sheer black Hermit shale, others of lava with slick obsidian seams. At one time, the canyon had grass as well and a people, ancestors of the Hopi, who raised corn and grazed goats in this impenetrable natural fasthold. Then, slowly, the wells died and the thin soil dried and blew away and the ancestors disappeared. Anyone lost in this forgotten home was accounted dead by the Hopi, who retreated across the desert to the Black Mesa; by the Navajo, who could find more grass among sand dunes; and by the pahans of Washington, who willingly ceded an outcrop of hell.

Until Landsat. The Landsat satellite was launched by the National Aeronautics and Space Administration on January 2, 1975. Since then, fourteen times a day, the satellite circled the earth measuring the radiation inten-

199

sity of the ground in 1.1-acre units. Within its multispectral scanner an oscillating mirror reflected light to detectors which converted the light into electrical voltages. The voltages were in turn converted into number values ranging from 0 to 63. Landsat beamed its data to a Goldstone, California station where the data was recorded on tape and shipped to the Goddard Space Flight Center, where the number values were reconverted back into black and white film, which was then printed through filters into color photographs. The photographs were stored at the Department of the Interior's Earth Resources Observation Systems Data Center in Sioux Falls, South Dakota. Although the photographs were costly, they were much in demand by developing countries eager to find signs of mineral deposits, by meteorologists mapping weather patterns, by civil engineers responsible for highway planning, and especially by petroleum companies. A group of such companies based in Houston noticed that one photograph of generally oil-dry Arizona displayed an almost insignificant and inexplicable leap in radiation intensity. Night photographs of the area, a stretch of the Painted Desert held jointly by the Navajo and Hopi tribes, showed an even sharper "dot" of radiation. Contact was made with the more progressive Navajos and helicopters were loaned for purposes of closer aerial study with infrared film. The cause of the radiation leap, they found, was not radiation at all but fire, a fire in a stark series of canyons that looked from the air like interlocked teeth, canyons with no trees or anything else to burn. Except oil. From deep underneath the surface, from an unsuspected oil pool, there was a seep. At some time, lightning had struck the seep and set it on fire, a fire that could have been burning for hundreds of years without anyone knowing. The burning seep was unusable, but where there was one there were likely to be others and there was sure to be oil.

From a distance of a mile, in the desert's midday, Maski Canyon looked like the remains of an enormous creature that had fallen, burning, to earth. Instead of the flat top of a mesa, angular crags jutted at the sky. Through a shroud of dark lava broke seams of rust-red Supai sandstone and streaks of dull mica. There was no vegetation and, except for a flock of carrion crows, no life.

"Stop," Youngman said.

The Land Rover rolled to a halt.

No reflection and no shadow, Paine thought as he stepped out of the truck. As if the canyon absorbed all light or cancelled it out.

Youngman climbed down, staring at the cliffs ahead. In a way, he was very amused. But Paine was heading in this direction when Youngman ran him down the day before. Youngman should have guessed.

"You know these canyons?" Paine asked him.

"He does." Anne joined them. "All the Hopis do."

"Give me your glasses," Youngman told Paine.

Paine gave Youngman the binoculars and the deputy focused on the face of the mesa, sweeping slowly from left to right.

"It has religious significance," Anne said. "I didn't know the place actually existed at all."

"Superstitions," Youngman cut her off. "Ignorant witch stories. Nothing to concern you. You say the bats are up there?"

Paine pointed to a ragged gap in the cliffs.

"They fly through there. If we can get the truck up that far, we can go the rest of the way on foot."

Youngman studied the walls of the gap and let the field glasses fall slowly to the base of the mesa, to a stripe of brick-red sandstone where he found what he had been searching for, a black double spiral about ten feet across and twenty feet above the ground.

"There must be a thousand caves up there, Paine. How are we going to find the right one?"

"They'll lead us to it once we get the truck up—" Paine became aware of Anne's concentration on Youngman. "Is there something about the canyon I should know?"

"You worry about the bats." Youngman handed back the glasses. "I'll handle the rest. What about the truck?"

"Okay." Paine opened a map on the Rover's hood. "According to this aerial survey Chee gave me—"

"You got it from Chee? Interesting," Youngman remarked.

"There is a path wide enough for a truck in this sector."

Youngman glanced at the map and back at the canyon.

"Not a path. That's a stream of volcanic dust. You'll sink up to your windshield."

"Well, the only other map I have is a satellite photo."

"Then bring it out. Let's see it," Youngman said when Paine hesitated.

Paine did as Youngman said, laying out the yard-wide acetate satellite photo on the ground. Hues of computer-emphasized color seemed to melt into the sand.

"These are hard to interpret," Paine began.

Youngman turned the photo around.

"Sun here," he held a finger up. "Sandstone canyons are the pink blotches. Shale is orange, lava collected the most heat so it's red. These darker spots are exposed obsidian." Youngman went on for a minute translating the shades of color into ridges, canyons, cooler dry wells, and turquoise fields. "This dot is the burning oil. I spent a year looking at this kind of photo, except they were taken by reconnaissance planes. We always looked for burning oil." He ran his finger along the eastern

202

edge of the canyons. "There are two ways up to the ridge. Maybe both blocked, maybe one. You and Anne take the truck half a mile west along the base of the canyon, you'll find a break. Go slow. The only danger is volcano dust on your way but you don't want to get trapped. I'll go east. There's a faster way there, but it's usually blocked by rocks."

"She was right," Paine said. "We do make a good team."

Youngman said nothing but waited for Paine and Anne to get into the Rover.

"I wish you'd come with us," Anne said.

"Later."

He waited until the Rover grew small along the western base of the canyon and then he began running east, towards the double spiral on the sandstone.

Paine downshifted and turned the Rover up the path Youngman had told him about. Except for a rubble of loose mica-bright slate, he couldn't see any obstacles ahead and he was encouraged.

"The Indian was right. Youngman, I mean," he looked at Anne to see whether he'd offended her. Her mind was elsewhere. He said louder, "Youngman's quite an interesting guy."

"I suppose he is." She watched the path. The Rover was steadily climbing, shooting slate from all four wheels. The walls ahead were pale, ossified sandstone.

"But he doesn't have to be," she added. " 'Interesting' is really a very small word. A bored word. Vampire bats are 'interesting,' plague is 'interesting,' Indians are 'interesting.' All of them are, from a distance, as a thrill. Life is 'interesting.' "

"Death is, too," Paine said firmly.

Anne glanced at him; there were times when she glimpsed more than the gulf in communication between them.

For an hour, the Rover picked its way into the canyon and then the path turned slowly, inexorably back down to the desert.

Under the double spiral drawn on the canyon wall, growing as the only vegetation on a small hillock, was the datura. Almost as tall as a man, the plants bore pale violet, trumpet-shaped flowers. Youngman sank to his knees before them.

Right where Abner always said they were, he thought. Because no Hopi could enter Maski Canyon without datura in his mouth. It was the "way," as much as any road.

All his life, he had turned his back on the "way" and everywhere he turned the "way" was in front of him. His manipulation of Paine and Anne, sending them on a useless road so that he could be alone, was minor in comparison to what Abner had done to him. Because here he was; after everywhere, he was here. But, he told himself, he still didn't believe.

A black-and-white shrike feather vibrated among the coarse leaves of the datura.

Still, a person had obligations. Youngman tore up one of the plants and hacked off a yellow-white root. He cut off a button-sized segment from the root and stuffed the rest in his pocket. He put the button in his mouth, and gagged. The taste was alkaloid and bitter, and at first he thought he was going to throw up, but after he rolled it under his tongue the nausea ebbed. Youngman got to his feet, turned right, and ran along the base of the canyon to where sheets of pocked lava came down to the desert in overlapping folds which hid a road of graded earth and mica. Without breaking stride, he turned into the canyon.

The datura, he noticed with relief, had no effect. He breathed the thin air comfortably and watched the sky narrow by steps into blue wedges between canyon walls.

The road was torturous, a series of seeming cul de sacs, and cruelly steep. There was shadow but no shade. The walls radiated an enervating heat that seared the windpipe and lungs. Youngman breathed through his nose at the start of the climb, but after a half an hour the oxygen demands on his legs were too much and he opened his lips. In minutes, his tongue thickened into a wooden lump, while the datura button swelled. His eyes fell from the sky to the vari-colored walls, and from the walls to the ruts that marked the road.

It was the Castillo priests who built it three centuries ago, their ox carts burdened by double loads of flammable stone that had bitten into the road. Their knotted whips that came down on the Hopis struggling to control the overloaded carts, because oxen were valuable and souls were cheap. For fifty years, until the priests were killed and whips burned, their bells melted, their mission razed, and their road abandoned.

Sunspots danced over Youngman's eyes. As he dropped to rest he saw waiting for him, sitting high on a sandstone outcrop that jutted over the road, the silhouette of a small man wearing nothing but a ragged cape.

"Hello, Flea," Abner said.

"Hello," Youngman pulled himself to his feet and walked under the outcrop. Looking up at Abner he was looking directly into the sun, but he could make out dimly the features of his old friend and the dried blood on Abner's chest. Abner had been smoking mesa tobacco and listening to a transistor radio. He put out the cigarette and turned off the radio.

"Surprised to see me," he asked.

"Not really." Youngman spat the datura from his mouth. "Since I was stupid enough to eat that, I expected to see something."

"You can't see anything here without datura," Abner reprimanded him mildly. "You shouldn't fight it."

"I'm fighting you, uncle."

Abner cocked his head and smiled.

"It was a real powerful painting, wasn't it, Flea? Swastikas backwards, spirals backwards, everything in reverse to start all over again. Letting Masaw out of the fire. You were in it, too, remember, Flea?"

"Why me?"

"You're Coyote Clan."

"That's not why."

"Then," Abner granted, "because you're the only one I can trust. You hate the pahans."

"I hate too many people, but I don't kill them."

"The same thing, Flea, if you know how to put your mind to it. You will. You have to."

"No."

"Why," Abner asked slyly, "do you think you're here?"

Youngman stared up without an answer. Sunlight clung like dust to Abner's blanket. This wasn't happening, Youngman reminded himself.

"Sorry about the priests in the kiva," Abner changed tone. "They wouldn't let me have the Fire Clan tablet, Flea."

"You were dead before they were."

"It was their fault, they should have helped me out. It's important when you end the world, and you have to have the tablet. Harold understood."

"Harold's here?"

"No."

"Any bats here?"

As the silhouette on the rock shifted, sunlight ran like liquid down the blanket. A change in the wind brought the stench of ammonia. Abner ignored Youngman's last question.

"It makes my heart glad to see you again, Flea. You know why I'm ending the world."

"You told me before. The strip mining on the mesa. The Indian Bureau. Navajos."

206

"Masaw says they're coming here."

"Masaw said that to you?"

"You know, if the headpounders want to sell their part of the Black Mesa to rip up and carry off, that's okay. You can't expect much religion from a Navajo anyway. But, you know, we're the only real people in the world and Masaw is the only real god. This canyon is his home. The first thing you ever learned is how he came out of the fires here to watch over us. Isn't that the first fact you learned in your life, Flea?"

"It's what I heard." That was true.

"Then you agree, the day a company can buy Maski Canyon, it's time to wipe everything out and start all over again."

"You mean, wipe everybody out."

"Not everybody. We'll go underground again, the way we always do between worlds. And when everybody else is dead, we'll have plenty of room when we come back up. Masaw promised."

Youngman thought about it.

"Let me tell you. An hour back, when I saw where I was, I would have killed Walker Chee. If he had been there with me, I would have done it, because one thing I never thought I'd be doing is helping him take Maski Canyon. He's going to get it. You're right about all that, uncle. They'll take it if it kills us, and it probably will. They'll kill Masaw for sure. They'll blow him up with blasting powder and bury him under oil rigs. I felt that. But now. Now, I just feel sad. You know, my life has just been one circle. Starting here, going out, so far out I never saw the curve, and then ending here. A circle. What's funny is that I even thought I could get away again, and I can't. So, I'm here with you, uncle. And what are you, uncle, but a dream, a ranting nightmare trying to scare away all the rest of the world."

"Masaw said you'd be like this at the start, Flea."

"Stop it! Masaw isn't killing people. Bats are. The

plague is. Hopi people are dying. What kind of a god kills his own people?"

"It's not unusual."

Youngman thought he could make out a smile again on Abner's face. The image vibrated.

"The reason you're here," Abner went on, "is that Masaw wants you to help kill the pahan."

"You're not here at all, uncle. I'm just imagining you."

"You don't need to kill the pahan yourself," Abner said, soothingly. "Only keep him out of the cave until the sun goes down. Then Masaw can come out."

"What if I want Masaw to tell me all this himself?"

"You have the datura. Let your mind open and you will see."

Youngman backed away from the rock.

"No. I see you, but you're not there. I'm talking to myself, you're not there."

"You're a good boy, Flea." Abner started to make a cigarette. "We know you'll do what you should."

"You're not there!" Youngman shouted. He picked up a rock and threw it at the outcrop with all his might.

A large crow flew into the sky, screamed over Youngman's head, and dived away, out of sight.

The outcrop was bare.

Long after the desert below was ocean dark, the promontories of Maski Canyon stood in the sun. Looking away from the desert into the canyon, Anne saw a labyrinth not so much of other ridges and canyons as of shapes. Of canyons that flying sand had scooped out of sandstone, leaving them as clean and round as shells, of rivers of volcanic ash, of lava chimneys that twisted up by the hundreds.

Medical bulletins were coming more frequently now over the Rover's AM radio.

We have good news for folks in the plague area. Public Health authorities have informed us that the plague situation covering the southwest corner of the Navajo and Hopi reservations is now under control. A state and federal effort to bring in vaccine by helicopter is being mobilized at this very hour. Health facilities at Ship Rock and Window Rock are being expanded to treat the sick. If you are outside the plague area and you think you may be infected, do not, repeat, do not go to Tuba City. Stay where you are. The growing coordinated effort is being personally led by Navajo Tribal Chairman Walker Chee, who emphasizes that cooperation between the two Indian nations is essential. Rebroadcasts of this bulletin in Navajo and Hopi will follow. If you are in the plague area, it's probable you can carry on life as normal with certain precautions. Do not approach any wildlife that appears sick. If any livestock appears sick, kill all your livestock and pets by rifle at a distance not less than thirty feet. Under any circumstances, continue to wash twice a day with green soap, use insect repellents, and fumigate your house. Do not go out after dark for any reason. Avoid caves. Keep your windows and doors bolted at night. Most important, do not try to leave the plague area. State troopers stationed along Route 89, on the approaches to Flagstaff and Winslow, along the Black Mesa and east along Oraibi Wash have orders to turn back evacuees. Anyone not obeying their orders will be shot. . . .

As the tide of shadow rose, Youngman and Paine finished the erection of the wire mesh tent from the back of the Rover. When he'd pounded the last stake into the ground, Youngman ran his fingers along the fine metal wires of the tent.

"They can bite through this."

"Yes." Paine set a heavy battery next to Youngman. Together, they attached two wires to the mesh wall. Youngman noticed that where the walls joined the back of the Rover was an insulating collar of thick rubber. When the attachments were complete, Paine set the battery at 115 volts and threw a switch, setting off a deep tocking. "Now they can't."

Youngman's quickest touch of the mesh sent an electrical jolt up to his elbow.

"I know what I'm doing." Paine turned the battery off.

. . . a change in previous announcements. For precautionary reasons, the northern limit of the plague alert area now includes these pueblos on the southern rim of the Black Mesa: Hotevilla, Bacopi, New Oraibi, Oraibi, Toreva, Shongopovi, and Walpi. Also, the towns of Moenkopi and Tuba City are now considered in quarantine. Again, these are precautionary measures and not reasons for alarm—

Youngman turned the radio off. As darkness swung over the ridge, Paine slid into the driver's seat. The unidirectional microphone was already set up on the roof and the oscilloscope glowed green next to Paine. Youngman and Anne crowded into the rear of the truck. Paine checked his watch.

The first stars began to appear, growing in intensity every second. Hotomkam in Orion's Belt. Choochokam, the Pleiades.

"I've got their flight pattern down pretty pat."

Paine turned the microphone grip back and forth in an arc of 15 degrees. He wiped the palm of his other hand and fine tuned the amplifier, and tuned it a second time.

Anne had grown used to the sounds of the desert at night. There were none on the ridge or from the canyon. Not an insect or a bird.

The oscilloscope's white line was straight. A string of ice.

"If they moved to a new cave—" Anne began to say.

The line shivered. A faint pattern emerged. Three harmonic lines slashing from one octave to another.

"Under three minutes after sunset," Paine looked at his watch. "We're very close to the cave. To," he checked the compass reading on the microphone shaft, "west-northwest, and bearing straight at us. They're packed tight, very tight."

Youngman heard nothing, but the oscilloscope line shook violently. He looked at Paine, whose face was triumphant.

"Listen." Paine snapped off the scope.

There was a wind, Anne thought with surprise. No, rain, she corrected herself, but no rain was falling. A milling of wings, she realized, but sharper. Wings without feathers.

Youngman thought they sounded like steps in the sky.

"Look," Anne said.

From west to east the stars were vanishing, eclipsed by a whispering tide that swept over the ridge at a height of thirty feet. It moved over the Rover, blotting out starlight. They were faster than Youngman had expected, more than he had thought possible and he cringed reflexively, bowed by their shadow and the close and heavy strokes of wings. A minute passed and the bats were still coming overhead. Paine closed his eyes; for a moment the old panic was back burning like a red bulb but he mastered himself and the panic faded. Anne concentrated on the blind eye of the scope. Youngman watched the last of the bats funnelling down into the desert, a sinuous line dipping and curling into the night wind.

"When will they return?" he asked long after the bats had disappeared and Anne was making a supper of powdered egg tortilla on a hot plate.

"I don't know." Paine laid his air gun, three darts, and a pocket-sized radio receiver on a table. "It all depends how quickly they find food out there. A couple of hours at the least but they're bound to find some abandoned livestock. I've set the beeper on the microphone so we'll know when they get close."

"They may find something besides livestock. Everyone in the quarantine area is abandoned."

"True, but that isn't what you asked. Anyway, we'll be ready for them when they return."

"We will?"

"This," Paine held up one of the darts, "contains a miniature radio transmitter. It weighs about a gram and only throws a signal for two hundred yards, but I think that'll be sufficient to find a cave as close as theirs. The trick will be to plant them on the backs of the bats so they can't bite them off." Paine slid the receiver's button to ON, checked three frequencies of tones from the darts, and slid the button back to OFF, speaking softly to himself, " 'Where the bee sucks, there suck I. There I couch when owls do cry. On the bat's back I do fly.' "

Supper. Paine ate his spongy tortilla voraciously and with great good humor. Anne busied herself in a charade of domesticity. The bright light of the Coleman lamp dissolved the fine mesh of the tent, so that the three seemed to be having a picnic in the open air.

"Now that we're all in this together," Youngman pushed his food aside, "I think it's time you told us just what we're up against, Paine."

"You know. Infected bats."

"I know from what I've seen so far that I don't think we're going to come out of this."

212

"Youngman—"

"Wait a second, Anne." He considered telling her and Paine about his hallucination of Abner, but there was no point. He wasn't going to eat any more datura. "If we're going to die up here with Paine, I want to know why. I want his reasons. I want to understand. I want to understand everything."

"It's very complicated," Paine said.

"You said the same thing the first time we met. You were lying then."

"All right," Paine conceded. He shifted uncomfortably, searching for words.

"It's like a war," Anne suggested. "That's obvious enough."

"No," Paine shook his head, "not in a biological sense. It's simply a meeting. A meeting of life forms."

"A competition," Anne said.

"No. An interdependence. Vampires and plague and man." He looked at their faces. "You did want the truth, didn't you?"

"Go on," Youngman said.

"It could be argued that the two dominant life forms on earth are bacilli and mammals." Paine chose his words slowly. "The three most successful forms of these groups are the plague bacillus, man, and bats. Functioning together. The plague, to begin with. The plague bacillus has always been here. As a minor disease."

"It wasn't as dangerous?"

"To the caveman who caught it, yes, but how many other men could he infect? Or a farmer? Or a hunter? Do you see what I mean? There was plague, but there were no epidemics, not one in the history of the world until the coming of higher civilization. Until men got together in cities, until men traded, until men congested. Then starts the reign of the plague above all other diseases. Because of man, nothing else."

213

"The plague does okay," Youngman said. "What do we get out of it?"

"Unions. Before the Black Plague hit Western Europe, the majority of the population was in servitude. When the plague passed and half the population was dead there was a labor shortage. Men who had been slaves could sell their labor. Individual rights began. Democracy began with the plague."

"Then public hygiene is the end of democracy, according to you," Anne said.

"Sewage disposal and rat control didn't stop the plague. The first pandemic of the plague killed a hundred million people in the sixth century. Seven hundred years later, the Black Plague killed a quarter of the world's population. In between? Believe me, there was no great improvement in open sewers. The plague has its own pulse, its own cycle. It rests in places like this and waits."

"Bats," Youngman nervously felt for a cigarette, "what about them?"

"What about them? Don't be angry, but what do you know about bats? Little, fluttery creatures, flying mice, freaks of nature? Not vampires now, just bats in general."

"Something like that," Anne acknowledged.

"Because you don't know how wonderfully successful a life form they are. One out of every five mammals on the face of the earth is a bat. Bats are more widespread over the earth than any other mammal, except man. We rule the day, not the night."

"Aren't they related to rodents?" Anne exchanged a glance with Youngman.

"Someone else. The two glorious specimens descended from tree hopping insectivores are man and bats. We climbed down and they flew out, although we share the same hand in different forms. For twenty years, Leonardo da Vinci tried to design wings for a
214

man to fly like a bird. His perfected design was the bat wing. We share more. More than twenty kinds of virus. The human bed bug first came from bats when we shared the same caves. And the closest of all bats to man is the vampire."

"Well," Youngman sighed, "I know you're a super exterminator of bats but your humor is a little strained."

"Not humor. Irony. It's true. You see this is an amazing concept, the vampire bat. Incredibly advanced. Of all bats, it's the only one that mates the year round, like humans. Of all bats, it has the longest gestation period. Eight months. Of all bats, its children take the longest to develop and teach. It's the only bat that can jump or run. The only bat that cannot live in harmony with any other animal, including other bats. Need I add, also the only bat unafraid of man. The first western scientist ever to see the vampire feed was Charles Darwin. He didn't know what to make of it."

"So," Youngman finally remembered to light his cigarette, "know your enemy."

"Know your cousins. And since a vampire can live close to twenty years, a fairly long-lived cousin. So, don't call me a super exterminator. You exterminate fleas. You kill bats."

"All of which shoots your theory of interdependence to hell, right?"

"No. The vampire lives off large mammals that sleep in herds. It lives off cattle and horses. There weren't any cattle and horses in the New World until the Spanish brought them. What do you think the vampires lived on before then? Name me the one large American mammal that slept together in herds, or villages."

A light-headed sensation came over Anne.

"You mean, people?"

"Yes, that's exactly what I mean. People. Which is why all the old vampire roosts were found next to villages. Of course, we can only speculate on the details of

215

this relationship. Whether one vampire colony would establish territoriality over a particular village and defend its feeding ground against other colonies."

"What did the people get out of it?" Youngman asked.

"Gods."

He knows about Masaw, Youngman thought.

"What kind of gods?" Anne picked up.

"The Mayan gods, for example," Paine said, to Youngman's relief. "You can still see the statues in the Yucatan. Statues with the heads of vampires. The curved incisors and the long tongue are very well represented. No one knows quite why the Mayans deserted their cities. Maybe it was the collapse of their slash-and-burn agriculture. Maybe it was simply enervation, a loss of blood. Wherever there were more vampires, there were more bat gods. More public sacrifices, more ritual bloodletting, until Aztecs paste their hair with blood and cut their ears into a vampire's fringe and wear a cape of bat skins. Maybe cattle herds are a secondary form of sacrifice for us."

"Then, what you're telling us," Anne said, "is that we can't change anything? There should be plague and there should be vampires?"

" 'Should' isn't the issue. The only thing that will ever eliminate plague or vampires is the elimination of man. We'll go together."

"Then what we're doing here is pointless," she said. "In the long run, in your biological scheme, we mean nothing. Then why are you here?"

"Because," Paine couldn't think of a better explanation, "it's what I do."

There was a long silence before Anne commented. "Good Lord."

For a long time, no one said anything.

Slowly, the star Hotomkam wheeled upside down over the canyon. Choochokam slid over the horizon. Youngman smoked, wishing he had some mesa tobacco.

216

Exhausted, Anne slept in the middle of the narrow tent. Paine methodically unloaded and reloaded his dart gun.

"Maybe we should be listening to the news," Youngman suggested.

"Why?" Paine asked. "They're broadcasting nothing that you couldn't predict."

"I predict they'll start bombing caves," Youngman lowered his voice.

"They will," Paine agreed, "for a cave or two. Until they find out they're only scattering bats. We want the vampires together just two more nights—"

"Speaking of that, Anne's not going into the cave with us tomorrow. Just you and me. She can't carry anything in her condition and she'd only be in the way."

"Okay."

"No, I want more than that. Your promise Anne stays with the truck, or you go alone."

"Very well, you have my promise she won't go into any cave." Paine put the dart gun down. A moth had been circling over the tent above the light. Suddenly, the insect began to fly erratically, zigzagging and dropping. Paine turned his head to the amplifier's beeper even before it sounded.

"Wake her up!" he told Youngman and dived into the rear of the truck.

"Anne," Youngman shook her shoulder. "They're here."

"Three hundred yards off," Paine returned. In one hand he held a thin, five-foot wooden pole. In the other, a two-ounce vial of defibrilated blood.

"You're sure they're going to stop," Youngman took the pole. The last two feet of the pole were wrapped in calf hide.

Rubbing her face, Anne was already beside the battery.

"They didn't see us in the truck before. This time

we're out." Paine poured the blood over the calf hide. "Be careful you don't tear the mesh."

"I know what to do."

"When I say 'Juice,' " Paine snapped his fingers at Anne.

Youngman realized that he had yet to see the bats close up. Paine had, Anne had. The deputy inserted the pole through the mesh so that the blood-soaked calf skin was outside the tent. The mesh was incredibly frail. He felt his heart pumping blood and adrenalin, and had a sense of the frailty of his own skin. He couldn't remember ever being afraid of an animal before.

The amplifier beeper became louder and more insistent, turning into one sustained whine.

Paine stood in the middle of the tent, calmly waiting. Anne stared upwards.

First, they heard the whisper of the false wind, then a leathery rustle. A shape flashed overhead, through the light before Youngman could make it out. Two more shapes. Ten. Eye reflections like candles. A hundred, more than Youngman could see. Anne stared, transfixed. The walls of the tent swayed. Youngman couldn't hear the beeper's cry any more for the wing beats.

"They're going past!" he shouted.

"No." Paine pointed with the gun to a dark shape scuttling along the ground.

The river of bats poured overhead and curved, turning into a whirlpool of dipping wings. The whirlpool flattened into a tremendous wheel spinning over the tent. Youngman found himself crouching. Paine seemed to stand taller, turning on one heel. Anne looked into a face two feet outside the net. Bristles marked each cheek. Its dark eyes were slanted on either side of a squat nose with double-folded nostrils. Its ears were long and ribbed. Youngman saw that the top of the Rover was covered with bats. One, its wings wrapped into two long "arms," jumped onto the mesh directly over

218

Paine. More bats appeared all around the edge of the tent. Two leaped from the ground and agilely climbed the tent walls. More jumped from the Rover and others landed from the air on the tent. Youngman's arm jerked. On the bloody end of the pole was a bat. Its incisors sliced off a half-dollar-sized patch of hide. A long red tubelike tongue curled and delicately lapped the pole. He heard the soft explosion of the air gun beside his ear and saw the fin of a dart protrude from the back fur of the bat. Forty or fifty bats crawled on top of the tent, and more climbed up the walls using thumb claws as hooks. A quarter of them had face fur matted with dried blood. The pole Youngman held bowed with the weight of three more bats. Paine pushed the dart gun's muzzle into the mesh and fired again. The top of the tent sagged. More bats climbed up from the ground, bringing a retching smell of ammonia. Youngman heard the lowest register of their excited screams, a distinct clicking in his ears. Inches from his shoulder, they started sawing through the mesh with their teeth. Paine took his time aiming his last dart, knocking a bat out off the wall to pull the trigger on one with a strip of hide hanging from its mouth. As he lowered the gun a bat landed between his shoulderblades. Without thinking, Youngman ripped the bat off Paine and crushed it under his boot.

"Juice!" Paine shouted.

The tear was at the far end of the tent. Another bat was coming through when Youngman reached the rifle in his bedroll and blew it apart. Blood, bone and gristle splattered the inside of the tent. He shot two more coming through before Paine slid the wooden pole through each side of the rent and twisted it shut.

"Turn on the battery!" Youngman shouted at Anne, who knelt beside the battery, her hand limp on the starter knob.

The bats were cutting through the roof and the walls.

Youngman emptied his rifle on them and picked up the handgun he'd brought from Momoa's. A rip three feet long appeared down one wall. Youngman walked into the bats flooding through, using up his bullets until he reached the mesh and gathered it shut in his hands. As he watched, his hands became covered with bats.

Then a thrill of electricity washed through his body, leaving his brain a darkness surrounded by convulsions.

CHAPTER EIGHT

A blue sky surrounded Anne's face.

"How are you feeling?" she asked.

"Grand," Youngman muttered.

"Pretty good for a man whose heart stopped."

"Is it going, now?"

He raised himself from her lap and winced. His hands, he noticed, were bandaged to the wrists. The mesh tent had been taken down and the red canister of poison was gone. Paine, also, was gone.

"Where is he?" Youngman asked.

"Paine left to look for the cave. You saved our lives last night, Youngman."

"I don't remember a damn thing."

"It was my fault," she said. "I was scared, I couldn't turn on the battery."

He pulled himself away from her arms and stood. The ground swayed slightly under his feet. Youngman squinted at the sun; it was close to noon.

"But he should have waited. He can't carry all the stuff alone. And he didn't take the Rover?"

"He waited until he was sure you were going to come around. Youngman, he left the truck for us to leave. He never wanted us along. In fact, he took your rifle and he said he'd shoot you if you tried to follow him. I think he would. He's crazy."

Youngman slumped to one knee as much from surprise as weakness.

"You didn't know that?" he asked Anne.

He turned his stare from Anne to the road, where Paine's footprints led up the canyon.

"When did he go?"

"An hour ago, maybe more."

"He should have left at dawn." Youngman shook his head. "He doesn't know where he's going. Not enough time."

"Youngman, let's go home. He's a professional, he can do the job by himself. He's the only one who can."

"One of us is." Youngman still looked in the direction Paine had gone, where the road screwed through the dull-red walls of the canyon.

"So, we'll wait and see," he said.

Paine set the grinding weight of his pack down on the road, leaving the Cyanogas, rolled mesh, battery, wires and tools in the pack and taking only his receiver, rope, axe, and rifle. He was a mile from where he'd left the Rover and he assumed Anne and Youngman were now well out of the canyon. No more repeats of his father and Ochay. He was alone and free and his mind was clean.

The abandoned road continued to work its way through the canyon and under overhanging lava formations that had obscured it from aerial photographs. Steep walls of rust-colored sandstone crowded in on either side of the road. Occasionally, the sandstone would part to reveal a raw seam of shale that glittered like sequins. Or a strip of chalk-white limestone. And sometimes Paine would step back from the shadow of a man's torso and look up to see only a still figure of lava poised on a rim. Of this geological richness, all that interested Paine were signs of limestone which would be most likely to lead to a cave adaptable to bats.

The radio signals weren't coming. He was sure that the darts were good hits and the bats were close but the

222

walls of the road muffled any kind of transmission. Unless he left the road and got up higher he might miss the cave completely.

He moved slowly until he came to a ragged shank of basalt that ran forty feet up the fifty-foot wall. Paine scaled the basalt and from it chipped handholds that carried him to the top of the wall. All his skills were with him. He pulled himself up to a view of the entire eastern half of the canyon.

Maski Canyon defied the usual arid cycle of land erosion. Instead of uniform canyons and buttes, the varied rocks of different hardness created a bewildering, serrated puzzle. It must have begun as a volcanic eruption, he thought, been covered by sedimentary rock and then torn apart by winds that left gaping mouths of stained sandstone, dikes of basalt uplifted like teeth and, where sandstone had been stripped away from rivulets of lava, those upright almost human figures of black rock. The eastern half of the mesa covered about five square miles, he estimated, and the western half, a higher plateau of the same sort of formations, seemed nearly as large. The burning oil seep was in the western plateau.

Like Milton, he thought. "A dungeon horrible, on all sides round as one great furnace flamed, yet from those flames no light, but rather darkness visible."

Paine smiled to himself. He felt great, the way he always did when he knew he was right. On top of the world.

He moved from one cliff to another, jumping deep fissures, hauling himself by rope where a glassy wall of obsidian offered no holds. Wherever he found limestone he followed it until it either vanished or hollowed into a cave. There were caves, hundreds of them just as the Indian said, but none big enough or damp enough to support a colony of bats, and no signals reached his receiver. Paine was undiscouraged. There were bats and he was close to them.

From time to time he glimpsed shapes slipping through the basalt dikes. Crows. Beside a high nest, he found a dung beetle regally surveying a mound of bird droppings as high as a man's waist; Paine had seen storms moving across the desert, but when rain last fell here he couldn't even guess. There was no apparent plant life and, except for the solitary beetle, not even insects.

He crossed a natural bridge of gutted sandstone and discovered thirty feet below, sunk in shadow, the same road he had been on before. Paine was surprised it came so far. He checked his watch. Five o'clock; two hours to sunset. It was much later than he'd thought. He was confident, though. He still had time.

On the other side of the bridge, the composition of the rock changed to basically volcanic. Paine had to thread his way through fields of lava chimneys and arms that snagged his clothes. At one point, at his feet, he discovered a crude double-spiral scratched through the dark lava to an underlying level of white limestone. How the Indians had known there would be a different kind of rock beneath the lava he didn't know; that was a problem for anthropologists. For him, the limestone was a good sign.

As he emerged from the lava field, he got his first signal. The signal grew stronger as Paine continued moving. He tried the other two frequencies of the receiver; the second could barely be heard, but the third was the clearest of all. Paine followed it through a series of basalt dykes. He jumped from one side of a crevice to a stone chimney and landed running excitedly on the other side of a crevice. Before him loomed a huge white dome of limestone.

All three frequencies were coming in loudly; he turned the receiver off. The limestone dome was fifty feet across and in the middle of it was a sinkhole twenty feet across where erosion had broken through. The edge of the sinkhole was green with lichen and moss. On his stomach, moving with great caution, Paine crawled up the dome to the hole and looked down.

He'd found them. The shaft of light that slanted down through the sinkhole into the cave dropped into a tarry pool two hundred feet below. The pool was shallow, a new one, but the unmistakable odor of ammonia rose into the air. Paine switched his receiver on for confirmation, just for a second. The short, raucous tone brought a stirring of claws six inches beneath his chest on the thin underside of the dome. All three tones from the same cave. He had them all.

As his eyes became accustomed to looking down into the dark of the cave, Paine saw that it was circular, about three hundred feet wide, with the general shape of a natural amphitheater. From the level floor, all the walls arched smoothly to the dome. If there were a thousand bats in the colony now, the cave would accommodate three times as many. Somewhere on the floor was a spring or access to a water table. Paine sniffed. Because the ammonia was not overpowering, he smelled another faint but familiar odor. Oil. Another seep. Chee would be overjoyed.

The irises of Paine's eyes continued to dilate. The vertical lines on the cave floor near the pool were not irregular. They were straight. They were crude ladders, maybe ten, with most of their rungs broken. More shapes emerged. In the deepest shadow of the cave was a slightly darker shadow. A square. More squares spread around and above it, reaching halfway up and a third of the way around the wall of the cave. Windows. Windows and doors for five stories of adobe houses, an enormous underground gallery. The reason Paine hadn't seen it sooner was not only the dark. The houses themselves had disintegrated almost into rubble. Roofs were crushed, walls had fallen in, dust lay like a heavy shroud. Paine reasoned that to escape enemies a people might hide for a short time in such a place. This was not the construction of a short time, though. This had been a small city.

Intrigued and puzzled, Paine edged around the entire lip of the sinkhole, spreading his arms and legs to minimize his weight. He'd thought he would have to lower the Cyanogas canister through the sinkhole from a piton driven into the dome, an operation that risked breaking through the flimsy limestone shell or, at least, scattering the bats. If any point of the ruins, however, came within a hundred feet of the cave ceiling, he could place the canister there. The ruins told him there was another way into the cave because there had to be human access.

But no point on the ruins was high enough for the gas spray to be totally effective. Which satisfied Paine well enough; it was usually a bad idea to change methods, and one misstep among ruins as ancient as these could mean disaster.

The sinkhole it would be, then. Right on top of the bats.

He left the way he'd come, through the lava field to the sandstone bridge, where he descended by rope to the road. By now, he was asking himself questions.

The road comes all this way? To what?

He didn't want to stop, but his habit of thoroughness was too strong. A trap was no good if there were two exits, and somehow people had gone in and out of the cave.

As Paine reversed himself and ran up the road in the direction of the cave, his receiver came gradually alive again. Not as loud as the signals above the cave, but distinct.

Youngman knew about the canyon and the road. Paine's face flushed. The bastard must have known about the cave all the time.

The road ended directly in front of what seemed to

be an entrance to a mine. A cart wheel of solid wood that had been slowly decaying for hundreds of years lay beside an opening eight feet high and wide enough for two carts to enter abreast. The signals came from inside. He checked his watch. It was getting late, but he had to be certain.

As Paine stepped in, he touched the walls. They were cool and damp and left his fingertips black. One sniff explained all. Oil-saturated shale, that was what the mine was for. Soft shale so pregnant with oil it could be hacked into bricks that would burn brighter than coal.

The mine burrowed ahead and with each step the signals grew stronger. This had to be the other way into the cave. One hundred and fifty feet in, though, the mine came to a dead end. Yet the signals were stronger than before and Paine could smell ammonia. He pushed tentatively against the end wall, and it disintegrated in his fingers. His arm went through the rotting threads of a hanging blanket that had been the only separation between the shale mine and the limestone cave. Carefully, he pulled his arm out and peered through the hole he'd made. Before him, lit by the sinkhole, stretched the gigantic hall of the cave, the shallow pool of digested blood, the ghostly ruins of the pueblo and, overhead, both deadly and vulnerable, a ceiling of bats. They didn't use the mine.

Paine broke into a run when he reached the road. It was six o'clock, not enough daylight left for him to poison the bats before they flocked. In fact, there was just enough time to retrieve the backpack and escape from the bats' usual flight pattern towards the desert.

The road wasn't straight for more than a hundred feet at a time. To Paine, it seemed to wind malevolently, as if it were trying to slow him down, but at last he saw his pack sitting where he'd left it. A crow flew away from the pack as Paine approached.

From habit, Paine checked the pressure of the Cyanogas canister as soon as he reached his backpack. The tank was good. The battery had its charge and the wire mesh was rolled as neatly as before. The crow had been searching for food, that was all. Paine slipped the pack onto his shoulders and started his return to the dome.

In spite of the uphill grade and the weight of the canister Paine maintained a rapid walk. The road was a murky blue under the sunlit tops of the walls, though rarely the low sun did penetrate a gap and throw Paine's hunchbacked shadow high up a wall. Once, a second shadow joined his and Paine looked up to see a crow running along the cliffs.

Paine cast his rope over the sandstone bridge and hoisted himself up from the road. From there, he worked his way through the lava field and circled to the west side of the sinkhole, where he huddled beneath a stone shelf and watched the last rays of the sun burning out on the dome.

Now that he knew exactly what he was going to do, Paine felt a rising confidence. He opened his pack and laid out his helmet and wire clipper. He wouldn't need gas mask or gloves. An easterly wind rose, driving his smell away from the cave. Everything was going well.

As the sun set, the eastern horizon turned a fleshy pink shading into purple. No bats emerged from the sinkhole. Other bats might greet the dusk, but vampires waited for true night. Then Paine heard them, the sound of their stirring, of wings and the rain of nitrous urine lightening them for flight. The distant mesa tops lived briefly as golden clouds, stars swam into sight and, in seconds, the world tipped into the dark.

Paine held his breath. For a final minute, the air above the canyon was still, and then the first bats rose from the sinkhole, spiralling up like leaves from a fire. The rest came like a black pillar mounting five hundred feet into the sky.

His bats.

Paine held onto the rock as if he were going to be sucked into the swirling column. Part of him was. Along with his father, Ochay, the years in Mexico. You are what you kill, Joe Paine had said. Too true. The bats and Paine had joined, become the head and tail of a single creature leading and pursuing itself. One beast conceived in death and nurtured by obsession. Mantled in evil. He'd lied to Anne. There was, past biological frameworks, a sense to everything. There was a mutual grace in nature. The carnivore eliminated the weak, the herbivores and birds transmitted seed, insects cleansed the soil, flowers lent beauty. Each in turn lent something in return for its life, all but one. There was that single instant, a freak, which gave nothing in return for its all-consuming thirst. The vampire, alone. Claustrophobia was not what Paine had suffered, it was a shudder in the presence of evil. He'd come to understand that but what he hadn't foreseen was that evil had its own gravity. Not until it had drawn him in and used him to push the bats where they had never been before, and multiplied a thousandfold its own energy and horror. Apocalypse needed no pale horse or fiery dragon, not with the bats as its engine and the plague as its seed. All thanks to Paine. All due to him.

But the end of the chase had come, and after the end he would be free.

Flattening into a cloud turning again and again into itself, spreading into a crescent until the center moved forward and then forming one swift and undulating line, the bats flew east into the desert.

Paine gave the bats ten minutes before he unrolled the wire mesh and cut it in equal sections with the clipper. He wanted a snug fit over the sinkhole, no slack. One section of mesh he neatly re-rolled and carried to the far edge of the sinkhole, where he hammered a side of mesh into the dome with pitons. On all fours, he moved to the lip of the sinkhole nearer the rock shelf and tapped in more free pitons. He didn't need to drive the L-shaped pitons deep, just enough to keep the mesh tautly in place when it was spread. Underneath, he heard the anxious shifting of baby bats clinging to the ceiling. He knew of but couldn't hear the high-pitched distress calls of the babies, calls that were too weak and too far behind the hunting wave of bats. Paine attached two electrical wires to the rolled mesh and led them back to the battery under the rock shelf. He set the battery voltage at 300, turned it on long enough to listen to one tock, and switched it off. That part of the trap was set.

The rock shelf itself was granite, harder than limestone. With a piton, Paine searched out a vertical fissure and then hammered the piton into the fissure. He tied his two fifty-foot ropes together, making a single hundred-foot length. One end, he tied to the piton. The other end, he knotted in a bowline through the canister handle. He twisted the timer on the canister valve. Every complete revolution set back the Cyanogas spray sixty minutes; he gave the timer twelve full turns, its limit.

Then, he turned the canister on its side and, lying on his stomach, started to roll it up the dome to the sinkhole. The granite shelf was fifty feet from the sinkhole; the tank would hang fifty feet below the sinkhole into the cave, well out of the bats' way when they returned, and when Paine would spread the net and throw the battery switch and wait. Until 7:45 AM, to be precise, when the first lethal vapor of the canister would rise. Nothing could be simpler.

Stars came out in clusters of light. Paine rolled the canister slowly up the dome. At the lip of the sinkhole, he gave the tank a final push that tilted it into the cave. He grabbed the rope and let it play through his hand gradually, lowering the tank. Cautiously, he moved
230

away from the sinkhole, halfway down the dome, before he played any more rope through his hand.

The rope stopped. The heavy tank was only about ten feet down into the cave, Paine estimated, but the rope must have snagged on something at the lip of the sinkhole. He tugged the rope. It wouldn't move.

Paine crawled back up the cave dome. Underneath his hands and knees, he felt the anxious scuttling of the infant bats, unsettled by the ominous appearance of the tank. "Patience," he whispered to them.

At the sinkhole, he found the problem. The rope had cut into and stuck in the soft limestone of the lip. He didn't like resting all his weight on his knees, but he pulled the rope free and raised the tank to set the rope at a different place.

There was another problem he saw as the tank rose. Somehow, the rope from the handle had twisted around the valve and jammed the timer. Paine lifted the canister gently out of the cave and set it on the edge of the sinkhole.

A single yank loosened the rope and Paine freed the valve. He lowered the tank into the cave again, watching with satisfaction as it descended into the dark, playing the rope tenderly until the canister had vanished, gently swinging in the shadows.

Paine leaned back and took a deep breath.

He heard the dome crack around him. He was already twisting as the sinkhole widened and the limestone under him dropped away. His hands clutched at rocks that crumbled with each grasp into a pale sand that streamed over him.

Paine fell. Feet first, to begin with. Then he spread his arms and legs like a man soaring and dark blew into his face. In front of him, he saw the canister rope measuring his dive.

He stopped short swinging fifty feet below the sinkhole. His wrist was tangled in the rope at the canister handle. The canister rocked coldly against his cheek, which was crushed over an eye. He tried to raise himself, but the arm caught in the rope was pulled out of his shoulder socket. His other arm couldn't reach around the canister.

He dangled.

The babies scuttled around the ceiling. In time, though, they settled down and waited.

Along with Paine.

CHAPTER NINE

"He didn't make it," Youngman said. "He'd be back by now if he made it."

The two stars of Natupkom, Castor and Pollux, swung high overhead. Rising from the earth was Talawsohu, the Morning Star. Twice during the night, he and Anne had followed the flight of the bats. Their departure by sight. Their return, five hours later, by Paine's oscilloscope. That was five hours ago.

"I told him to wait."

"Paine knows what he's doing. Here, eat something, you look terrible." She offered him a slice of bread smeared with margarine. "I'm sorry that's all that's left. And some beers."

He shook his head. Even in the green glow of the scope, his skin was tinged with the ash of fatigue.

"He would have shot us if we went after him."

"He won't shoot any more, he's past that."

"He's all right. The best thing we can do is get to the highway so Chee will know to send a helicopter here and pick Paine up."

Youngman turned the radio on again. The stations in Tuba City no longer played music. Long periods of dead air were punctuated by bulletins. Tuba City was nearing its second day of quarantine. . . . Fifteen dead at Shongopovi, twelve at Walpi. . . . Utah and New Mexico state lines were closed. . . . the evacuation of Flagstaff was orderly. . . . the situation was in hand. . . .

"I'm going out to watch." Youngman kissed Anne's hand. "Let me know if you see anything on the screen."

He got out and stood in back of the Rover, looking up the road. Paine wasn't coming back. Instead of leaving for the cave when he should have, Paine had overstayed on the ridge. Even asleep, Youngman had done as Abner had asked. As Abner had predicted, how long ago? A week? Only that long? And a week from now, who or what would be left? What would have happened to anyone if a week ago a deputy had been able to read a dead man's sand painting?

As Youngman felt for a cigarette, his bandaged hand fell on his pocket. He drew out the datura root.

On his own, Youngman knew he didn't have the strength to go to the cave. He could barely walk and his hands were almost useless.

If only Paine had been right. If Paine had been the one man who could stop the bats.

Youngman bit into the root. The largest bite he could manage, although he didn't know how much he could handle. If he poisoned himself, Anne would drive him out of the canyon. If it was narcotic, they could go after Paine. What was there to lose? He let the bitterness pour down his throat.

After Talawsohu came Ponochona, the Dog Star, and night was complete, darkest before dawn. All night ceremonies ended with the appearance of Ponochona, and then the priests would wait for the sun to tell them whether the ceremonies had been carried out correctly. One error would cause the rising sun to bring in its right hand a rainbow of reversed colors. Youngman waited, his arms and legs rigid, his mouth open, his heart slowing with every beat. His head lolled against the truck and his eyes followed the course of the stars, bright bats wheeling in a middle distance. The lights were all colors

234

and in between were mixed auras, like colored grains of sand. He measured out minutes to the rare beats of his heart. A morning breeze blew on the left side of his face and traced its way with infinite slowness to the right. Showers of turquoise obscured the stars and then the desert burst into flames that leaped from end to end of the eastern horizon. The canyon began sailing into the flames.

The flames covered Youngman and warmed him like a light blanket of gold. His body burned up and released him, letting him float upward. For a long time, he enjoyed nothingness, and for a long time he felt consciousness returning. Below him he found the world spinning slowly between two kachinas, one with a face of clouds and the other tarnished brown by the sun. They bowed to Youngman and gave the world a push.

The world was different. An ocean lapped against a canopy of trees. Between the trees he could see familiar rows of corn and elsewhere were square obelisks and temples like statues alive with stone faces of tigers and snakes and bats writhing, their mouths gaping. The corn was fat and the wells were full of clear water but the people were leaving, walking along the axis of the earth for hundreds of years until they stopped at an inland sea surrounded by volcanoes. On the sea islands grew pyramids and on the pyramids formed steps mounted by blood-encrusted priests and guarded by soldiers dressed as animals. Yet some of the people left again, again walking the world's axis north until they reached the edge of a desert. Under his eyes new cities grew. Mesa Verde, Aztec, Wupatki, Keet Seel. Each built and at the height of its prosperity abandoned until the people were gathered for their last great migration into the desert itself. Into four groups they divided themselves and in four directions they left, making a cross over the land until more hundreds of years passed and they wheeled right, forming a swastika. As this

235

swastika wheeled, they broke into smaller groups, all returning but all moving in circles until the land was a giant's pattern of moving swastikas and serpentines. A pueblo would live for an instant. Another group would find it and a spiral map of their predecessors' path and then turn in the opposite direction, one eddy twisting from another, yet always directed to the finally permanent gathering at the center of the world. And there at the rim of the Black Mesa they finally did appear, at Oraibi and Hotevilla and Shongopovi, without water, without fertile land, without friends, at the mercy of their gods.

Youngman saw himself, on his back, hands and feet outstretched, and covering the desert spinning slowly within a nimbus of yellow light.

He had finally arrived. He was ready.

"Feeling better?" Anne joined him.

"More myself."

He took a deep, comfortable breath. The breeze of the dawn swayed a ringlet of soft hair at her temple and the slanting rays of the sun made her blue-brown eyes luminous.

"You know, you're very beautiful." He got up.

"Yes, that's more like yourself. Come on, we'd better get ready if we're going to go."

She climbed on the hood and handed down the unidirectional microphone to Youngman, who stowed the mike, amplifier, and oscilloscope in the rear of the truck. The equipment was almost weightless to Youngman. He looked at his hands and peeled off the bandages.

"What are you doing?" Anne saw the open cuts.

"Anne, I know how to stop them. I'm going to the cave."

"You don't know where it is."

"I have an idea."

"Paine is—"

236

"Paine is dead. It's day, Anne. He's not back because he's dead. Isn't he?"

"If he is," she faltered, "it's all the more reason for us to go. I'm sorry I got you into this."

"You didn't. Believe me, you didn't."

Two hours before, he'd been almost in shock. The Youngman she saw now was casually using mutilated hands to remove his shirt.

"That was a very fast recovery, Youngman. Just about unbelievable. What is your idea?"

"Abner opened the ring. I'm going to shut it again."

" 'Shut the ring?' That doesn't make any sense to me, Youngman. You're talking like a medicine man. Make sense."

"You mean, something called Cyanogas made sense." Youngman ripped the back from his shirt to tie it Hopi-fashion around his head.

"Yes."

"Paine made sense?"

"Yes."

"And Paine is dead."

Anne caught her words behind her teeth. The raw light of the rising sun threw blue shadows of the Rover and Youngman and her from the edge of the ridge to across the road. Youngman was talking suddenly on different levels.

"I don't understand," she said.

"Don't understand. All I want is your trust."

"But how can I trust you when I don't understand what you are doing?"

"That's why it's called trust. Your trust in something unscientific and unwhite. Don't you think it's about time we found out whether you do?"

"This is a good time," she agreed. "It's very unfair. We could hardly stay together if I say 'No' right now. It's unfair because I love you."

"Sometimes love isn't enough."

Anne walked away so as not to see him. He decided to give her five minutes to make up her mind. She returned after only one.

"Let me put it this way," she said. "At the moment, for asking me a question like that, I don't love you, I hate you. I'll go with you, though. I wouldn't let you go without me."

Which was not the same thing as complete trust, Youngman knew. But, a start.

The road had been built for high-wheeled Mexican ox carts, not a Land Rover. Although Youngman released some air from the tires and gained a couple of inches in roof clearance, hours were lost hacking with a shovel against crowding sandstone walls and low natural bridges. He didn't care how slow their progress was, how much backing up and road clearing they had to do; if Anne was going with him Youngman was determined to bring the shelter of the truck as well.

It was midday, halfway to exhaustion, when they came to the end of the road.

"What is it?" Anne pulled the hand brake.

"A mine."

"I never heard of a mine up here."

"Well, it hasn't been used for a while." He intercepted the question in her eyes. "About two hundred years."

As they got out of the Rover, Anne began to call for Paine and Youngman stopped her.

"We'll find him."

An ancient wooden wheel rested by the mouth of the mine entrance. There was no sign of Paine and the ground was too hard to pick up tracks. Anne looked anxiously around the cliffs that crowded against the narrow road. Along the edges of the cliffs, dark lava outcrops looked down.

"A mine and a road only Hopis know about? What's

the secret?" she asked. "What makes you think the bats are here?"

"I could be wrong. Want to stay here?"

"Together." She fell in behind him.

As they stepped into the cave, black wings bolted over their heads. Youngman put his hand over Anne's scream and they watched four crows climbing into the sky.

"You okay?"

"A little edgy."

Youngman took the flashlight away from her.

"Stay here."

He went in alone.

It was as cool as a tomb. Not uncomfortable, though. Just as Abner had described it so many times. The walls of dank, velvet-black shale that the Castillo priests had valued higher than any Hopi slaves. The ruts of overloaded carts. As Youngman went deeper he heard his footsteps resounding and muffled by the sweating walls. The entrance, and Anne, faded into a blur. Youngman swept the mine floor with his beam, looking for Paine. Nothing.

As he came to the end of the mine, a breeze tinged with ammonia drew by him. When he turned off his flashlight, a fainter light glowed on the end wall. The wall was a rotting blanket and the light was a hole. Youngman took one look before he ripped the blanket apart and stepped through.

He could see he was in a tremendous limestone cave lit by an exposed sinkhole in its ceiling. Youngman had to crane his neck to see all of the ceiling and everywhere he looked were bats so thick they seemed to hang in layers, and as one bat shifted all the bats around shifted so that their daytime languor was marked by constant ripples. Over the floor was a brackish pool of urine and feces. And there was the pueblo. And, beside the pool, a man clutching a red canister.

Youngman emerged from the mine ten minutes later dragging a rope. At the end of the rope, still locked together, were Paine and the canister. Paine's red-headed scalp hung slightly askew, like a cap, over his raw forehead. Stripes of pitch marked his shredded clothes. In the daylight, he seemed out of place, bizarre as a nightmare. Grotesque and reeking of ammonia. Youngman cut the wrist free and laid the dead man beside the cart wheel. Only then did he dare look at Anne.

"They're here." She was staring at the mine.

"Oh, yeah. The bats are here."

He watched her start to fall apart and pull herself back together. The dead-white pallor of her face turned into tears of anger.

"How did it happen?"

"There's a sinkhole over the cave. He fell in, tried to catch the rope and got his arm caught." Youngman held up the frayed end of the rope. "Maybe the rope broke before the bats came back, maybe he didn't feel a thing."

Youngman doubted it. A good rope didn't saw itself apart, not unless there was something at the other end struggling and twisting for a long time.

"The tank, he didn't use it." Anne wiped her eyes. "It's the Cyanogas. We can use it for him. See, Youngman, we'll do what he was going to do."

"No."

"What do you mean?" Anne righted the canister. "He told us all about it. He said it was foolproof."

"Anne."

"We'll do it his way. Just set the timer. It's easy."

"Anne," he knelt beside the canister with her and slapped the timer on the valve. It spun around. "The fall broke it. It won't work."

"Then how, damn it! What's your great idea? What did you bring to use?"

"Nothing, Anne. It's all here."

240

While her eyes followed him furiously, Youngman went to the Rover for a blanket, which he laid over Paine. The smell of ammonia didn't only come from Paine any more, the mine was breathing it.

"You saw the bats." Anne controlled herself.

"They're in a big cave at the end of the mine." Youngman nodded at Paine's body. "He had a lot more gear in his pack than the canister when he started out, you said. I think I know what he was up to at the sink-hole."

"Can we reach the bats, that's all I want to know?"

"We can kill them. Isn't that enough?"

Youngman climbed onto the roof of the truck, from which he saw a lava torso jutting from a cliff twenty feet above. He lassoed the torso.

"I'll be back," he called.

He pulled himself up the wall to the cliff, where he stopped to rest out of Anne's sight. The narcotic datura was wearing off and his hands burned from the short climb. He bit off more of the root. Just enough to dull the pain, he hoped. When he'd licked his fingers with his dry tongue, he started scrambling up the dome of the cave.

Before he was halfway up the dome, he felt better, stronger. At the sinkhole's edge, he found metal mesh rolled over pitons and ready to be spread. Electrical wires and a severed rope led to a rock ledge, where he discovered Paine's battery and backpack of equipment. Youngman spread the mesh tight on the pitons, covering the hole, and started the battery going to electrify the mesh. From the backpack, he selected only the pick axe.

As he straightened up, the datura rushed to his head and he saw the sky become choked with clouds. All the clouds were red, spewing blood.

Youngman had been expecting something like that.

241

He turned his back to the clouds and, his eyes down, worked his way to the road.

Anne was gone when he lowered himself onto the truck. She came out of the mine before he had a chance to call for her.

"There you are," Youngman was relieved. "I blocked their way out of the sinkhole. Paine had everything set up."

"I saw you. I went in the cave."

"Okay, good. Then you saw the bats."

"I saw the houses, too. Youngman, those tales you told me about an underground city, they weren't just tales, were they?"

"Ruins of a pueblo, that's all. The desert is full of them."

"Not in a cave. And the story about that flaming pit. If we went on another hundred yards would we find that, too?"

"What would it matter? So we found some ruins. We came here to find the bats and we did. You're not going to be scared of some old Indian witch stories."

"It matters," Anne said, "because you knew what was in there and you didn't tell me. Do you believe in those stories? Do you?"

Youngman took a long time answering because he wanted to lie, it would have been such a comfort to lie, for her, for him. But Anne would hear the lie and despise him for it, as she should. So in the end, he didn't answer her at all.

"We're wasting time," he said instead. "Get all the blankets you can find in the truck."

They hung a new blanket from the crossbeam that divided the mine from the cave, not only to block the light of the flashlight but to muffle the sound of their work. While Anne held the flashlight, Youngman swung the pick axe into the mine wall.

"See this," he picked up the first chunk of shale dislodged. "Saturated with oil. It'll burn like charcoal if we get it hot enough."

"We're going to smoke them to death?"

"No. There's an oil seep somewhere in the cave, I smelled it. If we hit the seep, we'll get more than smoke."

"That's going to take an awful lot of shale."

"That's right." Youngman dropped the rock on a blanket.

He dug the pick axe into the wall again. Again. And again. The shale was soft and absorbed the blows rather than split. But a small pile of glossy chunks accumulated on the blanket. The pile grew. Holding the flashlight so that its beam was a target for the axe, Anne felt her resentment breaking down under the blows. Youngman took his shirt off. He didn't swing the axe as much as attack the wall with it. She watched the muscles of his arms and back jump with each stroke.

"You almost died two nights ago, Youngman. How can you do this now?"

"Well, hard labor's a funny thing," he said between swings. "You never forget how."

The datura was working for him now. He was in control.

Anne took over with the axe while Youngman dragged the first blanket load of shale from the mine into the cave. By the angle of the light from the sinkhole, he could tell it was about two o'clock. He dragged the blanket across the cave floor to the pueblo ruins. His first step on a ladder rung splintered the entire ladder, but he was able to scale a mound of debris onto the remains of a plaza above the first-story houses. A vapor of dust swirled around his feet. In the curve of the wall, four more stories of ruins loomed over him. Youngman let the rocks spill from the blanket. A ring was what he needed, a solid ring of fire within the cave.

"Flea," one of the doors whispered to him.

Youngman stumbled down from the rubble. The bats ignored him.

He went on with the digging, deliberately concentrating on the task at hand. The ring would have a circumference of 150 feet and he'd need fourteen piles of shale about ten feet apart, each pile about a foot high. His body became covered with black dust striped by rivulets of sweat. The same dust Abner had used. When he looked down on his chest he saw himself painted in spirals.

After carrying three more piles to the ruins in the cave, he was on the point of collapse. While Anne went to the truck for the last bottle of beer, he choked down more datura.

A cold sweat of shock poured from him. Within his head, he felt the datura coalescing bright and hot, like a second brain.

"Let me do some of the work," Anne offered when she returned. "You're going to kill yourself at this rate."

"We're doing fine," he said calmly.

"Youngman, let's run. Get out of here while we can."

Pain and feeling drained from his hands, and he took the beer.

"Just don't go in the cave," he said. "Even if I call you, don't go in."

He was done with the ruins. The next load of shale he dragged to the foot of the rubble, the sort of detritus of adobe and stones marked by an occasional pot shard that some people called history. The light from the sinkhole had swung high onto the plaza of the ruins, illuminating a standing tablet with the figure of a headless man. One corner of the stone tablet was broken off; it was the Fire Clan tablet stolen from the kiva of dead priests. Youngman was unsurprised until he started to gauge the time from the angle of the beam from the sinkhole, when he realized the tablet and the plaza were

244

at the western end of the cave. The sun had moved to the east, backwards.

"Check the time on the truck clock," he told Anne when he returned to the mine. "Don't go by the sun, just the clock."

"It's six o'clock," she reported a minute later. "But it's very light."

Ninety minutes to sunset.

"Take the blanket off Paine," he said.

He filled two blankets for a double load before he went into the cave again, where he started to widen the circle of piles around the pool on the cave floor. So far, he still hadn't seen any clear signs of the oil seep and he no longer smelled it. Overhead, the roof showed no more than a slow rousing of the bats, but he dumped the first pile as quietly as he could.

The second load of shale hissed out of the blanket as red sand. He felt the datura surge through his head.

"Flea. Flea, what are you doing? You have the datura. We can talk. You're one of us. What are you doing now, Flea?"

The voice wasn't Abner's.

Youngman returned to the mine. Numbed, his body was starting to fail him and each blanket took longer to fill. The wounds on his hands were long since split open, making the axe hard to grip.

"Stop. There's only an hour left," Anne told him. "There must be enough shale in there."

"Has to be a ring."

"Why?"

He missed the wall and the force of his swing threw him against the shale. He fell on the blanket, blind until Anne wiped blood and sweat from his eyes.

"There's a towel in the Rover. I'll be back in a second."

Alone in the mine, Youngman ate more datura and rubbed some into his hands. When Anne returned, he

245

was hard at work again. The new cut on his brow had stopped bleeding.

"At least, let's bring the Rover in here and use it to cart the shale," she said. "The truck will fit."

"It won't go under the beam into the cave, not unless we let all the air out of the tires."

"Then, let's do it."

"No." Youngman continued slashing at the glow of her flashlight on the black wall. "You're going to get out of here in a hurry. You don't want to steer down that road on wheel rims."

"You mean, *we're* going to get out of here."

Dragging the next two blanketloads, Youngman found the mine corridor becoming longer and narrower. His legs moved stiffly until he reached the cave, which was suffused by a cool, water-blue light.

Instead of shale piles, one great double serpentine covered the entire floor of the cave. The coils shifted with the lazy power of a huge snake, a snake without a head.

"I watched out for you, Flea. For her, too. For your sake. For the new world I'm making for you. That's why I'm doing all of this. For you."

I understand, Youngman thought.

One spiral of the serpentine uncurled and reached out for Youngman to draw him in.

"Let me show you the new world, Flea. Let me show you."

I'm sorry, Youngman thought. It's too late.

As the spiral coiled around him, he picked up the sharpest rock in the blanket and twisted its point into his bloody palm. He ground it into his hand, probing until the jagged point found the last neurons of pain, and then he clutched the rock tight in the open wound. The spiral receded and the whole length of the serpentine faded. He looked up through the blue mist to the
246

ceiling of the cave, where a thousand hanging faces looked down.

Youngman emptied the blankets and hurried back to the mine. A wind followed and Anne's flashlight went out, plunging them into darkness.

"It didn't even dim," she said. "What do we do now?"

"Bring the truck up to the mine entrance and turn on the headlights. Run them on the battery."

In the glare of the headlights, Youngman carved out two more piles of shale. The axe became too heavy to lift and in full view of Anne, he lifted the last of the datura root to his mouth. She shouted at him from the Rover, but her voice echoed confusingly through the mine.

"Getting dark," he finally understood.

The two piles of shale he dragged into the cave were the last, the ring was complete. The voice was silent, but the ceiling had changed. There was a steady simmering among the bats, waves of arousal and short flights from one part of the roof to the other. He could hear the "clicks" of their lower pitched chatter.

Youngman went out of the mine to the Rover. The road was dark under the cliffs barely trimmed in orange.

"The sun's going," Anne said.

"Where's the siphon?"

"You didn't ask me to find it."

"I know, but where is it?"

Youngman's face was black with dust, except for the red of his eyes. He was unrecognizable. Anne found a kit panel in the back of the Rover and in the panel a siphon tube with a bulb. Unasked by Youngman, she also took out two empty jerry cans. She was halfway through filling up the second can when the siphon tube went dry.

247

"Nothing more in the tank. It's empty. How do we get out of here?"

"Roll. There's enough in the fuel line to get us started."

"Okay," she agreed. "Be careful. I love you."

"Yes. Keep the lights on so I can see my way out."

"I'll be here."

Youngman picked up a can in each hand and was about to go when he remembered something.

"Have you got a match?"

She put a book of matches in his pants.

"Good luck."

He went into the mine. At the midway point, the mine curved and he left the illumination of the headlights behind him. The mine had been straight before. The jerry cans grew heavier. Youngman could lift his feet no more than an inch. He reached the cave and, between the pool and the ruins, started pouring from the heavier can a line of gasoline connecting the ring of shale piles.

The sinkhole was a halo of light around which the cave ceiling vibrated. By the hundreds, bats spread their wings in anticipation of sunset and a steady rain of urine sprinkled the floor. Youngman concentrated on drawing his steady line of gasoline.

"Flea, look."

Smoke drifted from the chimneys of the pueblo. The ladders stood strong and upright and poles with clan feathers marked the handsome houses. Up five stories, windows were lit in welcome and on the inside walls Youngman saw the shadows of people. The smell of bread and the sounds of life spread through the cave.

"Stop, Flea. And look."

The halo around the sinkhole diminished to a crescent. Around it, bats gathered so thickly they hung from each other and beneath the sinkhole massed a stationary

248

cloud of wings. The musical laugh of a woman came from the pueblo.

He retraced his route across the pueblo. He could hear children, the sound of men gambling, the gossip of girls, the boiling of stew in an oven. Each pile of shale was a bough of cottonwood and the broken Fire Clan tablet was whole and surrounded by prayer sticks. Gasoline hit the ground as blue cornmeal. From one house came a song he hadn't heard in years. "Somewhere, somewhere, far away, Sibopay. What was I at Sibopay? When was I born? Where did I come from? Where am I going? What am I? I asked myself at Sibopay." Out of the corner of his eye he saw people at the windows, faces that vanished when he looked up and reappeared as he looked away. After a day without food, the aroma of fresh piki bread was overpowering.

"Join them, Flea. They wait for you. Your people, Flea. Waiting for you."

A white-bellied shrike flitted over Youngman's head and flew towards a row of stars. When it reached the stars, the bird's wings turned to leather and the stars became the last drops of sun on the rim of the sinkhole.

Youngman stumbled down from the pueblo. He only had to finish dousing the shale piles leading back to the mine.

"Flea, stay with us."

Gasoline spilled over his pants. The more he poured, the heavier the can grew, until he was dragging it along the ground.

Wingtips grazed walls, roof, and cave floor. By the hundreds, more bats dropped and spread their webbed hands. The cave was filled with the thousand of them, a wheeling, living shadow going round and round, color-blind eyes fixed on a final candlelight of sun on the sinkhole, waiting for their moment of emergence. Wings, eyes, mouths flashed past Youngman, rose like a wave to the sinkhole and fell away from the light.

Youngman poured out the second can of gasoline in a straight line in front of the mine exit. He'd light the ring of shale piles first and ignite the exit as he left. A bat flew over his shoulder. He didn't hear the bat's whisper or its change in tone. Two more bats flew by his face, their eyes turned on him. Another went by. He felt a slight nick. Blood flowed from his ear. A whisper spread through the cave up to where the hanging, pink newborn cried. Youngman shook his head at another bite along his neck. It was too dark now to see the bats coming at him anyway.

He pulled out the book of matches. As he started to light one, a wind knocked the book out of his hand. He went down on his hands and knees and felt the ground. Wings and teeth landed on his back. Something scuttled towards him along the floor. His fingers closed on the matches. Deliberately, he peeled another match from the book and struck it. A bat darted away from the flame and Youngman threw the match. He rolled away, crushing the bats on his back.

From the first burning shale pile, two blue flames raced to the other piles, meeting on the ruins. From each pile rose a flame thirty feet high. A new line of fire appeared and shot into the pool in the center of the cave, which ignited into flat, glassy flame. A line of red swept into the ruins. Others blossomed into life from the ring and zigzagged over the floor and up the walls. Behind him, blocking the mine, was a sheet of fire.

The bats that weren't burning rose to the sinkhole and the electrified mesh. As a cloud, they boiled over the flames. Youngman turned in amazement. The entire cave was on fire, a palace of lights. More oil seams erupted in flame from the walls and the shale fires grew, spewing dense, black smoke.

For Youngman, bats and smoke became one, a one that took the shape of a giant crouched beneath the roof, a face of flames in agony over a ragged, black cloak. Blind, milky eyes stared in disbelief.

"FLEA! . . . WHY? . . . IT WAS FOR YOU . . . FOR YOU!"

"I know!" Youngman cried. Tears started from his eyes.

"EVERYTHING . . . FOR YOU!"

A truck pulled in front of Youngman and its door swung open. Anne was at the wheel, shouting.

"Youngman! Youngman, here!"

Through the fire, he saw the pueblo melting. Adobe walls split into red dust. Windows raged. Inside, figures of flame danced wildly, running from room to room without escape.

"Youngman!" Anne screamed.

He fell into the truck and at once she swung the Rover around, clumsily on slashed tires.

She aimed directly for the fire blocking the mine and broke through. Within the mine, the Rover caromed off the walls. The last gas in the truck's fuel line ran out as they crashed onto the road, and from there they rolled, down, down, almost to the desert when the dome of the cave rose on a fireball into the sky.

CHAPTER TEN

The explosion ran like a pulse through a subterranean network of seeps and around the cave smaller caves erupted in series. Along a tracery of shale seams on the surface, blue flames spread like couriers, running parallel, converging and spreading again. Where vertical seams met, flames spewed through the canyon walls in search of more shale, which cracked and exposed rich veins of oil. Fire licked its way up the higher western plateau of the canyon, touching off fireballs that dwarfed the first, that rose into the night to rain fire onto the canyon. So the fire continued to spread, by the blackened teeth of basalt mines and across lava fields of twisting forms. The first fire engines and mobile lab from Tuba City tried to fight their way to the bat cave, only to retreat when the fire began to cut off the road behind them. They pulled back a full mile from the base of the canyon as Parks Department helicopters cruised overhead to release trails of phosphate-enriched water.

In the minutes before dawn, the fire subsided even as it widened. From one end to the other, Maski Canyon was lit by blue flames.

Youngman and Anne watched from the fire engines and emergency vehicles that huddled on the desert floor. Standing on the hood of his car, Piggot watched the flames' progress through field glasses.

"That first explosion lit up the mesa. Sounded like a

bomb." Walker Chee stepped on a cigarette butt. "Whole canyon must be laced with oil and shale."

Like campfires, Youngman thought. The canyon was alive with blue campfires. His face was blistered. His neck and ear were bandaged and a blanket covered his back.

Another oil seep erupted, orange turning to blue. Turbines wheezing in desperation, a helicopter peeled away from the rising flame.

"Useless. Absolutely useless." Piggot jumped down from his car and threw his glasses onto the rear seat. "That'll burn for years, maybe forever. Kiss it good-bye, Chee."

"Where're you going?"

"Venezuela, Indonesia, Alaska." Piggot got into the front seat. "Somewhere, someone wants to do business. All I gotta do is find him."

"We have a contract!" Chee shouted after the moving car. He watched the rear lights of the Cadillac vanish before he turned back to the canyon, where he could watch $2 million going up in smoke.

One of the Disease Control mobile labs took the space vacated by Piggot. A young investigator in vinyl coveralls, his fresh cheeks dusted with soot, eyed Youngman and Anne curiously before reporting to Chee.

"There's no way of telling when we can check out that cave. The main thing is, are all the bats dead?"

"Ask him." Chee shrugged and walked away in disgust.

The investigator was eager but tentative about approaching Youngman. The Indian he saw was dark, as red-eyed as an animal, and naked to the waist.

"They're dead," Youngman said.

"I hope that's correct. If they are, then the major vector of the disease is eliminated and the rest will be basically a quarantine operation." The investigator studied Youngman more carefully. "If you understand what I mean."

The investigator's uncertainty reminded Youngman of Paine.

"I try," Youngman said.

"And I hear that a man was left in the cave?"

"In the mine."

"A friend?"

"Yes." Youngman looked at Anne. "The Hopi people owe him a great debt."

The investigator made notes. He asked Anne about the fire, the cave, and the bats; she answered that they'd set the fire with gasoline, the cave was ordinary in all respects and that there was no chance of any of the bats escaping. While she talked, she slipped her arm through Youngman's. When he closed his notebook, the investigator was very pleased.

"Thank you. There's an ambulance on the way for the two of you. You'll be in a hospital for a couple of days of observation but I bet you can use the rest. You've had an amazing escape."

"Do you think so?" Youngman asked flatly.

"Well . . . yes," the investigator blurted. "Unbelievable."

"Good."

The investigator went in some confusion back to his truck, and drove off to the rank of fire engines sitting out the dawn.

Youngman spread his blanket over Anne so that they could lean together. Around the canyon the sky paled.

"You're going to make Paine a hero, aren't you?" Anne said.

"He was."

Or Abner was, and Harold, even Chee. Give them their due, everyone was right, Youngman thought. All but him, perhaps.

"But you did it," she said.

254

"I don't know what I did. I hope no one ever knows what I did."

The features of the canyon began to emerge in the morning light. The different colored sandstone walls were all charred black. Cliffs, gutted, hollow-eyed, disjointed, wore a mask of black. Black smoke rode over the morning wind without moving.

"I hope I never know."

The flame lights looked like the stars of a universe that had died and collapsed upon itself. As the sun rose at Youngman's back the stars faded and, one by one, disappeared.